Formula for a Perfect Life

Formula for a Perfect Life

CHRISTY
HAYES

ISBN
Paperback: 978-1-62572-018-4

Book Cover Design by ebooklaunch.com
Edited by Iola Goulton, Christian Editing Services
Proofreading by Paula Bothwell
Interior designed and formatted by: E.M. Tippetts Book Designs

Chapter One

Kayla Cummings stared at the two lines so long her vision blurred. Her breath came fast and faster until her lungs felt too full, too thick, too heavy to function. Her mind whirled, her neurons firing through a maze of wrong turns and dead ends. She dropped the stick with the prison-bar stripes onto the counter and fell back against the bathroom door, freefalling in the void of denial.

No. No. Just … NO.

Kayla swiped the evidence into the trash with the back of her hand and stared where it landed, nestled between used tissues and a discarded tube of lipstick. She kicked the trashcan to move the stick, forcing it deeper into the bin. When that didn't obscure the proof of her life-altering mistake, she pulled a length of toilet paper from the roll and balled it in her fist, lobbing it onto the pile. She exhaled when she could no longer see the stick, but she couldn't force her shoulders to lower from their perch around her ears.

If only she could discard the news the way she discarded the messenger. Those prison-bar stripes were branded to her forehead, tattooed on her arms, a neon sign blazing in the dark. She washed her hands, scrubbing them raw. Her pulse echoed between her ears. *What have you done? What are you going to do? How could you be so stupid?*

She looked into the mirror and blinked at her reflection, disgusted. How could she look the same—same cornflower-blue eyes, same ragamuffin blonde hair, same pixie face that earned her the nickname of Tinkerbell—when everything had changed. She'd always loved her nickname and the idea of staying forever young. Like it or not, her youth had crashed and burned with the appearance of those two lines.

Kayla stumbled into her bedroom, crumbled onto her bed, and clutched her stuffed bear to her chest. She nuzzled the musty and matted fur and tried to accept what her brain rejected. A baby. How could she have a baby? Some girls hooked up all the time and never got pregnant. She did it once—one stupid, careless time—and made a baby? She couldn't make sense of the senseless.

She should have listened to her gut—churning with more than lust, more than excitement—while he dug through the console and glove compartment in search of a condom. How many times had her mom told her that sinking, buzzing feeling was her internal meter signaling danger? More than enough times for Kayla to heed the warning and stop. She distinctly remembered his satisfied, relieved look as he held up the foil package—to the victor go the spoils.

He was the victor and she'd gotten spoiled.

She pinched her eyes closed and choked back the memory, slapping a PG rating on her X-rated night.

Beckoned by the intoxicating lure of sleep, Kayla lifted the pink and white blanket from the foot of the bed and yanked it over herself, tucking it under her chin and around Mr. Snuggles. She might not be able to face the truth, but she could hide from it in her dreams. Maybe this was the dream, a nightmare she could laugh about with her roommates. Exhausted and nauseated from the scent of her candy-apple candle, Kayla plunged into sleep.

Two numbing days later, as Kayla's religion professor lectured on the historical influence of Jesus Christ in the modern-day calendar, she stared into space and realized she too would classify everything in her life as before or after. Before she knew, after she knew.

She longed to go back to before.

Someone tapped her arm, drawing her attention to the present. She turned her head and blinked at the cute boy next to her.

"Hey," he said. "I dropped my pen and it rolled under your seat. Would you mind handing it to me, please?"

Kayla flinched. It was the first and only time he'd spoken directly to her and the cadence of his voice, the earthy depth of it, spurred her into motion. She looked down, spotted the pen on the dingy marble, and leaned over to pick it up. She winced when she squashed her tender breast. His fingers brushed hers in the transfer, and his smile sent his dimple quivering like a coy heroine in the romance novels she devoured.

"Thanks."

Before, Kayla would have felt hyperaware of him beside her. That Kayla would have obsessed about her hair, her outfit, her makeup or lack thereof. She would try not to fidget in her seat, sneak him glances, or spin fantasies in her mind. Old habits were hard to break. For a moment, Kayla mourned the loss. His broad shoulders would never absorb her tears, his fingers with the neatly clipped nails would never hold her, his mouth—that wide masculine mouth—would never utter the words she longed to hear.

But this was after.

She couldn't muster the energy to smile back or say, "You're welcome" or even care. The cute boy next to her and his deep voice and dimply smile mattered little now. After.

Sighing, she tried to zone back into the lecture. Her grades were one of the only things she could still control. She couldn't afford to get behind in school. Not now, not when it took every ounce of energy to pull herself out of bed, dress, and get to class. Her education—her graduation—depended upon paying attention and finishing strong. Her future, on the other side of those pink prison-bar stripes, seemed as uncertain as a few days ago when she'd discovered the truth.

When the other students shoved laptops into backpacks and stood to leave, Kayla followed like a catatonic robot. She had to snap out of her funk, face reality, and make plans. She couldn't continue to wade through the quicksand of uncertainty. Doing nothing, pretending she didn't have a ticking time bomb within her, was as irresponsible as the act that put her in this predicament.

At first, she hadn't seen the harm in taking time for introspection, weighing her options, tossing around possibilities. Now, the harm was her total lack of concentration on anything but her situation. With finals fast approaching and the lengthy Christmas break that followed looming, she couldn't waste valuable time on what-ifs. She had to face what was.

She pushed out of the building, squinting her eyes at the blast of sunlight through December's barren trees, and gulped cool air into her lungs. She had to start talking. Rip off the Band-Aid and deal with the fallout. She cut across the quad, leaves crunching under her feet, and tried to set an agenda.

Who would she tell first? Who would share her burden, give her guidance, and hold her hand? Which of her roommates could she trust not to judge? Her emotions were so raw, she could bleed to death from a sarcastic quip.

Just a few months ago, Kayla would have gone straight to Reagan. Sharp and determined, Reagan would've been able to drill down to the heart of the problem and help Kayla figure out her next move. But with Reagan and boyfriend Dash building a life together based on their mutual faith, she seemed a risky choice.

Emily had endured her fair share of drama—breaking up with one brother to date the other. Since none of her roommates liked Zach, none of them cared when Emily tossed him aside for Dylan. Emily and Dylan had floated through life in a bubble of happiness ever since, and spending their lives together seemed a foregone conclusion.

Kayla knew what perma-single Shelby would say. But Kayla wasn't ready to make a decision before weighing all her options, and she worried about Shelby's lack of patience for Kayla's wishy-washy ways.

Her conscience nudged her toward the other person she had to tell—the only person who needed to know her condition, the only one who mattered, the only one who deserved a say. No.

She'd tell her roommates first. If she didn't, she feared the truth would burst forth in class or in casual conversation with one of her sorority sisters or friends. Like a tire filled to bursting, she had to relieve the pressure in order to think.

Reagan, Emily, or Shelby? She'd leave it to chance and tell the first person she encountered at home. Like it or not, she couldn't spend another moment keeping her secret to herself.

Ben Strickland hitched his backpack onto his shoulders and walked across campus, inhaling the crisp winter air. The late afternoon breeze nipping his neck had him tugging the collar of his pullover, wishing he'd grabbed a jacket on his way out the door. His walk home tonight promised to be chilly.

He despised spending another evening in the library. While all his friends breezed toward the finish line of college, cramming for senior finals and anticipating Christmas break, he'd been in study mode. His finals came a distant second to studying for the Law School Admission Test, or LSAT as most called it. While everyone else would go home, catch up with friends and family, possibly travel over their lengthy break, he'd be holed up in some library, studying for the test that determined his future.

Ben frowned, feeling as lost as the leaves flittering from

the trees bordering the quad. He'd had three and a half years of messing around, taking school only as seriously as necessary, getting by with decent grades and good times. He'd known he'd blown the November LSAT before he'd even left the room. The shame of having to tell his parents the pitiful number as soon as the scores posted along with a good dose of guilt, propelled him to the library every night to study for the January sitting.

Going to law school and following in his father's footsteps had always been the plan, but now it was time to forgo the parties, hangouts, and usual college fun and spend the next three years living and breathing the law, he felt … ambivalent.

Ambivalence wasn't much of a motivator.

"Strick!"

Ben turned at the sound of his nickname and smiled at his friend, Ryan, who was dressed in sweats and holding a football. "Hey, man. What's up?"

"I'm headed over to the intramural fields for a football game. You didn't respond to the group text."

Ben rubbed the back of his neck, tried to keep the annoyance from his voice. "I turned off my notifications so I wouldn't be tempted."

"Tempted to what? Come on, dude. When was the last time you let loose and had a little fun? Your studies will improve if you blow off steam."

Easy for Ryan to say. He had a job secured and nothing to do but mark time with friends until graduation. Ben's mind flashed to the last time he'd let go of the reins and acted on impulse. He spent most days hoping to catch a glimpse of her blonde hair and listening for the perky laugh that had entranced him into a night of debauchery. He should have felt guilty for the cool November night he'd done something unpredictable and wild and seriously out of character, but he didn't. Instead, he spent most days reliving the memory with reverence. Yeah, he'd been stupid and rash, but she'd made him laugh. She'd made him forget.

"I can blow off steam in January—after the LSAT."

Ryan scoffed. "Whatever, dude. But think about it this way. You won't remember another endless night in the library, but you'll sure remember the night we kicked serious butt on the football field."

Ben squeezed Ryan's shoulder. He wasn't trying to pour salt in a wound. He couldn't see or understand the pressure and panic tracking Ben like a stalker. "You will live in infamy. Go forth and conquer."

Ryan shook his head. "You already sound like a lawyer. Tell you what. I'll conquer the football field, and you conquer the library. We'll meet again in January and decide who made the better choice."

"A wise compromise, my friend. Now go kick some butt."

With a salute, Ryan jogged away from the quad, leaving Ben to stare after him and stew in his wake. Would time spent in the library feel like a victory or time spent in prison? Despite his misgivings, he turned back to the building. Victory or not, he'd already tempted fate once that semester and walked away unscathed. He refused to tempt fate again.

Kayla opened her apartment door and found all three of her roommates in the den, staring at her as she entered. Her stomach toppled and the saliva in her mouth turned to sand. Seated on the couch, Emily dropped a strand of long blonde hair and clasped her hands between her legs. Reagan stopped pacing in front of the TV and turned around to glare. Shelby sat up from a yoga pose that had her flattened to the floor, her brows arching in line with her movements.

"Hey." Kayla could feel her roommates' eyes on her, sharp and seeking. She shut the door with tingling fingers and dropped her backpack, her movements halting and sluggish. Sure, she was ready to tell one roommate her troubles. But not all three at once. Her breath came in short, stuttered gasps. "What's going on?"

Reagan folded her arms against her chest and stuck a confrontational pose. "Why don't you tell us?"

Kayla smelled her own fear, thick and acrid like burnt hair. She choke-coughed and tried to act indignant, but it came out flat. "What do you mean?"

Emily pointed a manicured nail at a magazine on the ottoman. Lying across the face of an up-and-coming actress sat a thin white stick. A thin white stick with two pink lines. "Shelby found this in your trash can."

Kayla's heartbeat boomed in her ears, the vibration quaking through every vein and along every nerve ending. She tried to swallow the dread coating her throat. Anger was the only emotion strong enough to pierce her shock. "What were you doing in my trash?"

"Seriously?" Shelby rose to her feet in one fluid motion. "That's all you have to say? I was taking out the trash!"

"Okay, fine." Kayla tore her coat from her shoulders, sweating from heat and embarrassment. She tried to remember what she planned to say, how she planned to spill the beans. Their accusing looks erased her mind. She tossed her coat along the back of the couch and dropped onto the edge. She didn't have to tell because they already knew. "I was going to tell you."

"You're pregnant?" Emily's voice was little more than a whisper.

"When?" Reagan asked. "How long have you known?"

Kayla blinked back tears. She'd done her best to ignore the truth, but the albatross sat front and center for her friends to see. She stared at the carpet, barely able to breathe through the lump in her throat. "A couple of days."

Reagan's feet appeared just moments before she wrapped Kayla in a hug. "Honey, why didn't you tell us?"

Kayla clung to her friend, tears blinding her vision. She squeezed her eyes shut and let them fall. Within seconds she felt arms and hair around her shoulders, whispers and shushes in her ear. Coconut and lemongrass tickled her nose. It was like getting hugged by a fragrant octopus.

Her sobs subsided to a hiccupping ache, leaving her face bloated and hot. Her friends stepped back as Kayla sank back into the couch and used her palms to dry her cheeks. She struggled to catch her breath. "I was … going to tell … whoever I found … at home today. I just needed … I needed a few days to let it sink in."

"Kayla." Reagan gripped her knee. "We love you. Whatever you need, we're here for you."

"Of course we are." Shelby crouched at her feet. "Whatever you decide, we'll support you."

Emily scooched closer and rubbed her back. "We'll get you through this."

Their unconditional support rent the ache in her chest wide open. The tears she thought she'd shed dry threatened to return. Kayla bobbed her head and sucked in air to regain her composure. "I love … y'all, too." Her breath hitched. "I'm sorry … I didn't say … anything sooner." She stared at her friends, their faces etched with worry, and added guilt to her litany of sins.

Reagan cleared her throat, drawing everyone's attention like a trumpet in a crowd. "Now that it's out in the open, what are you going to do?"

Kayla picked at the skin around her thumbnail and averted her eyes. Now that they knew, "tell you" didn't seem like much of a plan. She opted for honesty. "I don't know."

Her roommates sent curious glances between themselves, mentally tossing the question she most feared around the room. Kayla knew what they wanted to ask—she could tell from the bugged eyes and the you-do-it look on each of their faces as they lobbed the hot potato between them.

Kayla saved them the trouble. "You want to know who's the daddy?"

Reagan fluttered her arms as if revving herself up to speak. "Between school and Dash, I haven't been around much, but are you seeing someone?"

Starting with those who loved her was supposed to feel like dipping her toe into ice-cold water, but the chill running through her veins came from a head-first plunge. She shook her head and studied her shoes.

"You hooked up with someone?"

Kayla hated that phrase, hated the casualness it denoted, but didn't detect an ounce of condemnation in Emily's voice. "Obviously."

"Does he know?" Shelby asked. "Have you told him?"

"I haven't told anyone."

Standing next to Kayla, Reagan folded her arms across her chest, but her voice held no judgment. "How far along are you?"

"Six weeks."

Shelby blew out a breath. "That's good. It's still early."

"Good? I don't see anything good about this situation."

"I just mean it's not too late …"

Kayla bolted to her feet. She regretted it the moment the room tilted, and her head spun. She grabbed the arm of the couch and closed her eyes.

"You okay?" Reagan clutched Kayla's arm.

"Yes. Sorry. I stood up too fast."

Shelby got to her feet. "I wasn't implying anything. I just meant you have time to make decisions."

"I don't want to make any decisions! I don't want to be pregnant!" She walked around her friends and sat on the other end of the couch, scrubbing her hands over her face. She couldn't think, couldn't breathe, couldn't stop her hands from shaking between their prying eyes and probing questions. "If I knew what I was going to do, I would have done it by now." She dropped her hands into her lap and lowered her voice. It wasn't Shelby's fault Kayla didn't have any answers. They were asking the same questions she'd been asking herself for days. "It doesn't seem possible. How am I supposed to make decisions about something that doesn't feel real?"

Reagan cleared her throat and sat on the arm of the couch, leaning forward. "Maybe the first thing you should do is make an appointment with a doctor. The test could be wrong."

"I called. I can't make an appointment until eight weeks."

Shelby scoffed. "So you're just supposed to assume the drugstore test is right?"

"I did a lot of research." She pointed to the offending object on the coffee table, glanced away. She couldn't look at it, couldn't face the evidence of her idiocy. "The tests are only wrong when the line is faint. It wasn't faint when I took it, and it isn't faint now."

"But—"

"No buts, Em. My period comes like clockwork. It never showed. My breasts are tender and I'm so tired I want to crawl into a ball and never get out of bed. That's not like me. I don't lounge around in bed even when I'm sick." She stared at her friends, willing them to believe her. "Trust me, I've tried to convince myself it's not true. But it's true. I'm pregnant. I know I am."

"Okay," Reagan said. "You're pregnant. Now what?"

"Now … I don't know. The only thing I decided so far was to tell y'all. The next logical step is to tell him."

Another pause and another round of triangular stares had Kayla shifting on the couch. Once again, Reagan drew the short stick. "I'm not trying to pry into your personal business, but—"

"Ben Strickland."

"Is he a student?" Shelby asked.

Kayla rolled her eyes and shot Shelby an accusing glare. "You think I hooked up with a professor?"

"Of course not, but …"

Kayla rubbed the bridge of her nose. "I'm sorry. I'm sorry I snapped. This is awkward. It's bad enough I hooked up with a guy I barely know. Talking about it is more than a little embarrassing."

"If you think you're the only girl on this campus—in this apartment—who's hooked up before, you're wrong," Reagan said. "What you're going through now could have happened to any of us."

The weight of her statement settled in the room like an unwanted visitor. After a lengthy pause, Emily's quiet voice rose above the clamor of introspection. "I thought I was pregnant last spring. My period was late. It scared me to death even though it was Dylan."

Yeah, it could have been Emily. It should have been Emily.

But it wasn't. "This is different. I'm not pregnant by my boyfriend and future husband."

"So ..." Shelby sat on the floor. "Who is this guy? Can you trust him? Have you seen him since you ... ?"

"Hooked up? No. I thought he'd call. We had fun. I thought we had a connection. I was being stupid—again—about boys. I'll never learn. Ha. Maybe now I will."

"How well do you know him?" Emily asked.

"He was in one of my classes freshman year. We'd see each other out sometimes and we'd flirt. We kissed once. Before. I've always had a thing for him."

"Ben Strickland." Reagan's brows furrowed and she pinched her lips. "That name sounds familiar."

"He's pre-law." At least that's what he'd told her. "You may have had a class with him."

Reagan narrowed her eyes. "Tall, floppy brown hair, bedroom eyes, preppy hunting style?"

Before Kayla could answer, Shelby rolled her eyes. "You just described half the guys on ASU's campus."

Half the guys? Maybe. Ben Strickland. Absolutely. "That's him."

"Do you want us to go with you when you tell him?" Emily asked.

Kayla stared at the carpet. Her face boiled. She lifted her shoulders as much as she could, given the cloak of shame weighing her down. "I don't even know how to get in touch with him."

"Where did you see him?" Emily asked. "Where did you ... ya know."

"I went out with some sorority friends and ran into him at a bar. We went to The Cow Bell to get something to eat, and then we drove around talking. We ended up at the river." She squeezed her eyes shut, as if that could shut out the memory. Glossing over the sordid nature of their time together was like putting lipstick on a pig. Underneath the pretty shimmer, she was still a pig. And so was he. "We did it in his car. He drove me home after." She lifted her eyes, saw the pity on her roommates faces, and let them fall. While face down at rock bottom, she may as well come clean. "I foolishly acted on a longstanding and obviously unrequited crush. I thought I'd see him again."

"Of course you did." Emily said it fast—too fast to sound anything but sincere. Her fellow cheerleader always had her pom-poms at the ready. "You're awesome. Why wouldn't he call."

"Because he's a guy." Shelby used her don't-mess-with-me voice, the voice that held her legions of admirers at bay. "A selfish jerk who used Kayla and tossed her aside when he was done."

"Okay." Reagan, always the litigator, held her hands in the air. "Making assumptions about this guy doesn't help Kayla."

"Who's making assumptions?" Shelby crossed her arms. "I'm stating the obvious."

"Stop," Kayla said. "Just stop. Jerk or not, he deserves to know." Bashing Ben was as useless as bashing herself. What was done was done. She looked at Reagan while smoothing the lines in her forehead. "Do you have any idea where he lives or how I can find him?"

"No, but I think Dash's keyboard player is in his fraternity."

"Don't tell him why, okay?"

"Of course I won't. But … if Dash asks me why I'm looking for some guy in Jacob's fraternity, I'm not going to lie."

Of course Reagan wouldn't lie to Dash. Dash would know before the end of the day, and so would Dylan. Thank heavens Shelby remained blissfully unattached, or the whole campus would know. “I don’t expect you to lie. I know you’re going to tell Dash, and Em, I know you’re going to tell Dylan. But please ask them not to say anything. If this gets out …”

“Dash won’t say anything,” Reagan said.

Emily put her hand on her heart. “I promise. Dylan won’t say a word.”

Kayla, swamped with love and gratitude, nodded at her friends. They were there for her like she knew—hoped—they would be. “Thanks. I don’t know what I’m going to do, but I know I won’t get through it without you.”

“Have you told your parents?” Shelby squinted her eyes and chomped her bottom lip as if in pain.

Kayla pictured their faces—her mom’s quivering lips, her dad’s rigid jaw, her brother’s disgusted flinch—and choked. “Uh, no. I can’t even think about that until I tell Ben and we’ve made some plans. They’re going to be horrified.”

Reagan squashed Kayla into a bone-crushing hug before pulling back and gripping her shoulders. “One step at a time, okay? Let’s find Ben. You can deal with the rest later.”

Chapter Three

Ben glanced around his apartment and found his phone on the kitchen table under a notepad. He answered the squawking duck on the third ring. "Hey, Mama."

"Hey, Benji. How's it going?"

"It's good." He lifted his backpack onto the chair. "Busy."

"You ready for finals?"

"Getting there." He gathered his notes and shoved books into his backpack before zipping it closed. "I'm about to grab some food on the way to the library."

"I won't keep you, honey, but I wanted to let you know Darcy will be in town this weekend."

Ben rolled his eyes. His ma kept pushing him to officially get back together with Darcy. Although they'd broken up freshman year when they'd gone to different colleges, they were still a couple in every way that counted. Everyone—his parents, Darcy, her parents—still thought of them as a couple. It was only a matter of logistics. "That's nice. Give her my best."

"No, silly. She's going to be at Addison State."

His stomach glazed with ice. "Here? It's the weekend before finals." And why hadn't she given him a heads-up?

"You know Southeastern State gets out early for Christmas. She's visiting friends and I told her to give you a call. Last time we talked, you didn't have a date for your spring formal."

"Mama …"

"Do you think you can do better than the runner-up in the Miss Georgia pageant? Someone who's been more than loyal to this family?"

Ah, there it was. The nudge that was more like a shove. "Thanks for the vote of confidence."

"You know what I mean. She's gorgeous, she's still single, and she's still interested in you. Why you aren't falling all over yourself to get her back is a mystery."

He wasn't tripping all over himself because they'd never really stopped seeing each other. Sure, she'd taken a few guys to formals at SE State when he couldn't get away, and he'd done the same at ASU, but their dates were placeholders. With everything that hung between them, they both assumed he'd propose at the end of college.

"Spring formal is months from now. I spend all my time studying for finals and the LSAT. I haven't had time to think about spring formal." And he could find his own date. Spending his life with Darcy was pretty much written in stone. Did he have to spend his senior formal with her, too?

"Honey, I shouldn't have to remind you everything the Kellers have done for this family. And if the rumors are true, Henry Keller is on the governor's short list to replace Judge

Milford. Bless his heart, he's got cancer. Having a judge in the family would be quite a coup for your law career."

Like he needed reminding. Ben cleared the grit from his throat. "You're jumping the gun a little."

"It's not like I'm asking you to go out with some random girl. You and Darcy dated for three years. I still don't understand why you broke up."

They broke up because being with Darcy felt like an arranged marriage—and every moment he spent talking to his ma confirmed it. "We broke up because we were at different schools and we both wanted to see other people." Even though that never really happened. Being together was a harder habit to break than swearing.

"What people? You haven't dated anyone seriously since Darcy."

It was easier to keep things going with Darcy than face the wrath from his family. Besides, falling for someone other than Darcy wasn't exactly an option. Half his high school friends went to SE State. If he traveled to see his friends and hooked up with Darcy on a regular basis, what did it hurt? His parents were hardly going to object.

"Mama, I gotta go study. I love you. Do me a favor and let me handle my love life."

"Fine, but you know as well as I do, she's the perfect girl for you."

Ben scrunched his face and bit his lips until each tooth left an impression. Maybe three more years away from his hometown wasn't such a bad plan after all. "There is no such thing as the perfect girl. Trust me, I've looked."

"Joke all you want, but you'd better scoop that girl up before it's too late."

Ben stared at the wall and imagined working alongside his dad and spending weekends at the club with his parents and in-laws. He shook the thoughts from his brain and tugged at the collar of his too-tight shirt. Scoop her up, or tie them both to a predictably boring life?

Kayla put the finishing touches on her makeup as Reagan peeked her head into the bathroom. "Are you sure you don't want us to go with you?"

"I'm sure." Kayla capped her lipstick with unsteady fingers and stared at her reflection in the mirror. If she had to face Ben, she'd do it looking her best. Or the best she could muster under the circumstances. Despite the makeup she'd meticulously applied, she looked like a waxed version of herself—vapid and vacant. She could barely swallow through the cotton in her mouth. Her stomach felt as if it had been shoved through a wood-chipper. Twice. She had to focus on putting one foot in front of the other to leave her bathroom.

Kayla's roommates had been more than supportive since she'd told them her secret. They were driving her crazy. Asking if she was okay every five minutes, tiptoeing around her as if she were a porcelain doll, treating her as if any moment she would break down and cry. If one of them gave her another sympathetic shoulder squeeze, she was going to scream. And did they really think it was a good idea for all four of them to show up at Ben's doorstep to announce her pregnancy?

"I need to do this myself." She pushed past Reagan and gathered her coat.

She felt bad enough about confronting Ben at home. Reagan

had secured Ben's address in two maddeningly short days, and now she had to face him—her one-night stand—and tell him his life was about to change forever.

The timing couldn't have been worse. The weekend before finals had everyone vying for a spot in the library and surviving on caffeine and protein bars. She'd be lucky to catch Ben at his apartment—a small complex a mile away—but she had to try. If he wasn't home, she'd bring her studies and wait in the parking lot for him to return. She refused to let the sun rise again before spilling the news. If she waited much longer, she risked him leaving town for Christmas. As hard as it would be to show up on his doorstep, it would be a hundred times worse to do so at his parents' house.

When she turned to leave, each roommate greeted her in the hallway.

Reagan opened her arms for a hug. "I'm praying for you," she said, passing her off to Emily.

"You look pretty," Emily said. "You got this."

Shelby's brow furrowed. "No matter what his reaction, you're not alone." With a final squeeze, they ushered her out the door.

Descending the stairs, she dissected their words. If she had this, as Emily said, she wouldn't need Reagan's prayers. If she looked pretty, why did she feel as if she was about to puke? If she weren't alone, how come she'd never felt more alone in her life? Kayla shook her head clear.

If she were going to get through this, she had to take one step at a time—literally. She got into the car, placed her backpack on the passenger seat, and started the engine. She took a left onto the road heading away from campus and rounded two bends before signaling a right turn into Ben's complex.

Not three minutes after leaving her apartment, she located

his building and parked across from six matching navy doors. Ben lived in the bottom middle unit. Three minutes from her apartment. She tried to blink away the sting of shame. He passed her apartment every day on his way to class. Every. Single. Day.

Kayla couldn't give her emotions an inch of space to thrive. She had to stifle every tear, shove the hurt and embarrassment aside, and focus on the facts. She was pregnant. He was the father. They needed to talk. She inhaled a deep breath, let it out with a groan, and exited the car before she chickened out.

Kayla's stride felt stiff and awkward as she crept up the narrow walkway and swayed when her toes brushed a worn welcome mat. She inhaled, mustering courage, and rapped on his door. Her heart thundered in her chest and the vibration had her fidgeting from foot to foot. She pinched her cold fingers into fists. Seconds passed. A blackbird's shrill squeal sliced through the silence. She knocked again. Her knock went unanswered.

Kayla dropped her head and sighed, her lungs deflating like an air mattress under the weight of an ASU lineman. A hearty brew of relief and impatience propelled her back to her car to wait. No matter what, she was telling Ben tonight.

Chapter Four

Ben snuck a glance at his watch and cringed. Quarter past seven, and he and Darcy were still waiting on their food to arrive. At the rate they were going, he'd be up all night. Fantastic.

"Everything okay?" Darcy placed her hand on his arm. Her silver nail polish sparkled in the muted light of the restaurant.

"How long does it take to make a couple of pasta dishes?" He blew out a breath. "I knew we shouldn't have come here."

Darcy flipped her hair behind her shoulder and gave him a practiced look of appeasement. "I'm sure it won't be long. It's a Saturday night. They're busy."

Which is exactly why he'd suggested the sandwich shop around the corner from campus. His plan was to grab a quick bite before he dropped her wherever she wanted to go and headed to the library. In typical Darcy fashion, she gave him some sob story about craving chicken parmesan. As usual, he'd caved because he didn't want to listen to her whine. Would he ever learn? He scanned the restaurant for their waiter. "Why didn't you tell me you were coming this weekend?"

"Because I knew you'd tell me not to come."

Ben drummed his fingers on the table and didn't try to hide his frustration. How could someone so aware of her priorities care so little for his? At times like this, she reminded him of rainbow candies, pretty on the outside but sour in the middle.

"Oh, come on. Stop being such a stick-in-the-mud. I missed you. I wanted to see you." She kicked her lips to the side and raised her brows. "Didn't you want to see me?"

"I'll be home in a week."

"Yes, but we can't sleep together next week—or any week we're home."

Ben choked on his water, coughing into his fist. "Darcy, we've been sleeping together for years."

"We've been having sex for years. We can only sleep together at school."

"There'll be no sleeping together tonight. I've got to study."

"All night?"

"Since you insisted on coming to the world's slowest restaurant, yes."

She huffed out a breath and rolled her eyes. A few silent minutes later, their food finally arrived. When the waiter walked off, she picked up her fork and knife. "Fine. Go study. I guess I'll just entertain myself." She cut a bite and slid it between her teeth. "In your bed." She chewed and swallowed. "Alone."

"Darcy ..."

"What?"

Ben took a bite of his lasagna, the steaming pasta burning

the roof of his mouth. He gulped water and crunched the ice. “That should have come with a warning.”

“Poor baby.” Darcy leaned across the table and licked her lips like a snake ready to strike. “You want me to kiss it and make it better?”

“No.” He set his glass down and glared at her. He was done playing games. “I want you to eat so we can get out of here. I’ve got to study.”

“You’re no fun.” She buttered a piece of bread. “If I’d known you were going to be this grumpy, I wouldn’t have come to see you.”

“If you’d called, I’d have told you not to come.”

He cursed himself when she set her bread down and crossed her arms over her chest. At the rate she was eating, it’d be midnight before he got to the library. “You don’t have to be mean.”

“I’m sorry, Darc. I’m stressed out, okay? Because of the LSAT, I’ve let my classes slide. I’m in danger of blowing my finals if I don’t spend some time with the books.”

“Fine. That’s all you had to say.”

Ben grit his teeth and bit back a sarcastic retort. That’s all he’d been saying since she arrived on his doorstep, complaining because her girlfriends had to study and couldn’t hang out. If he didn’t calm her down soon, she’d make a scene and he’d spend all night soothing her and getting nothing done. “My lasagna’s hot, but it’s good. How’s you chicken parm?”

She glanced at her plate as if seeing it for the first time and wrinkled her nose. “It’s okay.”

Perfect. Ben shoved his hand in the air to wave down the waiter. If her food was only okay, she wouldn’t mind boxing it up and eating it cold.

The sound of a car door slamming startled Kayla awake. She jerked upright and blinked her eyes, lifting her hand to her cricked neck muscle and massaged the stinging knot. She glanced out the windshield into the inky black of night. When had it gotten so dark? And when had she fallen asleep? She gathered the notes from her lap and placed them in the passenger seat. Her stomach slid to the floorboard when she recognized the car pulled in front of Ben's apartment as the car in which she and Ben had created a life.

Ben emerged from the sporty sedan looking as handsome as ever, wearing jeans and a vest over a button-down. He shook the windblown hair out of his eyes and hightailed it around the hood to open the passenger door.

Kayla bit back bile as a girl unfolded from the car and reached for Ben's hand in one fluid motion. When they passed in under the street light, Kayla noted their linked fingers a second before scanning the girl's face. She was gorgeous—Shelby Zurlo gorgeous, all dark hair and long legs. She strode confidently next to Ben before they disappeared into the bottom middle apartment.

From the way they touched to the way they walked, it was clear this wasn't a first date, or the awkward beginning of a new relationship. They were a duo—an Ashton Kutcher and Mila Kunis, a Will Smith and Jada Pinkett-Smith, a Tim McGraw and Faith Hill kind of couple. Brilliantly shiny, oozing intimacy, a power couple for Generation Z. Tears welled in Kayla's eyes, blurring her vision.

She'd never considered he'd have a girlfriend. Not once.

She felt ten shades a fool for being so naïve. Of course he had a girlfriend. No wonder he never called or stopped by or made any attempt to see her.

All this time she thought she'd said something wrong or not been pretty or smart enough to warrant another meeting. Even though they'd spent the better part of the night talking and laughing. What an idiot she'd been to believe they'd made a connection that night that might carry them through the most devastating news of their lives. Just the brief glimpse she'd caught of Ben and his girlfriend confirmed she had more than his shock and disbelief to deal with. There was also a longstanding relationship that trumped their one-night mistake.

Shame stained her resolve. Her throat cinched tight as a fist. No matter how broken she felt, if she didn't calm down and get some air into her lungs, she was going to pass out. Lightheaded with fear, she took panting breaths, squeezing air in and out of her lungs until the dizziness subsided and her pulse calmed.

Kayla closed her eyes and took stock. Finding out about his girlfriend was the swan song of a one-two punch that left her reeling, but it didn't change the facts. She was still pregnant. Ben was still the father. Girlfriend or not, they had decisions to make.

Chapter Five

Ben refused to feel guilty. Just because Darcy showed up unannounced and demanded his attention at the worst possible time, just because he snubbed her seduction and she'd stormed out, didn't mean he was to blame. Sure, he'd pay for it later. And pay dearly. But for now, the only thing that mattered were his finals and the ticking clock on the wall.

Desperate not to waste a moment, he'd forgone the library and decided to study at home. His roommate was gone, Darcy was on her way home, and who knew how long it would take him to find a parking spot on campus. He'd just settled at his kitchen table with his laptop and notes when there was a knock on his door.

Ben rolled his eyes and stewed. Couldn't she leave well enough alone? He stalked to the entrance and wrenched the door open. "Darcy, I told you—"

But it wasn't Darcy standing on his welcome mat whining for him to let her in, but the startled face of a pleasant memory. "Kayla? What are you …"? He looked over her shoulder into the shadowy stillness of the parking lot and the empty space where Darcy's convertible recently sat. "What are you doing here?"

"Hi, Ben."

Her breathy high-pitched voice had memories flooding his brain. The lushness of her lips, the raspberry scent of her skin, the faint taste of onion rings, the minty gum she'd chewed after eating. All the times he'd scanned campus for a glimpse of her forbidden fruit, and here she stood on his doorstep, wringing her hands and blinking her pretty blue eyes. "Hi."

"Can I come in?"

"Uh … sure." He took a step in retreat and held the door open wide. When she entered, the scent of raspberry cream filled his nose. His pulse spiked. He closed the door and turned to face her, his tongue coated with unease. He'd wondered if what happened between them that November night was a figment of his imagination. But here she stood in his apartment, petite and blonde, like a sexy little fairy in her jeans, boots, and a furry black jacket. He'd always liked the open way she smiled with her whole body and her penchant for casual touches. But she wasn't smiling or touching him now. "Can I get you something to drink?"

She sputtered a nervous laugh. "No, thank you. But, would you mind if I used your bathroom?"

"Uh … sure. It's …" She scrambled down the narrow hall before he could get the words out. "Down there, first door on the left."

"Thanks."

As soon as the door closed behind her, Ben closed his eyes. What in the world was she doing here? He couldn't wrap his mind around the strange turn of events. First Darcy, now Kayla. Thank goodness Darcy left before Kayla knocked on his door. How would he have explained that one? And how did he explain her showing up weeks after they'd shared an unforgettable night together? What could she possibly want from him now, the weekend before finals? He—they—should be studying.

Kayla emerged from the hallway, her shoulders back, her chin lifted. When she stopped a few feet from him, he noted her glassy eyes and pale skin.

"I'm sorry to barge in on you like this."

"No, it's …" Weird. Unexpected. Confounding. "It's fine."

"I wouldn't have come. I know it's a busy weekend, and you've got a mountain of studying to do before finals, but …" She took a deep breath and let it out through her nose. "I need to tell you something."

Ben had one of those out of body experiences, like a slow-motion video of a bullet hurling toward its target. Whatever she'd come to tell him would blast through him and leave a path of carnage in its wake. He could tell from the way her breath caught, her lips shook, her eyes blinked furiously. He swallowed. His muscles tensed for impact.

"I'm pregnant."

Her words slammed against his solar plexus, each distinct syllable vibrated between his ears, but he could only stare. She was pregnant. Kayla's pregnant. Kayla was having a baby. "I … that's …"

"It's yours." Kayla obviously mistook his lack of articulation for confusion over why she'd tell him this very personal thing about herself.

"We … used a condom. Right?" He remembered fumbling through the glove box in search of something—anything—that would allow him access to her sweet offering. He'd found it behind a stack of fast food napkins and a disposable razor. Lord only knew how long it had been in there.

"We did."

"But you're pregnant?"

"Yes."

"You're sure?"

"Yes."

"And it's mine."

"Yes."

"I …" He shook his head, tried to clear the molasses from his brain. "I don't understand."

"Look …" She clasped her hands in front of her as if in prayer.

Yes. They should pray. Pray this was some kind of joke.

"I know this is a shock," she said, her eyes huge. "I was shocked, too. I'm still shocked, and I've known for a few days." She spoke quickly—too quickly—as if she had to get it off her chest before she exploded.

"How … how do you know? How did you find out?"

"I felt off, tired and cranky. I thought maybe it was mono until I realized my period was late."

"Have you seen a doctor?" he asked.

"Not yet."

He grasped that lifeline and clung with hands and feet and teeth. "So you're not sure?"

"I'm sure, Ben. I took a test. I took another test yesterday to confirm."

"But if you haven't seen a doctor …"

"The doctor does a pee test. I took two pee tests and they both say I'm pregnant." She stepped closer and he retreated. "I never would have come here and told you if I weren't absolutely sure."

He whirled around and stalked into the kitchen. She wasn't freaking out. Why wasn't she freaking out? Pregnant? With a baby—his baby? There had to be some kind of mistake.

He was Ben Strickland, second-born son of Wade and Anna Strickland and future attorney. God knew he wasn't perfect, but none of his silly, immature, irresponsible antics had ever caught up with him before. Why now, when his entire future lay in the balance?

This couldn't be happening. There, on the table, sat his laptop and notes—the most important, most pressing issue in his life until he'd opened the door to Kayla. He needed to study. He had to study, or he was in jeopardy of failing two required classes for his degree. If he didn't pass, he wouldn't graduate on time, he wouldn't pass the LSAT, and he wouldn't start law school in the fall. His plans, his carefully laid plans, plans he'd recently begun to question, seemed the only safe place to land.

"I have to study," he said to himself before turning around to find her steps behind. The dazed look on her face, as if he'd slapped her, almost pierced his resolve. "I can't think about this until after finals. I can't. I just can't."

Kayla took another big breath before letting it out. Her shoulders drooped and she watched him with sad wary eyes. "Okay ..."

"Give me a week." He rubbed his temple and tried to think. "Give me a week to get through finals and then we'll figure this out. We'll talk all of this out. Okay?"

Kayla weaved where she stood, her face slack, before bracing herself against the wall. "Ben, I know this is hard to wrap your head around. Trust me, I know. But we don't have a lot of time.

We need to talk about this. We need to make some decisions."

The pressure built in his chest as if his pectoral muscles were being sandwiched between the jagged claws of a metal vise. He glanced at the clock on the wall. He didn't have time nor the bandwidth to make decisions. He barely had a second to spare with his first final in fewer than twelve hours. "I know, and we will. After finals. You have to study, and so do I. Let's get through this week before we try to tackle anything else."

Kayla's expression went slack and she glanced away. When her eyes met his, he felt as if she looked straight into his soul and found him lacking. She wouldn't be the first. "Fine. If that's what you need, I'll give you a week."

He nodded. Ben couldn't think about her right now. He could barely look her in the eye. All he could think about was himself and how he'd get out of this mess before anyone found out and ruined his reputation and his future.

When he said nothing, Kayla sighed. "I need your number."

"What?"

A flush stained her cheeks. She cleared her throat. "We need to exchange phone numbers."

"Oh, yeah, right." He picked up his phone and opened his contacts with shaking fingers. Little wonder, since his frenzied blood jackhammered through his veins. He entered the number she recited and hit call as a way to share his number with her.

She created a new contact for him—probably labeled "jerk" or "loser"—and tucked her phone into her coat pocket. "I'll be in touch." She scanned the table, his kitchen, his face before turning to leave. He watched her open the door, close it, and fisted his hands in his hair. A baby? What in the world was he supposed to do now?

Chapter Six

Every step Kayla took felt like schlepping through sludge. The sludge of streets slick from a passing shower. The schlep up the slippery steps to her apartment. Schlepping the key into the lock. Schlepping the door open.

"Are you okay?" Reagan didn't schlep. She bounced off the couch with a puppy's excitement. "You've been gone so long." She wrapped Kayla in a hug and pulled her to the couch where she could finally schlep into softness.

"Fine, I guess." Kayla pulled a throw pillow into her arms and cradled it like she would a baby. Her baby? "Reagan, it was awful."

"How?" Shelby came from her room.

"What happened?" Emily trailed close behind. Any other time, it would be a typical Saturday night gab session. Who hooked up with who, who drank too much, who wanted chocolate chip cookies. Now it was all about her. Kayla. Single mother to-be.

"He needs some time." She kicked off her boots. "He asked me to give him a week to get through finals."

"Give him time?" Reagan asked. "Does he think the baby will stop growing to meet his schedule?"

Shelby scoffed. "What a jerk."

Emily grabbed a throw from the back of the couch and draped it over Kayla's legs, piercing Shelby with a pointed glare. "Kayla, you look exhausted. Can I make you a cup of tea?"

At that, Kayla rammed her knees to her chest and burst into tears.

"Oh, honey." Emily rubbed her back.

"It's going to be okay," Reagan said.

Shelby knelt at her feet and wrapped her hands around Kayla's socked feet. "We're here for you, sweetie."

Kayla cried harder at their kind words, burying her face into the pillow. How could they be so nice, so supportive, when the only person who could truly share her burden practically threw her out of his apartment because he needed time to study?

"I'm sorry." She hiccuped and wiped her cheeks. "It's not you. I'm tired. Just tired. Tired of being tired." She grabbed the tissue Reagan offered and wiped her nose. "He just stood there and looked at me like I'd sprouted another head." She blew her nose.

"He's being a guy," Shelby said.

"I can't really blame him," Kayla said. "I showed up on his doorstep and sprung it on him without warning."

"How were you supposed to warn him?" Reagan asked. "You didn't have any way to contact him."

"It doesn't matter. He knows now. I guess we'll figure it out after finals." Except a few more days sounded like torture. She thought she'd feel relieved after she told him. Instead, she felt numb. Numb and ashamed. "Oh, and the best part? He's got a girlfriend."

"He told you?" Emily asked. "After you said you were pregnant?"

"I saw them. He wasn't home when I got there, so I sat in my car and studied until I fell asleep. When I woke up, they were walking to his apartment, hand in hand."

Her roommates exchanged worried glances.

"That's his problem," Shelby said. "Not yours."

"Was she there?" Emily asked, her voice quiet. Kayla knew Emily was playing out a different version of the scene in her head, with someone showing up on Dylan's doorstep with similar news. "When you told him."

"No. I waited until she left." Kayla covered her face with her hands and tried to rub away the sting of shame. "I don't know what I expected him to do or to say, but I never expected him to blow me off the way he did. I mean, really? He's going to sit down and study now that he knows I'm pregnant? Who does that?"

"A slimeball," Shelby said. "A class-A slimeball."

Reagan sneered at Shelby before sitting beside Kayla. "He may be a slimeball. He may be in shock. He probably needs some time to process the news—just like you did."

"I know." She stretched her legs out and sighed. "I can't believe I slept with someone's boyfriend."

"You didn't know," Shelby said. "That's on him. It's not like he brought her up when you were together, right?"

"Of course he didn't, but that doesn't make me feel any better." She glanced at Emily. "How would you feel if some girl turned up pregnant with Dylan's baby?" Kayla turned her head to stare at Reagan. "Or Dash?"

Emily flinched and clutched her neck. "I'd probably punch him and then … I don't know. I honestly don't know what I'd do."

Reagan patted Kayla's leg. "You don't need to think about her right now. She can't be your concern."

"She wouldn't be if I hadn't seen them together, the way they were with each other. It wasn't a new relationship."

"How do you know?" Shelby asked.

Kayla jerked her head at Emily before answering Shelby. "You know how Emily and Dylan look when they're together? You know how it's different than the way Reagan and Dash look?"

Shelby nodded. "Yeah."

"What do you mean?" Reagan asked. "How do Dash and I look?"

"You look sweet—kind of starry-eyed and new. A little careful with each other."

Emily folded her arms across her chest. "Do Dylan and I look like an old married couple?"

"No. You look comfortable and in tune. Like a unit. Anyone who sees you knows you're together."

"Aww." Emily sighed. "I like that."

"I didn't think it was possible to feel worse than I did before telling him, but now I do. Now I feel like a homewrecker."

"The only homewrecker in this scenario is Ben," Shelby said. "He's the one who slept with you and conveniently forgot to mention his girlfriend." She tapped Kayla's leg before getting to her feet. "Let him sit with this for a week. It sounds like the punishment he deserves."

Kayla was grateful for her roommates' support, even if it did feel a little mean-spirited. When she thought of Ben—dazed, confused, and alone in his apartment—she shivered. He probably leaned on his girlfriend when life turned upside down.

Now Kayla had dumped the biggest problem of his life on his doorstep, and he might not have someone who'd listen.

Her roommates went back to studying. Kayla opened her backpack to try and do the same, but couldn't focus on her notes. Defying logic, she could only stare at the wall and pity the boy who'd knocked her up.

Chapter Seven

Ben's temple quivered. He ran his tongue along his teeth, swallowing the saliva pooling in his mouth, and fluttered his eyes. He shifted, wincing at the pain radiating from his collarbone to his skull, and blinked against the sun streaming through the kitchen blinds. Lifting his head, Ben rubbed the throb in his neck and stared at the notes scattered across the table.

His phone vibrated with an incoming text. He'd missed two messages from Darcy. The first was from three hours ago.

I made it home safe. Thanks for checking.

The second only moments ago.

Your mom's taking me to brunch today to make up for your behavior.

Ben dropped the phone and rolled his aching shoulders, tasting acid and cursing Darcy for acting like a spoiled baby. His body went rigid. The events of the night before slammed into him like high-speed train.

A baby.

Dread leeched from his pores, ice-cold liquid trickling through his veins and pooling at the base of his gut. What in the world was he going to do?

Footsteps sounded, and Ben glanced over his shoulder. His roommate and best friend entered the kitchen.

"You finally up?" Theo asked. "I didn't know if I should wake you or let you sleep."

"What time did you get home?"

"Around three. You were out cold."

Great. Just great. He'd laid his head down just before one. That meant he'd gotten maybe two hours of studying under his belt before he'd passed out cold.

Theo filled the coffee carafe with water and set the machine to brew. "I thought you were going to the library."

"I was, but Darcy wanted Grego's and it took forever."

Theo shook his head before pulling a mug from the cabinet. "When are you going to stop letting that girl dictate your life?"

Probably never. After what he'd just learned, he'd be kissing her butt from now until the end of time—if she let him. "Maybe I need to fail a class or two to get her attention."

"Your dad would love that. 'I'm sorry, Dad.'" Theo pitched his voice at Ben's baritone. "'I only did it so Darcy would learn her lesson.'" Theo chuckled at his impression. "Can I be a fly on the wall when you have that conversation?"

Ben scrubbed his hands over his face. "Why don't you be a true friend and have that conversation for me?"

"No way. Your dad scares me. I would have been a true friend and told Darcy to buzz off and let you study if I'd been here when she arrived." Theo poured a cup and sat down at the table. "Are you hungover? You look like crap."

"I wish."

Theo's forehead crinkled. "You wish you were hungover? That's a new one."

"Listen, Theo." Ben cleared the panic from his voice. "I gotta tell you something."

"Why are you whispering?"

"I don't know." Ben shook his head and scrubbed his palms against his cheeks, tried to warm his brain and kick his head into gear. "You can't tell anyone what I'm about to tell you."

"Okay, but make it quick. I'm meeting a study group at ten."

"I'm serious."

"Fine. I won't say anything. What's the big secret?"

"Do you remember back in the fall when I stayed out all night? You kept razzing me, asking who I was with, and I told you I passed out at the frat house?"

"Yeah. You were lying."

Ben nodded. "I was with someone."

Theo narrowed his eyes. "I knew it. You can't lie worth a crap."

"The girl, the one I was with, she showed up here last night and … she's pregnant."

Theo's jaw dropped and his eyes rounded into over-inflated basketballs. "Pregnant? It's yours?"

Ben glanced away. Theo's shock felt like a presence in the room, a live performance version of Ben's inner turmoil. His disbelief had turned to panic sometime before he fell asleep, and this morning it had morphed into a gaping cavern of fear. "What am I going to do?"

"Holy crap, dude. What did Darcy say?"

"She wasn't here. She got mad I blew her off after dinner and she went home. Thank heavens."

"What are you going to do?" Theo asked.

"I don't know." Ben shot up from the table and stomped to the window, squinting at the too-bright morning. The magnolia tree outside his apartment stood guard in the grassy area behind the building as it always had. Rubbery leaves fluttered and spiraled onto the lawn, propelled by a passing gust of wind. How could it look like a normal December day when everything in his life had turned upside down? He ran his hands through his hair and pivoted to stalk around the kitchen. "How could this happen?"

Theo followed him with bemused eyes. "If you don't understand how girls get pregnant, I think I found the problem."

Ben halted, thrusting his hands on his hips. "We were careful. I used a condom. And aren't most girls on the pill?"

"That might have a been a good question to ask before you hooked up." Theo sighed and splayed his hands on the table. "What did she say? Your … hookup?"

Ben cringed. He'd always prided himself on not being one of those guys who saw every girl as a conquest. With one impulsive move, he'd become a statistic. "She said we need to talk and make some decisions."

Theo blew out a breath. "Sounds like she's open to making this go away."

Ben dropped his arms and glared at his friend. An cold shiver ran up his spine. "You mean an abortion?"

"How else would a baby go away?"

Could she really go through with that? Could he? Ben slumped into the chair, digging his fingers into his disheveled hair. "I don't know, man. That doesn't sit too well."

"How does being a daddy sit? Because if she doesn't get an

abortion, you're going to be a daddy in a few months."

"I feel sick." He closed his eyes and prayed he was having a nightmare, but when he opened them again, Theo still sat gawking at him like he'd stripped. "I don't think my parents know me and Darcy have sex. How am I supposed to tell them I got some random girl pregnant?"

"You might not have to tell them—if she's willing to have an abortion."

"Stop saying the word abortion!"

"Dude." Theo leaned across the table and fisted Ben's wrist. "If you can't hear the word, then you'd better think about what it would be like to have a baby. A baby that's going to grow into a toddler, a kid, a teenager, and an adult. All the while, you're going to have to deal with this girl for the rest of your life—and I'm not even talking about marriage. Are you willing to do that? Because having this baby means a lifelong commitment to someone who's a virtual stranger. It probably means no law school. After everything you've been through to achieve that dream, are you seriously willing to give it up for one stupid mistake?"

Ben folded into himself, pelted by Theo's litany of Ben's mistakes and the ripple effects he'd yet to digest. Was he willing or able to take on the responsibility for a life when his careened toward disaster? "I don't know."

"You'd better figure it out."

Theo stood and squeezed Ben's shoulder before making a to-go cup of coffee.

Ben watched him, envied his immunity from overbearing parents and idiotic mistakes. "Hey, Theo?"

Theo paused on his way down the hall. "Yeah?"

"What would you do?"

Theo blew out a breath, considered him with sober eyes. "I'd talk to the girl and see what she's thinking. And I'd think long and hard about the options."

Chapter Eight

Kayla slogged through the motions of daily life. Crawling out of bed early, crawling into bed late, the hours in between spent with her nose in a book or taking an exam, all the while trying her best to avoid the life growing inside her as it clamored for attention, beckoning her to stop and give in to the lustful lure of sleep. The incessant queasiness that lurked beneath the surface repeatedly warred against her vertigo.

Every day her pregnancy got trickier to ignore. She kept crackers in her backpack to stave off the nausea, sipped ginger ale from a tumbler, and lumbered along with the weight of the world on her shoulders. Friends noted her lack of pep, asked if she were sick, and wrote it off as exam fatigue. It got harder and harder to paste a smile on her face and brush away their concern and her mounting fear.

Three days had passed without a peep from Ben. Seventy-two

agonizing hours of silence. If he were able to push her pregnancy aside and focus on studying, she envied his concentration. As it stood, she'd be lucky to hold onto the grades she'd gone into finals with and likely dropped a letter or two.

She couldn't bring herself to care. She'd still pass, no matter how poorly she performed on her exams. With one exam left, her mind and her conscience had more pressing issues to process.

When would she hear from Ben?

What would he say?

How would they proceed?

Lying on her bed, her laptop and notes scattered on the floor, her mind drifted to the future. With or without Ben, her options were few: have the baby and keep it, have the baby and give it up for adoption, or have an abortion. Each option gave her nightmares.

Kayla couldn't picture her life if she chose to keep the baby. Giving it up for adoption was the responsible thing to do, but that meant carrying and delivering a baby only to give it away. Abortion seemed the path of least resistance. Ben would certainly approve—then his girlfriend wouldn't have to know, and he could go on living his life as planned. But every time she contemplated making an appointment, her spine tingled, and her nerve endings fired as if flashing a neon warning sign. Could she end an innocent life simply because its existence was inconvenient to all involved?

Kayla rolled over and clutched a stuffed animal to her chest, folding her body into the fetal position. Could the baby hear her thoughts? Did it know she considered ending its life? Would the baby forgive her? Would she forgive herself?

A knock at her door had her sitting upright, her head

spinning, her stomach listing like after a tilt-a-whirl ride. "Come in."

Shelby appeared in the entryway, nibbling her bottom lip before meeting Kayla's eyes. "Ben's here."

Kayla fisted the comforter. Her pulse thrashed against her ribcage like a fuel-infused slingshot. She swung her feet to the floor, sucking air into her ice-crusted lungs. Ben was here. In her apartment. It was time to face her future.

Shelby hurried inside and shut the door, kneeling at Kayla's feet, her eyes huge. "Listen, I'm the only one here and I can leave if you want me to."

"I don't know …"

"I can stay in my room if it helps knowing you're not alone. Do you want to be alone with him?"

Did she? Would it be easier to face him knowing one of her best friends was steps away, or would that stilt their conversation? "I'm not afraid to be alone with him, if that's what you're asking."

"I'm asking what you want because I'll do whatever you want me to do to help make this easier for you."

Tears threatened and Kayla blinked them away. She wouldn't cry. She couldn't. The time for tears had passed. "I think we need to talk on our own. Are you sure you don't mind leaving?"

"Of course not. But I won't go far. If you need me when he leaves, you just say the word. In fact, I won't come back until I hear from you, okay? I'll text the others and give them a heads-up. No one will interrupt until you say so."

"Okay." Kayla exhaled. "Okay. Thank you."

Shelby stood and crushed Kayla in a hug. The ice in her lungs began to clatter. "You can do this. Talk to him. Be honest. Don't let him push you around."

"I won't. I promise."

"I'm a phone call away." Shelby slipped into the hallway and shut the door.

Kayla eased off the bed and shuffled to the door. She tortured herself by pausing in front of the full-length mirror, grimacing at her pale puffy cheeks, dull eyes, and rumpled clothes. The vain, immature part of her wanted to rush to her closet and change, sprint to the bathroom to comb her hair and apply a mask of makeup, but she couldn't muster the energy. What did it matter? Ben hadn't come for a social visit; he'd come because of the baby. Better he understand the reality of pregnancy than the prettied-up version she'd presented him last time. That version had ended with hurt feelings and rejection.

Kayla approached the door, straightening her shoulders, craving a resolution and answers to long-asked questions. The indecision, the waiting and pondering, was eating her alive. She swallowed her fear, took a cleansing breath, and left the sanctuary of her bedroom. Whatever they decided, whatever he wanted, she had a say in the matter—because she carried the life they created—and she stiffened her spine to voice her concerns.

Ben stood in her living room, tall and broad and lanky, his hands fisted in the pockets of his jeans. He stared out the window at the parking lot—probably ogling Shelby as she exited the building. His expression matched the mood of the room: somber, crackling with tension, reeking of fear.

Kayla cleared her throat.

Ben whirled around. "Hey."

His voice, that South Georgia drawl evident in just one word, sent memories flying. "Hi."

"Sorry for just showing up like this. I meant to call or text, but I didn't really know where I was going until I got here."

"It's okay." Kayla motioned to the couch. "Come on in and

have a seat. Can I get you something to drink?"

Ben chuckled. "A shot of liquor?"

She gasped.

He waved his palms. "I'm kidding, obviously, since that's partly to blame for me standing here. I'll take a water, if it's not too much trouble."

With one glib comment, her mouth turned sour. They'd been drinking, sure, but neither one of them were intoxicated when they had sex. However wrong and misguided, the act was a result of free will and not drunkenness. She'd remind him of that if he chose to force the issue. "Coming right up."

She moved into the kitchen to fetch a bottle of water, grateful for a moment to collect herself. Did he have to look and sound so helpless, a lost little boy in a grown man's body? Better to feel irritated at the outset and not fall prey to his innocent act. They'd done this together, for better or worse, a fact that remained unchanged.

She rounded the corner and stumbled at the sight of him lounging on the couch.

All knees and elbows, his gaze zipped around the room. The framed photo of Kayla and her roommates celebrating Shelby's twenty-first birthday. Emily's design magazines fanned on the ottoman. Her hand-knit throw puddled against the armrest. He linked his hands behind his neck, dropping his head toward the ground as if in prayer. Where was the guy who'd boldly approached her in the bar, made her feel like the only woman in the world, and eased her into a sense of completion with his touch?

Summoning courage she didn't feel, Kayla stepped into the room and bumped his shoulder with a bottle.

His head ricocheted, and he scooted back to let her pass.

"Thanks." Ben downed half the bottle in one guzzling gulp.

She sat far enough to face him but close enough to loiter in his masculine scent. "You're welcome."

"Look, Kayla, I'm sorry about how I reacted the other day. You took me by surprise, and I didn't handle it very well."

An apology was a good start, but her nerves would have settled if he'd sustained some kind of eye contact instead of glaring at his clasped fingers. "It's a lot to take in. Trust me, I get it."

He glared at her, nodding and grimacing. Her stomach shriveled to a raisin. Had she thought he'd ride in and propose marriage? Declare his commitment to her and the baby and erase her worries? There was no easy answer, and the uncertainty on his face was almost enough to send her screaming from the room. This was real. She was pregnant, and he didn't know what to do about it any more than she did.

"I've been mulling over the alternatives," he said. "The truth is, I don't know the answer. I guess I'm here because I need to know what you want." He sat back and ran his hands through his hair, leaving it sticking up on all ends. When his somber eyes met hers, her belly quivered.

He couldn't … he wouldn't expect her to decide for both of them what to do. Could he?

"We have to talk and come to some sort of agreement on the next step."

"I know." Kayla nodded and stared at her feet. Now he'd broached the topic, she could barely look at him without picturing their baby. Would it have brown hair and greenish-brown eyes like him, be blonde and blue-eyed like her, or something in between? She blinked the images away. "The truth is we have three options, and I don't know which one is best."

He speared her with a pained stare. "I don't think there is a best, but we need to figure out which one we can live with."

Kayla closed her eyes and exhaled a full breath. On that, they agreed.

Chapter Nine

The water in Ben's empty stomach turned to lead. Kayla squirmed in her seat, wringing her hands. He'd done his best to study and push her and the baby out of his mind long enough to scrape through finals. After his last exam that morning, he got into his car to drive home when he cruised past her apartment—and his—around this bend and that, his mind as unsettled as his destination.

The farther he got from home, the more the anvil in his chest ached. He'd turned the car around, passed his apartment, and driven to Kayla's. He hadn't called or texted or given her any warning. If he had to wait, he'd wait. Like it or not, they needed to talk.

Her yoga pants and ASU sweatshirt engulfed her small frame. Ben couldn't wrap his head around a baby growing in her belly. His baby. He scrubbed his hands over his face and waited.

"I have to be honest, Ben. I don't know which option I can live with."

The lead in his gut corroded at the hesitation in her voice. He thought of his grandfather. The crops he planted. The hours he spent nurturing them from seed to stalk. The anguish on his grizzled face with news of an imminent storm. "Okay. Why don't we go through them one by one."

Kayla nodded, as if yielding the floor.

Ben's scalp tingled. Anticipating the recoil, he lifted the pistol, took aim at the target. "What are your thoughts on abortion?"

She closed her eyes, lifting her chin as if asking God for an answer, his future clutched in her fists.

His pulse pelted his jittery nerves.

He waited.

"I … I don't know if I can do that."

Ben sagged against the couch, his legs heavy, his hope flattened. Moored by the weight of his mistake, he cursed himself, Kayla, and the innocent life growing inside of her.

"I'm a believer," Kayla said. "Killing a baby goes against everything I believe."

With one sentence, she blew his prospects to bits.

"But …" She swallowed.

His feet prickled.

She rubbed her hands back and forth against her pants. "Logically, it makes the most sense," she said. "There's still time to make an appointment. The only people who know are my closest friends and you, so it's not like our reputations would suffer. And not having to tell my parents is a huge plus."

The tightness in his chest eased. Feeling returned to his fingertips. "I agree." He expelled a full breath from his lungs.

"When you take emotion out of the equation, it's the reasonable decision."

"The thing is, I don't know how to make an unemotional decision about the future of a baby." She stabbed him with a glare. "Our baby."

Ben coughed, clearing the ammo from the chamber. If he pulled the trigger, he'd say something he couldn't take back. "Agreed. Let's table that option for now. What about adoption?"

Her shoulders relaxed. "It's a possible choice. We could go on with our lives and the baby could grow up in a good home where it's loved and wanted."

She shrank against the cushions, picking at her nails. Avoided his stare.

"But?" he asked.

She clutched her arms against her chest.

Ben held his breath, braced for impact.

"I'm not sure I could hear the heartbeat, feel it move inside me, deliver the baby, hold the baby, then give it away for someone else to raise. I mean, how do you go through all of that and go back to your life like it never happened?"

Ben rubbed the back of his neck, squeezed the nagging muscles. Her answers were clear as mud. "I don't know. I guess, if that's what we choose, we could talk to someone who's done it and see what it's like."

"I guess …"

"My grandmother was adopted."

Her eyes perked up. "Really? Did she ever look for her birth parents?"

"I don't know. If she did, I never knew about it." He tried to shrug away the unease that settled between his shoulder blades. What would his grandmother say if she knew he was thinking of giving his baby—her grandchild—away? "I guess I could ask."

Kayla huffed. "That might be an uncomfortable conversation."

"No more uncomfortable that this conversation."

Her smile faded like hot breath on a window, knifing him in the gut.

"Sorry, that was …" Stupid. Senseless. Hurtful. He wasn't the only one suffering. "Sorry."

"It's okay." She tugged the ends of her hair—"This is an uncomfortable conversation."—blinked her tired blue eyes—"for both of us."

Irritated, Ben stretched his neck from side to side, relished the crack. They weren't discussing options so much as kicking a flat tire. They could kick all they wanted, but nothing would change. "The only other option is to have the baby and keep it."

Kayla nodded.

Ben pried the words from his throat. "What do you think about keeping the baby?"

"Well …"

Ben leaned in, his breath shallow.

Kayla swallowed, played war with her thumbs. "I guess that depends on us and what our expectations would be." She glanced at him and quickly looked away. "It would be hard—"

Ben grunted. "Yeah."

She straightened. Her neck brimmed pink. "We'd have to figure out how that would work."

He willed his eyes not to roll. What did "making it work" mean? Marriage? Single co-parenting? It all seemed so preposterous they may as well debate an alien invasion. "I don't know how it would work. We're from opposite ends of the state. Neither one of us has a degree or a job."

"I'm going to finish my degree and get a job." Kayla sniffed.

She glared at him with her chin in the air. "I could probably get a job at the hospital where I did my internship."

"In Atlanta?"

Kayla nodded, jerked a shoulder. "Or wherever."

She resumed her thumb war, entranced by her fingers. "What about you?" she asked without making eye contact. "Aren't you planning to go to law school?"

Law school. The golden ticket. Not a day went by when it hadn't been his goal. "I was before …"—he lifted his hands, let them drop—"this."

She studied him with woeful curious eyes. "Have you gotten in anywhere?"

"I'm supposed to take the LSAT in January. I didn't do so hot the first time."

"Supposed to or going to?"

Ben sat forward, stared where his hands drooped between his knees. "That kinda depends on what we decide."

"Ben."

Her snap yanked his eyes to hers.

Her jaw clenched. "Don't tiptoe around. Just tell me. Law school or not?"

"I don't know!" He bolted off the couch, unable to sit as she shelled him with questions. He paced to the window, prowled around the room, tried to avoid her seeking eyes. "My parents were going to pay for law school. If I tell them about the baby, there's no chance that'll happen."

One step. Two steps. Three. The silence lingered. He stopped and faced her. At the startled look on her face, he tempered his voice. "I'm not tiptoeing around. I'm giving you the truth—it depends on what we decide."

Kayla covered her face.

Her chest expanded and caved. Her fingers trembled. Her sobs shook her small frame. He put one foot in front of the other and sat down before his knees gave out.

She dropped her hands revealing blotchy cheeks and red-rimmed eyes. "I never meant for this to happen."

Ben reached for her, felt the tears on her fingers. "Neither of us did." He glanced at her stomach, still as tiny as ever. Despite her pain, he had to be honest. He let go of her hand to rub at the ache in his neck. "It all seems like a really bad dream."

"I wish it was a bad dream. I can take another test if you want …"

"No, no, it's not that. I get it. I just don't get it in here." He jabbed a finger to his temple.

She sandwiched her hands between her knees, swaying back and forth, staring at his bottle of water. Back and forth. Back and forth. "I don't think I can have an abortion."

His chest squeezed. Pinched hard. Numbness spread through his veins like medicine through an IV. It would have been the easy way out—the coward's way. "I understand."

"I'm sorry. I know that would make everything so much easier, but—"

"It's okay." He rubbed his chest, tried to disperse the dread. "I'm not sure I could do go through with it either."

When she looked at him, scared and unsure, Ben slumped onto the couch and closed his eyes. For years, he'd wanted to get away from under his parents and their never-ending demands. Like it or not, having a baby meant more than breaking free from his parents. It meant becoming a man. A man with a baby. A man with responsibilities.

How many times had his dad told him, "Be careful what you wish for," whenever Ben complained about following rules he didn't understand? "You want to be on your own and make your own decisions," Dad had lectured over and over and over again, "you'll get there one day. Then you'll thank me and your mama for being so hard on you. If only I'd been a little harder on your brother ..."

His dad always stopped right there and let the rest go unsaid. Maybe Scott wouldn't have been so wild. Maybe Scott wouldn't have developed an addiction. Maybe Scott would still be alive. Ben knew the answer better than anyone.

"Okay." Ben sat up and slapped his hands on his knees. "We're having a baby."

When she moved a hand to her stomach, he tasted the sour bite of failure, but swallowed the fear.

"We're having a baby," she said.

Neither of them sounded convinced.

Chapter Ten

Kayla reached for a throw pillow and clutched it to her chest, hoping to quell the crickets pogoing inside her belly. Were they really going to do this? Could they? "So what's next?"

Ben sat on the couch, staring at the wall, his face an unreadable mask. When she spoke, he shuddered, as if coming out of a daze.

"My family's expecting me home tomorrow." His tone mirrored his expression, vacant with a trace of dread. "I suppose the next step is to tell our parents."

Kayla's jittery stomach spiked with panic. She'd annoyed her parents before—changing majors again and again, floating aimlessly through life with no better goal than to fall in love, get married, and live happily ever after—but changing majors was nothing compared to showing up pregnant. "I'm scared to tell my parents. They're going to be so disappointed in me."

Ben sighed and fell back against the cushions, rubbing his hands against his face. "That's the understatement of the century."

When he looked at her, it was the first time since she'd told him the news they walked on common ground. "Do you want me to come with you?" Telling his parents sounded a million times easier than telling hers, and she wasn't opposed to a dry run. "We can tell them together before I go home and tell my parents."

A muscle ticked in his jaw. "You have no idea what you're asking. I'd never subject you to that. It's not going to be pretty."

Visions of belts and chains floated through her mind. Ben dressed as a highlander. Sword in hand. She shook the image away and narrowed her eyes. "Are you … are you afraid of them? Physically?"

His mirthless chuckle didn't ease her nerves. "No, but there's more than one way to skin a cat."

"What do you mean?"

"Let's just say I don't think they're going to handle this well. They expect a lot from me, and I've pretty much put a fork in their dream."

"You mean *your* dream?"

Ben shrugged. "One and the same, I suppose."

He sat forward, dropping his hands between his knees. He looked so defeated, so exhausted, she resisted the urge to soothe the crease between his brows and ease the tension she could see in the rigid set of his shoulders. She couldn't justify the guilt that hung stiff and restrictive like a new coat on her back. She hadn't ruined his life—they'd both been willing participants—but she couldn't shake the blame.

His gaze met hers. "When are you going home?"

"My last exam is tomorrow. I haven't given my parents an

exact date, so I'll probably go in a few days. Do some laundry, pack, try to get my head in the right frame of mind to tell them."

"What do you think they'll say?"

Her dad would go quiet while her mom ranted and raved about how irresponsible and reckless she'd been. They would stew for a few days before coming to her with a plan they'd devised—without her input or consent.

"They were proud of me last summer, doing my internship, preparing to graduate on time. Neither one had high hopes of me finishing college. I suppose this solidifies my role as the family scatterbrain. They'll try to take control, fix the problem, and they won't give a hoot what I want." She shrugged the familiar sting of regret from her shoulders, but it clung like a wet blanket. "The usual."

Kayla snuck a glance at Ben. She'd revealed too much at a time when she needed to appear responsible and mature, but Ben seemed unfazed, watching her with narrowed, heedful eyes.

"You think they'll want you to get an abortion?" Ben asked.

"I don't know." Kayla rubbed the bridge of her nose and squeezed her eyes closed. She couldn't hear the word or think of the act another second. She prayed the baby wasn't old enough to hear them discussing the end of its life. When she opened her eyes, Ben waited, eyes intense, for her answer. "I really don't know. What about yours?"

"Well, I'm the one who toes the line, so there'll be a good bit of shock and a whole bushelful of disappointment. They'll try to fix it, but …" He stared at the window, his eyes as somber as the dogs on those animal rescue commercials, shaking, starving, begging. "There's no fixing this one. I'm basically ruined."

Kayla pulled her legs into her chest, tucking her face against her knees, choking on guilt and fear. She'd majorly screwed up, but this time she'd broken more than just her life—she'd broken Ben's. Ben sat inches away. Wilting. Steeped in misery. She pitied them both, but like it or not, what was done was done. The time for pity was over. Feeling sorry for themselves was a luxury they couldn't afford.

"The thing is, Ben, it's not about us. What we did was weeks ago, and no matter how much we want to go back and change what happened, we can't. It's about the baby. Everything has to be about the baby. Because intended or not, however we decide to move forward, there is a baby and we're both responsible."

He sat back and narrowed his eyes, studied her.

Seconds ticked by.

"You don't sound like a scatterbrain to me," he said.

Kayla chuckled. "You don't know me very well."

"True, but I think that's about to change." He shifted in his seat. "For both of us."

The thought of getting to know him better shouldn't make her stomach swell with excitement, not when it wasn't born of interest, affection, or desire. Her pregnancy would likely destroy any chance of a happily-ever-after ending. The swell surged into a tsunami when she remembered the relationship her pregnancy would most likely destroy.

He braced his hands on his knees to stand.

"And your girlfriend?" Kayla asked. "What are you going to tell your girlfriend?"

Chapter Eleven

Ben froze midway through standing as Kayla's question sucker punched his tenderized brain. "What did you say?"

"You heard me." Her voice may have been soft, but her tone was laced with steel.

Caught. His pulse clanged. His knees clattered. He dropped back onto the couch. He'd been so wrapped up in trying to pretend the baby didn't exist, he hadn't given any thought to Darcy or how the news would shatter her. He'd given even less thought to explaining Darcy to Kayla. "It's complicated."

"I imagine it would be. Why don't you un-complicate it so I can understand what I'm up against?"

"Kayla …" Ben tried to dislodge the words from his throat. "I … she … we …"

"What's her name?"

Defeated and more than a little irritated, Ben sighed. "Darcy."

"How's Darcy going to feel about my pregnancy?"

About like he did. Blindsided. Angry. He voiced the one that pinched the most. "Hurt."

"Hurt?" She stared at him, a little annoyed, a little disappointed. He'd recognize the look anywhere. "If I were her, hurt wouldn't even scratch the surface."

Ben rubbed at the knife stabbing the corner of his eye and stared at the pretty painting on the wall.

"How long have you dated?" Kayla asked.

"Three years in high school. On and off ever since. We're not technically together right now."

"But that's only a technicality."

It was a statement, not a question, but Ben felt obliged to nod. "Pretty much, depending on who you ask."

"I'm asking you."

He blinked at the rug under his feet, surprised he didn't see blood. Kayla's quiet interrogation chafed him to the bone. "We're bound by circumstances. I don't say it's complicated to skim the truth. It really is complicated."

"Okay." She relaxed against the cushions as if she had all the time in the world to listen. "I get this is the last thing you want to talk about. But this baby means we have access to each other's lives in ways we normally wouldn't. I need to know what's going on in your world every bit as much as you need to understand mine."

He stared at her, gnawing his bottom lip, trying to figure out what to say and how to explain.

"Come on, Ben. She's going to be furious with you and with me. If someone is furious and possibly going to confront me, the least you can do is give me a little background."

It shouldn't have rankled that she was thinking logically when all he could do was coast on the adrenaline high of emotion, but there it was. And she was right. Darcy would be furious. So would his parents. He couldn't predict what they'd do or say to Kayla when they found out the truth. Like a stone dropped into a still pond, the ripples would spread far and wide.

"We were tight in high school." When his life did a 180. "We broke up when we went to different colleges. She goes to SE State, but not much changed. Neither one of us broke the connection. We'd hook up if I went to State for football games or she came here to see her friends."

"I feel like there's more you're not telling me."

Scatterbrained or not, she could read him like a book. Unlike with Darcy, there were no tricks or tales to decipher. Kayla played it straight. He'd have to get used to her brutal honesty. "Her family's connected. Her dad's a judge. He could pave the way if I became a lawyer. It's kind of expected we'll end up together."

"Expected by whom?"

"My parents." He shrugged. "Hers."

"What about you?" Kayla asked, her voice small. "What about Darcy?"

What about him? He wanted to shout that very question at every family function where his future seemed locked and loaded. Kayla couldn't know the subject burned, but that didn't mean he could temper the anger in his tone. "My mom thinks of her as the daughter she never had. Darcy and my mom are close partly because her mom's ..." How could he explain the delicate tightrope of sanity Darcy's mom walked every day? "She's fragile. She's had some issues and Darcy's dad is a hard guy. Darcy depends on me and my family when things go south in hers." He'd welcomed the distraction from loss. They all had.

Kayla swallowed and shrank into the couch. Guilt pricked him for pulling her into his family drama, but she was the one prodding. If she wanted the truth, he'd tell her. Facing it live and in person would be a thousand times worse.

"You didn't answer my question," she said. "Are you planning to marry Darcy?"

Anger edged out guilt. "I don't know!" He ran his hands through his hair and yanked. "I don't know what you want me to say. I've never felt I had a choice."

Kayla sat forward and laced her fingers. "I'm sorry. I don't mean to upset you."

"It's not you." Ben dropped his hands and fisted them on his thighs. "Trust me, these are things I need to figure out." He stared at the shadows beneath her eyes, at fingernails bitten to nubs. She may have been scared to tell her family, but she sure wasn't scared to push him for answers. Her tiny frame, glossy mane of sunshiny hair, and big fathomless eyes hid pockets of strength. Someone like her, someone who wasn't afraid to be vulnerable, probably had more than her parents to disappoint at home. "How about you?" he asked. "Any boyfriends I need to dodge?"

She shook her head. "Nope. Just my mom and dad. Maybe my brother, but that's unlikely. He doesn't care what I do as long as I stay out of his way."

He'd had a brother once, a brother who sped through life like a hot knife through butter. Ben worked hard to do the opposite. He paid attention. He did the right things. He analyzed every consequence before making a decision. The one time he strayed to scratch an itch, he'd scorched his life to the ground.

Would he end up like a cotton field after burning—renewed and ready for a different crop—or like a dead possum, bloated and stinking in the heat?

Chapter Twelve

Ben signaled to pull off the highway when his mailbox came into view, the reflective numbers the only indication of a residence along the stretch of two-lane highway where loblolly pines stood guard for miles. The familiar sound of gravel pinging beneath his car's undercarriage announced his arrival home as much as the barking of the hunting dogs kenneled at the back of his property, their bays echoing across the still waters of the pond. He rounded the curve. His stomach clenched. His shoulders sagged. Darcy's car sat parked in the drive.

Perfect.

He hadn't spoken to Darcy since she'd stormed out of his apartment when he'd made the mistake of putting studying ahead of her. She'd done what she typically did—taken up residence at his house and waited him out with the loving support of his mother. He should have predicted her presence and been prepared. Lately, since Kayla and her bombshell, he'd lost the ability to sidestep life's landmines.

He didn't want to tell his parents about the baby with Darcy around. He wouldn't. Ben could only deal with one hysterical female at a time, and family came first. He needed to remind his mother that Darcy wasn't family.

Not yet.

Perhaps not ever.

Ben shoved the car into park and waited for the pinch of panic that preceded any act that might jeopardize his predetermined future. For the first time in a long time, it didn't come. Perhaps it was the numbness he'd embraced since leaving Kayla's apartment where his offspring grew inside her body, would continue to grow, and arrive around the midway mark of the upcoming year. What they did upon the baby's birth remained a mystery, but the facts remained unchanged. He'd knocked up a girl in a one-night stand. By the end of the day, his parents would know. By the end of the year, everyone in town would know.

He sat staring at his childhood home, the antique columns, the brick stairs and wide front porch he'd helped his father repair last summer, the twin chimneys bracing the sprawling roof like bookends. The scrolled iron railings and arched double doors welcomed all who meandered down their lane. He'd loved this place, the grandeur, the history, the land. So much had happened here in the belly of his birth. So much joy. So much pain.

Lost in nostalgia and avoiding a scene, Ben sat in the car until his father's hired hand, Nat, ambled around the side of the house carrying big-mouth pliers. Nat reminded Ben of a meerkat, with his thin-framed shoulders slouched beneath his old barn jacket and the sports sunglasses he wore year round. Nat lifted his free hand in greeting before setting the pliers aside to welcome Ben home.

"Hey, boy." Nat stretched "boy" into two distinct syllables. As a kid, Ben struggled to understand the man's vernacular while his dad routinely used Nat as an example of what an education could do for a man. "You gonna sit there all day or get out and join the livin'?"

"Hey, Nat." Ben climbed out of the car. "How's it going?"

"Aww, ya know." Nat fiddled with the brim of his ball cap. "Same ol', same ol'."

Nat pulled a can of snuff from his back pocket and offered the tobacco to Ben. Ben declined with a shake of his head, and retrieved his hanging clothes and leather duffel from the back seat. The old man placed a pinch beneath his front lip and remaining bottom teeth, reminding Ben of what chewing tobacco could do for a man.

"Your ma's inside. Been fussing up a storm since your girl showed up. My door's always open if you need a place to hide."

Nat's cackle brought back memories of bygone days when Nat used to shield Scott and Ben from their parents' ire when they were little and causing trouble. Later, when Ben would try to tag along with Scott and his friends and get rebuffed, Ben would retreat to the loft apartment over the barn and pout to the only man who'd offer sympathy. He'd spent more hot summer nights than he could remember learning to play poker and listening to Nat's stories.

For the first time in a long time, Ben considered the offer. He slung his clothes over his shoulder and grinned. "I appreciate that, Nat. Don't shoot me if I take you up on it."

His mama was in the kitchen, wearing a splattered apron and a scowl. The smell of fresh-baked bread perfumed the air. Ben's stomach rumbled. He couldn't recall the last time he'd eaten.

"You've lost weight." Anna Strickland squashed Ben in a hug, enveloping him in her vanilla and powder scent. Tall and lanky, they stood nearly eye-to-eye. "Good gracious, son, you're skin and bones."

"Finals week." He glanced around for Darcy. Her keys hung on the hook by the back door, and her purse sat on the counter next to his ma's. "Is Darcy here?"

"She's in the powder room. She saw you pull in and went to freshen up." His ma peered over her shoulder down the hallway before turning back to him and lowering her voice. "I should tan your hide for treating that girl so poor. She came home in tears and said you wouldn't give her the time of day."

Ben did his best to shuck off the burden. Darcy's made-up drama would have to wait. "She needs to go home. I have to talk to you and Dad. Alone."

"What's wrong? You fail a class?"

"Not that I'm aware."

She slammed her hands on her hips, lifting her painted on brows. "Then what is it?"

"Where's Dad?"

"Where do you think he is on a Wednesday afternoon? He's on the golf course. He'll be home by six."

Ben's gaze landed on the clock on the microwave. An hour until showtime and nothing to do but wait. Well, nothing to do but get rid of Darcy. He might need an hour to persuade her to leave.

Like clockwork, she sauntered into the kitchen wearing ripped jeans, heeled boots, an oversized sweater, and too much makeup to make this visit seem anything but calculated.

"Well, look who's home." She waltzed over and planted herself in front of him.

Ben stood with his hands jammed into the front pockets of his jeans, tried his best to keep his face impassive. Blank. Cool. He felt anything but. She was going to freak when she found out about the baby. "What are you doing here?"

"I came to see your mama. I certainly didn't come all this way to see you. Can't say your expression has changed since you tossed me out of your apartment."

"I didn't toss you out."

"You didn't make me feel welcome."

"I didn't invite you to visit the weekend before finals."

"I didn't think I needed an invitation."

They could go on, tit for tat, back and forth for an hour or he could swallow the ugly retorts and usher her out the door. He sucked in a breath, held it, and let it out with a whoosh. "I apologize for not making you feel welcome."

Darcy's head tilted, and her eyes popped. "That didn't sound very sincere."

He ground his teeth until his jaw ached. "Take it or leave it."

She wrapped her manicured hand around his arm and nuzzled into his side. Her sugary perfume grated. "I guess I'll take it, if that's the best you can do."

Ben shifted, dislodging her and reached for her purse and keys. "I'll walk you out."

"But—"

"You around tomorrow?" He held open the side door he'd just come through.

Darcy looked at his mama and shrugged. "Yeah." She followed him outside to the driver's side of her car.

"I'll pick you up at ten."

She played with the button of his Henley shirt. "To do what?"

"Talk."

She inched closer. Her eyes seesawed between his, her lashes gummed with kohl. Her fingers crept into his hair. "Talk? We can 'talk' now. Your dad won't be home for an hour."

Any other time he would have hauled her into the barn and taken what she offered, but not today. Today her suggestion irked. "I'll see you tomorrow."

Darcy huffed. "This is becoming a habit."

"What is?"

"You." She folded her arms against her chest. "Dismissing me. I don't like it."

He opened her car door, meeting her icy stare with one of his own. He wasn't in the mood for games. Their staring contest continued.

She finally gave in like he knew she would, bumping his shoulder on her way into the car.

"Fine. I'll see you tomorrow." She slammed her door shut.

Ben stepped back to avoid getting hit and watched her peel away. Blinking his eyes against the gravel dust her angry departure stirred, he heaved a cleansing breath. Now all he had to do was wait.

Ben heard Wade Strickland enter his house the way a king enters his castle, swaggering and ready for pampering. His mom waited, willing to oblige and fuss after him. He stood from the couch in the den where he'd been staring at the wall, refusing to answer Ma's questions. She'd eventually stomped back into the kitchen, slamming cabinets and drawers to show her frustration.

Now Ben was home, and he couldn't wait another second to rid himself of the news and deal with the fallout. Anticipating the anger and disappointment had to be worse than reality.

Ben shook his father's hand, smelling cut grass and whiskey when he leaned in for a hug. Despite spending the afternoon on the course, the collar of Wade's golf shirt peeked neatly out from under his pullover, and his khakis were perfectly pressed like he'd just left the house, a testament to his mom's ironing skills.

"One semester to go," Wade said in greeting. "How'd you do on your finals?"

"Kept my grades."

Wade eyed him on his way to the recliner. The leather creaked when he sat. Ben remained standing. "Do I need to remind you how important it is to finish strong since you bombed the LSAT?"

"No, sir."

Wade let out a breath and reached for the remote control on the end table. "Why are you standing? Have a seat. You're blocking the TV."

Anna stepped into the den clutching a dish rag to her chest. "He's got something to tell us."

Wade eased back against the chair, letting out a frustrated breath. God forbid he miss a minute of the news. "What's going on?"

"Mama," Ben cleared his throat. "You might want to sit down."

His ma walked to him, placed her hand on his chest. "Are you okay? You're not sick, are you?"

"Mama, please. Just have a seat."

He had their attention. Never had Ben come home and been anything but compliant. His parents stared up at him from their twin recliners, their eyes narrowed with nervous suspicion.

"There's a girl from school," Ben said. "She's pregnant. The baby's mine."

Dad's fingers dug into the arm of the chair, and his ears brimmed red. His gray eyes sharpened, turning stormy and cold. Ma's brows shot skyward and her mouth flopped open. She seemed unable or unwilling to close it with the hand that fluttered against her lips.

The silence hung between them. Heavy, dreadful silence.

"Who is this girl?" Dad asked through gritted teeth.

Ben had never heard that exact pitch in his father's tone—fury with a coating of fear. "She's a student."

"And the baby's yours?" he asked.

"She said so, and the timing fits." Embarrassment stung his cheeks. He flashed an apologetic glance at his ma. He shouldn't have bothered. She sat cold still and stared through him as if he didn't exist.

"The timing fits," Wade repeated in that same odd tone. "Some girl says you're the daddy, and you go along with it because the timing fits?"

"I … I mean …" Ben lifted his shoulders, stared at the design in the rug beneath his feet. Kayla wouldn't lie to him, but when his dad glared at him like he was the stupidest kid on planet Earth, his gut churned with unease. Could she have been with someone else? "I don't think she would have—"

Wade pulled himself to standing, shoved his hands under his armpits. "You don't think? That's the problem with you, Ben. You don't think!"

Wade took one long stride and stood nose to nose with Ben. The eyes that greeted Ben in the mirror each day stared back at him, flecked with gold, sharp with rage. "Do you have her contact information?"

"Of course I have her contact information."

"Call her. Demand a paternity test. You admit nothing. You say nothing. You do nothing until the results are in. Is that clear?"

"Dad, we've already—"

"You've done enough. Now you'll do what I say. Do you understand?"

Ben ran his tongue along his teeth, trying to moisten his desperately dry mouth. Even now, especially now, his father thought him a fool. "Yes, sir."

Chapter Thirteen

Kayla pulled onto her blacktop driveway through a line of barren cherry trees, their limbs outstretched. Entering this three-acre paradise, no more than a stone's throw from the heart of Atlanta, had always soothed her like an arms-open-wide embrace, a warm hug, a fond hello after time away even in the dead of winter.

Today, the manicured grounds left her feeling shunned.

The gated entrance snarled. The gnarled branches waved an angry warning. The meandering drive was never so short, never so hostile.

A day after her last final, twenty-four hours since her phone call from Ben, she left her apartment and headed home. When Ben called, she'd hoped to hear good news from him before approaching her parents. Words of wisdom. Assurance it would all be okay. A kind encouragement. His request cut her off at the knees. He wanted a paternity test. As soon as possible. She was to contact him with arrangements.

The silence between them reverberated like an unanswered shout.

She'd never felt more alone.

Exhausted to the core, Kayla pulled her car to a stop. His parents must think her a slut. Why wouldn't they? She'd slept with him. But still …

She lumbered out of the car, sliding her arms into her jacket. Rambo was the first to greet her. All wet tongue and muddy paws, he bounded around the bushes to wag hello, his shed-free fur snared with burrs from the creek bed behind their house. His carefree exuberance was a sworn enemy of her mother's latest decorating scheme.

"Hey there, boy." She leaned down and petted him. Her parents would expect her to see to his daily grooming now that she was home. He ran circles around her car while she unloaded the trunk, first her suitcase, then her makeup bag and accessories. Looping the bag over her shoulder, she zipped her down jacket against the cold air whipping her cheeks and started up the walk.

Mom stood at the side entrance, a knee-length sweater clutched around her tiny waist. Jessica Cummings monthly dermatology touchups and daily workouts attributed to her youthful appearance. In her jeans and Ugg boots, she and Kayla could pass for sisters from a distance. "I told you you'd hit traffic if you left too late."

Kayla tugged the heavy bag over the blacktop and up the side door stairs. "I know you did."

"Is the rest still in your car?" Her mom scooted back and held the door for Kayla.

"What rest?"

After shooing Rambo outside and closing the door, her mom turned to her and sighed. "Kayla Cummings. How many times did Dad ask you to start cleaning out your apartment and bring stuff home over break?"

Every time she called him, in the brief seconds before he passed his phone to her mother. Considering her current situation, packing up her apartment had been the last thing on her mind. She shrugged her shoulders and tried to appease her mother. "Sorry. I was in a hurry to beat traffic and I forgot."

"Your dad's not going to be happy."

He certainly wasn't, about that and so much more. "I'll bring stuff home over Easter."

After accepting a hug and a kiss to her temple, Kayla shed her coat and hung it on a hook in the mud room. She edged into the kitchen where the air reeked of rotten eggs. Her stomach rolled. "What is that smell?"

"Beef cabbage soup. It's a new recipe. Your dad and I are on the keto diet."

Kayla tried to escape to the adjacent keeping room where a fire warmed the stone hearth. She sat on the white linen chair, breathed through her mouth, and watched her mother stir the offending brew while trying to choke back the nausea.

"Are you okay?" her mom asked. "You look a little pale."

Kayla nodded, swallowed, and willed herself not to heave. "I'm just tired. When does Dad get home?"

"He's on his way. Your brother had a basketball game. I would have gone if I'd known you were going to be so late."

Kayla held her breath past the boiling soup and grabbed her suitcase. "I'm going to unpack."

Her mom huffed. "You can do that later. I wanted to catch up. You haven't called for more than a minute at a time in weeks."

Because the guilt of keeping her pregnancy from her mom meant she kept the calls home to a minimum. Besides, her mom had radar sensing whenever Kayla dodged. "We'll catch up later. I promise."

"Are you sure you're okay?"

"I'm good, Mom."

Kayla lugged her suitcase up the back staircase, marveling at how effortlessly she'd lied. So much had changed in the last few weeks—in the last few days—yet opening her bedroom door was like escaping into a time capsule when her biggest cares were what to wear to the high school football game and who would ask her to prom.

She collapsed onto her bed, simultaneously relieved and anxious to be home. She could still smell on her duvet the floral fruitiness of the Tommy Girl perfume she'd once used with abandon even though she hadn't touched the fragrance in years. The sheer pink curtains rustled when the heat clicked on, drawing her eyes to the window seat and the romance novel she forgot to pack when she left after Thanksgiving.

She flipped onto her back and stared at the chandelier hanging from her ceiling, watched the crystals refract the waning rays of sunlight. She'd been pregnant at Thanksgiving and completely unaware. She'd met a friend from high school for coffee, talked with Shelby about rooming together in Atlanta after graduation, made plans for her future. At graduation, she'd be as big as a bus, weeks from delivery, her plans unknown.

Kayla couldn't get the sound of Ben's voice out of her head. Defeated. Embarrassed. Determined. No questions about how she fared, how she felt, or how she did on her finals. He was all business. She hadn't even tried to talk him out of the test. Like it or not, he was the daddy, but she understood his need to confirm—especially since his tone implied the test was not his idea. She shouldn't feel insulted. Offended. Hurt.

But she did. How was he to know he wasn't one of many? They didn't know one another. Not really. She almost hated to get his hopes up when she knew they'd be right back to where they started—a baby on the way and decisions to make.

She heard the low ding of the alarm signaling an open door, followed by the deep bass of her father's voice regaling her mom with highlights from the game. Her brother's footsteps smacked against the stairs.

He stopped at her open doorway. "Hey."

Kayla envied the simplicity of Josh's life—school, sports, friends—rinse and repeat. His royal blue uniform reminded her of less complicated times. At his age, she'd longed to be where she was now—almost done with school and ready to set the world on fire. Little did she know her dreams would turn into a nightmare. "How was the game?"

"We won. I scored a couple, played good defense." Josh shrugged his bony shoulders.

"Good job." She drummed her fingers on her pant leg and studied her brother, considered warning him about the upcoming scene. "You have plans tonight?"

He whipped the shirt from his back, exposing a bulkier chest than she'd expected. Her little brother was growing up. "I plan to eat as little of that crap Mom made for dinner as I can get away with, and swing by a drive-through on my way to tutoring."

"Tutoring?"

"ACT," he said. "Some of us have higher aspirations than a second-tier in-state school."

"Snob," she said.

"Slacker." He slung his shirt over his shoulder. "Seriously, are you eating that crap? It smells like dog food."

"I don't think I'll eat much of anything tonight."

"You gotta talk to Mom. She ignores me when I complain about the food, but maybe she'll listen now that you're home."

Whatever pull she had with her parents would go poof with two little words. "I'll see what I can do."

He pushed off the doorway and headed down the hall to his room. Seconds after she heard his shower turn on, her mom called up the stairwell.

"Dinner's ready."

Kayla nibbled on the bread her mom served to her and Josh with a warning not to share with their dad, swirling the disgusting soup while swallowing back bile. The fact that she'd sat at the table without heaving for ten minutes took Herculean strength and certainly wasn't worthy of the scowl her mother tossed in her direction whenever they made eye contact.

"You're not eating," Mom said.

Josh kicked Kayla under the table, his brows lifting.

"I'm not hungry."

"This isn't exactly a heavy meal," Mom said. "After all the weeks you spend eating takeout and cafeteria food, you'd think you'd appreciate a little home cooking."

"I think Kayla would appreciate some home cooking, Mom." Josh scooted his chair back from the table. "Not some diet soup that smells like Rambo's dinner."

"Joshua …" Dad's tone sounded like Rambo's growl.

Josh stood and lifted his bowl.

"Where do you think you're going?" Mom asked.

"Tutoring. She threatened to charge you if I was late again, so I have to get going."

Mom crimped her lips and dropped her hands to the table. "It's not that bad."

"I think it's delicious." Gary Cummings patted his wife's hand, always the supportive husband. "It wouldn't hurt him to eat a little healthier. Avoid packing on the pounds like his old man." Gary palmed the belly beneath his crisp button-down shirt.

Kayla's dad had aged better than most. The laugh lines around his eyes and the salt-and-pepper coloring near his temple only added character to his classic good looks.

"See ya," Josh yelled from the kitchen before disappearing into the garage. The quiet thud of the door sounded alarm bells in Kayla's head. Her brother was gone. She was alone with her parents. It was time to confess her sins.

"Mom. Dad." Kayla cleared her throat and stared at her soup. The brown and green mixture was a perfect depiction of her revolting emotions. "I have something to tell you."

Gary dropped his spoon and swung his eyes in her direction. "If you're changing your major again, I'm liable to eat that whole loaf of bread."

Jessica moved the cutting board out of his reach, rolling her eyes in his direction. "What's going on?"

Every nerve in Kayla's body prickled, from the bottom of her feet to the top of her scalp. "I don't know how to tell you this without just saying it so …" She lifted her brows, dragged the words from her desert-dry mouth. "I'm pregnant."

The words seemed to suck all the air from the room. Her mom shrank back against her chair like a balloon pricked with a pin, her mouth working but silent. Her dad gripped the edge of the table with both hands like he was going to push back but didn't budge, his face somehow gaining and losing color.

"What did you say?" Her dad tilted his head in her direction as if "I'm pregnant" wasn't clear or self-explanatory.

"I'm pregnant, Dad. I'm so sorry."

"You're pregnant," Mom repeated, her voice low and leery. "How? Who?"

"A boy from school."

Jessica shook her head. "How could you be pregnant from a boy I've never heard you mention? I don't understand."

"We're not dating." The admission felt as dirty and distasteful as the declaration. Her stinging cheeks flamed. "We're not anything, really."

"Does he know?" Gary asked.

"Yes. I told him. We discussed our options. We haven't made any arrangements yet but we both agree abortion is off the table."

"You both agreed." Mom's voice oozed sarcasm, edging toward nasty. "How lovely. Perhaps you could have agreed to use birth control whenever you had sex with this boy you're not dating."

Kayla's eyes brimmed with tears. Even though she'd anticipated their reaction, every insult felt like tiny daggers to her soul. She knew telling them would be hard, knew their outrage would only magnify her shame, but the way they looked at her, their eyes cold, their faces drawn … She felt like a stranger who'd murdered the innocent daughter they once knew and loved. "We did."

"Oh, well." Mom stood, tossing her napkin onto the table. "You didn't do it right if you're pregnant." She cupped her mouth as if the words caused pain.

Kayla looked to her father, the most rational parent at the moment. "Daddy, I'm sorry. I never meant for this to happen."

Gary nodded, up and down, up and down, a bobble head with hollow eyes. When he looked at her, his pupils had shrunk to pinheads. "Why no abortion?"

"Gary," Mom said from somewhere in the room. Kayla, trapped in her father's stare, couldn't take her eyes from her dad and the curiously detached way he studied her.

"Why?" he asked. "Why is that off the table?"

"Well …" She hadn't expected to have to defend her decision. Out of all the screwups she'd maneuvered in life, this at least seemed like the right thing to do. "I don't believe in killing a baby. I didn't think you would either."

"I don't think it's right. In theory. But this is you. I don't think I want my baby having a baby."

"Dad, I'm not a baby. I'm twenty-one years old."

Her mother appeared, stomping into Kayla's line of vision. "Do you think—at twenty-one—you're ready to be a mom?"

"No, but like it or not, at twenty-one, I'm going to be a mom. I don't have much say anymore."

Her parents went quiet, sinking into their thoughts. Like a grenade with a pulled pin, her confession shattered their Instagram-worthy life. Kayla sat still and let them process. Lord knew it took her days to believe what she'd seen with her own eyes.

"Tell me about this boy," her dad demanded. "Where's he from? What's he like?"

"He's from a small town in South Georgia. Stokeville, Swanville …" She scrunched her nose and tried to focus. Ben had told her and she'd looked it up on her phone, but she couldn't recall the name. "It's about an hour from school."

"So he's from nowhere."

"He's from somewhere, Dad. I just can't remember the name of the town."

"The name doesn't matter." He pinched the bridge of his nose. "What matters is that some kid from nowhere planted his seed in your body."

Eww. Planted his seed? What was wrong with her parents? "He's as happy about it as I am. As you are." She looked down at her hands, realized she'd picked her nail bed raw. "He told his parents. They want a paternity test."

"A paternity test?" Her mom finally sat down across from Kayla in Josh's vacant seat. "Can that even be done before the baby's born?"

"Yes. I looked it up online. It's expensive, but it can be done."

"Have you been with anyone else?" her dad asked, smashing any shred of childhood beneath the heel of his loafer.

"No. No one else. Ever. He's the father."

Chapter Fourteen

Ben idled in Darcy's driveway at ten o'clock on the nose. Usually, Ben would have gotten out of his car, walked to the porch, rapped on the door, and let himself in to the delighted surprise of Darcy's mother. Priscilla Keller fought the daily battle of living life on the razor's edge of sobriety, teetering between lucidity and the depression that called to her like a siren's song. Darcy said Ben was the one person who could draw Priscilla out even on her worst days.

For Priscilla and her daughter, today was going to be a colossally bad day.

Ben honked the horn and watched the blinds in Darcy's second-story window crack open and closed. No use buttering her up before dropping the bomb. Better to usher her out of her house and away from her daddy's gun collection as quickly as possible. With Darcy's habit of keeping score, Ben stood so far in the negative that even a perfect entrance at her home couldn't bring him up to par. He wasn't in the mood to fake small talk with Priscilla while Darcy kept him waiting.

He tapped his fingers on the wheel, watched the numbers on his clock tick up and the needle on his gas gauge spiral down. At 10:14, Darcy opened the door, turned back and yelled something to someone behind her, and sauntered down the steps as if working a fashion runway. An argyle vest over a turtleneck and dark knee-high boots rimmed in fur gave the impression she was ready to mount a horse.

"What's with the outfit?" Ben asked.

Darcy got into the car. Her perfume, something floral and pungent, filled the interior. "You don't like it?"

He yanked the gear into drive and pulled onto the highway. "You'd be all set if we were going on a fox hunt."

"Don't be mean. It's called fashion." She eyed his jeans and flannel shirt. "You could try a little harder sometimes."

Why did he care how he dressed when he'd wrecked two women's lives without even trying?

"Where are we going?" Darcy asked, staring out the window. "We're headed away from town. And why do you look so grumpy?"

Ben pulled off the highway onto a side street. He didn't answer.

Darcy glanced out the window and back at Ben. "You made fun of me for wearing riding attire, and you're taking me to the arena?"

The blacktop gave way to a packed sandy road. Ben pulled to a stop in front of a line of empty horse stalls and killed the ignition. He drummed his thumb on the wheel once, twice, and watched the gravel dust dance in front of the windshield before turning in the seat to face Darcy. "We need to talk, and I didn't want an audience."

A tiny furrow appeared between her brows. "Why do you sound so serious? What's going on?"

Ben sucked in a breath, let it out. "I'm going to Atlanta next week."

Darcy stared at him, waited for the punchline. "Okay …"

"For a paternity test."

Her glossy lips squeezed. Her brows slashed and her eyes narrowed into angry slits. "A paternity test?"

Ben nodded, blinked his eyes.

Darcy tucked her once relaxed arms into her sides and clutched her fingers together. She slowly shook her head. "That's ridiculous. Ben, tell me how ridiculous that is."

Ben sat still in his seat, staring into her eyes, willing her to see the truth.

"Tell me!"

"It's not ridiculous."

"You fathered a child?" Her voice, high and shrill, cracked on the last word. "With someone else?"

He lowered his gaze. "Probably."

"Probably?" Darcy twisted her body and shoved the door open, slamming it hard before stomping along the front of the stalls at a breakneck pace, her arms swinging like the tail of a cantering pony.

Ben exhaled and watched her. He sucked his bottom lip into his mouth. Bit hard. Got out of the car. "Darcy! Wait."

She kept on marching, kicking up a billowing haze of dust in her wake. Ben, stiff after a sleepless night, took off at a jog. He caught up to her after a handful of strides and reached for her arm. "Darcy. Stop. We need to talk."

She flung her arm out of his grasp and turned to face him, her cheeks slashed with angry red patches. Strands of dark hair stuck to her lip gloss and she swatted them away. "How old is the kid?"

"What?"

"How old is this child you supposedly fathered?"

Ben sucked in a deep breath as he realized where her thoughts had gone. "There isn't a kid yet. She's pregnant. She just found out."

Her eyes grew huge, the white swallowing the brown. The first slap caught him hard across the cheek, surprising him into a stunned stupor. He watched the second one come, felt the itchy burn. When she attempted a third, he grabbed her wrist, tongued the inside of his cheek. "Enough. I deserve the first two, but that's enough." He let go when her shoulders drooped, and her arm went limp in his hand.

She stared at him without blinking, her breath escaping in short seething snorts.

"I hate you!" She lunged at him, fisting his shirt and shouting in his face. "How could you?" She let go only to pound on his chest.

Ben didn't dodge. He didn't evade. He didn't flinch. Even her best attempt at battery couldn't breach his bleak barrier. He clutched her wrists when the blows grew weaker and her screeches turned to moans. She wilted against him, sobbing into his chest. Every groan felt like a dagger. Every whimper left a gaping wound. He held her, absorbed her pain, took the punishment he'd earned.

When her cries subsided into hiccuping bursts, he wrapped his arms around her shoulders and let her regain her composure. When she jerked away, he led her back to the car, opening the passenger door and helping her inside. He rounded the hood and resumed his position behind the wheel.

She stared out the windshield with swollen saggy eyes. "When?" she asked, her voice thick like molasses.

"November."

Her eyes flicked to him. Held. "After we were together at homecoming?"

He rubbed his cheeks, felt the heat and the stubble. Said nothing.

"Nice, Ben. Really nice."

"Are you going to sit here and tell me you haven't been with anyone else? Ever?"

She drew her gaze away, lifted a shoulder. "I never got pregnant. It never meant anything. It never happened within weeks of us being together."

He had no answer. They'd both been with other people. They'd both expected to marry each other one day. He'd ruined them both.

"Who is she?"

"You don't know her."

"What's her name?"

Something twisted in Ben's gut, knifing into his spleen. "Why does it matter?"

"I'd like to know the name of the skank who's probably carrying your child. Is that too much to ask?"

Kayla's comment about Darcy popped into his mind. *If someone is furious and possibly going to confront me, the least you can do is give me a little background.* Boy, had she hit the nail on the head from fifty miles out.

"I'm not telling you her name."

"Why not?"

“Because if you know her name, you’ll stalk her online and in person. She didn’t do anything wrong.”

“Oh, really? She slept with my boyfriend. She conceived your child—probably on purpose—and she didn’t do anything wrong?”

It was like talking to his parents all over again. “She’s not like that, Darcy. She didn’t know about you. She’s not happy about the baby.”

Darcy scrunched her face and turned away from him, digging her nails into her arms. After a bloated silence that felt like a noose, she turned back, her brows lifted, her eyes filled with a cunning kind of hope. “Wait a minute. If she just found out she’s pregnant, she can have an abortion. This can all go away, and everything can go back to normal.”

He’d considered it. He’d talked it through with both Theo and Kayla. He’d felt an optimistic yearning to rub the slate clean before Kayla said she couldn’t go through with the easy fix. But sitting in the confines of his car, facing the girl he figured he’d someday marry, his stomach rolled with disgust as she casually and enthusiastically discussed killing his child.

“No. The one thing we agree on is no abortion.” For the first time since he found out about the baby, his heart and his head were in agreement.

Darcy exhaled on a huff, slapping her hands against her cheeks before gesturing palms up in his direction. “Are you kidding me? You’re going to have the baby?”

“What do you want me to do? I can’t force her to have an abortion. I don’t *want* her to have an abortion.”

“So you’re happy about this?

“Of course I’m not happy about this!” Ben took a breath, tried to mine a well of patience beneath the hard, bitter crust.

Darcy had just found out. She was angry. She needed time to digest. He let his breath out slowly. "She won't kill it, and neither will I. We'll deal with it. I'm sorry this hurts you. I never meant for this to happen."

"You're sorry?" Her brows were getting a workout, lifting up and down with every comment. "That's pathetic. You're pathetic."

On that, they could agree.

"Tell me the truth, Ben. Was this some elaborate plan to ditch me?"

Me, me, me, me, me. Ben's head fell back against the headrest and he closed his eyes. "This isn't about you." He opened his eyes and faced her, unable to mask the mocking tone of his voice. "It's about me and her and the baby. We're not going to murder an innocent child because it's inconvenient."

"Go to hell, Ben. You and your little whore can go straight to hell." She turned in her seat to face forward, reached for the seatbelt, and clicked it into place. "Take me home."

"Darcy …"

"I said take me home. Now."

He drove by rote, stopping at every stop sign, signaling before every turn, even waving at a passing car. Darcy seethed in the passenger seat, breathing fire. The rapturous heat of her rage magnified her simmering silence and the sound of his tires scarfing the pavement. When he pulled into her drive, she opened the door before he could even come to a stop.

"Darcy—"

His half-hearted attempt to stop her was cut short by her slamming door and the image of her running up the porch steps to the safety of her home. He stared after her as the car idled, her perfume still haunting the air. He shifted, ran his hands down his face, and reversed before she or her dad emerged with a shotgun.

Driving home, Ben tried to label his emotions. Not sorrow. Not relief. Not resentment. Contrary to all logic, in the midst of his biggest screwup, he felt nothing but numb.

Chapter Fifteen

Kayla sat in the plastic waiting room chair, wedged between her mother and father. Nervous. Nauseated. Afraid. Any minute Ben and his parents would arrive for their eleven o'clock appointment for the prenatal paternity test. It wasn't the blood stick she dreaded, or the harmless cheek swab Ben would endure, but seeing him again. With his parents. Angry. Accusing. Hostile.

Mom pulled Kayla's hands apart so she'd stop picking her cuticles. Her mom had tsked at Kayla's fingers more than once since she'd been home, as if the state of Kayla's nails were as offensive as the child she carried. Kayla sat on her hands, rocking back and forth, her gaze glued to the glass doorway and the parking lot beyond.

She and Ben had texted but hadn't spoken since he'd called and asked for the paternity test. She didn't know what to expect from him or his parents, so she anticipated the worst. Her father sat to her right, reading glasses perched on the tip of his nose, laptop open, emails dinging like an elevator changing floors. Even the receptionist seemed annoyed, casting frequent glances his way. In typical Gary Cummings fashion, he continued working, oblivious.

When a large four-door truck backed into the spot nearest the door and Ben's khaki-panted leg emerged, Kayla's stomach bottomed. She chewed the inside of her cheek.

"Ben's here."

Her father slapped his laptop closed and yanked the glasses from his face, tucking them into the pocket of his work shirt. Her mom fisted the decorative scarf around her neck and cleared her throat. "Here goes nothing," she muttered as she stood.

Ben entered first, then his mom and dad. The resemblance was striking. Ben stood taller than his dad by a couple of inches, but they moved with the same long lanky stride. Ben had his dad's eyes but his mom's features and coloring. His family's height made Kayla feel as if she and her parents were not only a different family, but a different species.

"Hi, Ben." Kayla stood and stepped forward. Like the night at the bar when he'd nearly knocked her over with the power of his stare, the zing of attraction buzzed all the way to her toes. She couldn't put her finger on what made her so aware of him, so pulled by his presence, but the way he looked at her with his amber eyes had her stomach quivering from something other than nerves. "These are my parents, Gary and Jessica Cummings."

Ben reached out to shake Gary's hand, and nodded soberly at her mom. "Ma'am."

"Mama, Dad," Ben gestured to his parents, his deep voice echoing in the tiny room. "This is Kayla. Mr. and Mrs. Cummings, these are my folks, Wade and Anna Strickland."

Everyone shook hands with grim, closed-mouthed smiles.

"Do we need to check in?" Ben's mom asked, her Southern accent as out of place as her green flats and oversized orange sweater. Kayla prayed her mom didn't comment or judge Mrs. Strickland on the unflattering combination.

"I'll let them know I'm here." Ben's departure left them standing in a semicircle, nothing to say, nothing to do but nod. Kayla felt as much as saw his parents' assessing gazes. From the sour looks on their faces she figured they found her lacking, especially compared to Darcy.

Her mother broke the uncomfortable silence. "How was your drive?"

"Wasn't bad 'til we hit the city," Ben's dad said. "I don't know you how y'all deal with this traffic day in and day out. It would drive me crazy."

"Price of doing business." Gary slipped his hands into the pockets of his slacks and rocked back on his heels. If her dad planned to answer mundane questions with that snarky tone, it was going to be a very long day.

Ben rejoined the group. "She said it won't be too long."

Everyone took a seat, Kayla and her family along one wall, Ben and his parents along the other.

Mom fidgeted in her seat and tapped her leopard-print loafer against the floor. She hated quiet, any quiet, especially quiet stretching across the waiting room like an ocean.

"Anna, I just love your purse."

Mrs. Strickland seemed surprised by the comment, staring down at the designer shoulder bag slumped in her lap as if it appeared out of nowhere. "Ah, thank you. I like your … earrings. They're so sparkly."

Jessica lifted a hand to her diamond stud and flinch-smiled. “An anniversary gift from Gary.”

“How lovely.” Anna sounded anything but impressed.

Kayla slumped in her chair and stared at the floor, praying the nurse would appear soon and put her out of her misery. As if summoned, the door to the back of the office opened and a woman in blue scrubs called her and Ben’s names. Kayla bolted from her seat. Ben hoisted himself from the too-small-for-his-frame chair, and they followed the nurse without a backward glance.

“That was awkward,” Ben whispered after the door closed behind them.

Kayla chortled, relieved he could make light of the train wreck in the waiting room. “I wonder what they’ll talk about while we’re gone.”

“Hopefully nothing.”

“Kayla.” The nurse stopped outside a small room with a blood draw chair. “Have a seat, and our phlebotomist will be with you in a second.” She waved at Ben to follow. “I’ll do your cheek swab in the next room.”

He lifted his brows at her, a here-goes-nothing smile tugging his lips, and disappeared down the hallway.

Kayla sat, fighting the urge to pick her cuticles. She smiled when a woman wearing purple scrubs and purple tennis shoes appeared in the doorway, saving her nail beds from torture.

“Hi, there. I’m Veronica.” She pulled a red-topped vial from a drawer and tugged on a pair of latex gloves. “I’ll try and make this as painless as possible. Do you have an arm preference?”

“No.” Kayla extended both arms onto the plank Veronica lowered.

Veronica examined the veins in each arm. “This one looks

good." She tied a tourniquet onto Kayla's left arm and rubbed the vein with an alcohol swab. "You'll feel just a pinch."

Kayla closed her eyes. She felt the prick of the needle piercing her skin and lifted her lids to watch blood flood the vial.

"Keep pressure right here." Kayla pinned the cotton ball to her arm while Veronica applied a Band-Aid. "You're all set." She lifted the desktop so Kayla could leave.

Kayla stood. The room tilted. She dropped her head and placed a hand on the side wall.

Veronica grabbed her arm and eased her back into the seat. "You okay, honey?"

The floor leveled and Veronica's face came into focus. Kayla swallowed, nodded. "Just got a little dizzy."

"Take your time getting up. You can sit there as long as you like."

Kayla heard the squeak of the nurse's tennis shoes followed by the clomp of Ben's boots. She glanced up in time to see him stop, pivot, and brace his hands on the doorframe, his forehead creased with worry.

"Are you okay?" he asked.

"She got a little dizzy," the phlebotomist answered. "Not uncommon for a blood stick in the first trimester. She'll be fine."

He knelt in front of Kayla, his knee popping on the descent, and caressed her arm with his thumb. His hazel eyes heavy with concern. "Have you eaten today?"

Kayla nodded. "Some toast this morning. It's all I could keep down."

"You need a solid meal. You're weaker than dishwater."

Her throat constricted at the thought of food, but she managed a wobbly smile. "What in the world does that mean?"

"It means you're pale," Veronica said with a grin. "I've got some crackers in the break room and there's probably juice around here somewhere."

"No." Kayla shook her head and gingerly pushed to standing. "Thank you, but I'm fine. I just needed a minute."

Ben steadied her with his hands, his long fingers circling her forearms. She could smell him, spicy, woodsy, clean. "You okay to walk?" he asked.

Kayla nodded, twisted away from his too-handsome face. She needed to remember why he was here, why he was being nice—circumstance and manners—and not get lost in the intensity of his stare. "Yep. Thank you."

His fingers brushed her waist as he escorted her to the exit.

Walking back into the waiting room was like walking into a death chamber. Both sets of parents scowled at one another and stood when Kayla and Ben entered. Four pairs of eyes stared where Ben's hand rested along Kayla's back.

Jessica stepped forward and clasped Kayla's arm. "Are you okay? You look peaked."

"I'm fine. Just got a little dizzy."

Her dad ushered them to the clinic entrance, grasping her arm and pulling her to the door. "We'll be in touch," he said over his shoulder before steering them outside and to his car.

"That was rude." Kayla closed the car door and clicked her seatbelt into place. Her father gunned the sedan out of the parking lot and into traffic. "I didn't even say goodbye."

Her mom huffed. "We'll save the pleasantries for later, like when the test results come back. The gall of those people."

Kayla's chest squeezed and she dug her fingers into the leather seat. "What happened?" she asked. "What did you do?"

"We didn't do anything," her dad said through clenched teeth. "They wanted us to pay for the paternity test."

"So?"

Her mother jerked around to face Kayla. "Honey, they think you're lying." She kneaded her dad's shoulder. "I thought your dad was going to lose it."

"What did you do?" Kayla asked.

"Nothing," he said. "I told them I'd be happy to reimburse them if the test comes back negative. We'll know in three days."

"Three days? I thought it took at least a week."

"He insisted on paying the expedited fee, and your mother and I agree. The sooner they have to swallow their pride, the better."

Kayla's heart sputtered to a crawl and her arms felt too heavy to lift. Her cheeks flamed with shame. "Mom, Dad, when the test results come back, I'm going to have to deal with them for the rest of my life. They're going to be the baby's grandparents, just like you. You couldn't play nice for five minutes while I was gone?"

"They called you promiscuous," her mom said. "As if their precious son had nothing to do with you being pregnant."

"Mom, please. Casting blame only makes things harder on everyone."

"Civility will ensue as soon as they apologize," her mom said.

"There's a time to be nice," her dad pulled into their drive, "and there's a time to do what's right. I'll never apologize for defending my daughter."

"And I'm sure they feel the same about their son," Kayla said. "You're both upset with your kids and taking it out on each other. Truth is, Ben and I are to blame. His parents are probably reeling from the news just like you are."

Her dad put the car into park but didn't cut the engine. "I'll be home for dinner," he said to his wife before staring at Kayla in the rearview mirror. "Get some rest and try and eat. The baby takes what it needs. You're too thin to support both of you."

Her eyes pricked with useless tears. For herself. For Ben. For everyone affected by their recklessness. "I will, Daddy."

Chapter Sixteen

Ben sat in the backseat of his dad's truck. Hackles up. Guard down. After finding Kayla slumped in the chair, dull as the gray clinic walls, any animosity he felt at being subjected to cheek swabs and paternity tests faded into compassion. He wasn't the only one dealing with ornery parents. He wasn't the only one suffering the consequences of a poor decision. He wasn't the only one whose future hung in the balance of some stupid lab test.

The baby was his. As much as he hoped Kayla had lied to him and slept with someone else, he knew in his gut she wasn't the type. The fact that his parents had tried to force her parents to pay for the paternity test meant they'd sowed the seeds of bad blood before the baby was even born.

"You'd better pray that test comes back negative," his dad said when they left the clinic. "If you've tied us to that pompous family, I have half a mind to set you loose to deal with them on your own."

"Wade," his mama hissed.

His dad lifted a shoulder in an angry, heartless shrug. "He wants to be a man so bad? I say we let him. He'll figure out soon enough he can't support a baby without a job." He speared Ben with a glare in the rearview. "You'll be responsible for child support whether you've got money or not. Don't count on her parents to come to your rescue. Him with his tailored shirt and her all decked out in diamonds. All that flash, and they wouldn't even pay for half the paternity test."

"They believe their daughter," Ben said. "Can you blame them?"

"You think you're so smart." His dad tapped an irritable thumb against the steering wheel. "I bet you had no idea an unwed mother has full custody rights in Georgia. If you're the dad and you want to see your kid without getting her say-so, you've got to file a legitimation action in court unless she's willing to sign a voluntary acknowledgment of legitimation."

Custody? Visitation? Legitimation? The ache behind his eye turned to a throb, pulsing into his skull. This was getting a little too real. Instead of feeling butt-hurt about Darcy and his future, he should have spent a little time preparing for his dad's legal argument. As it stood, he looked like a fool. "I think she'll sign voluntarily."

"You *think*? We're not going to stake our family's name and assets on your best guess. With a paternity test, we know for sure you're the father before she ties you and us to someone else's baby."

"I get that, but making her parents mad isn't going to help negotiations down the road."

"I don't care if they're mad. If that baby's yours, you've got as much right to it as she does. At least now they know we're not going to roll over and play dead." He braked, jerked around a line of cars into another lane, and cursed under his breath. "And if the baby's yours, we're going to fight for legal rights to custody and visitation, which means she either signs or you have to file."

"That's great, Dad. Now they'll lawyer up and we can fight this out in court instead of sitting down and talking like adults."

"The time for talk is over. Negotiating through lawyers protects both parties." Wade glanced out the window, shaking his head. "And I thought you'd make a good attorney. What a joke."

When all else failed, his dad went for the jugular. Ben's jaw ached from clenching his teeth, locking his comebacks inside. They all knew Scott was the natural lawyer. All that charm, all those smarts, wasted on the son who didn't live to see the end of high school. What good was a second-born son when he'd never live up to the first?

The interstate unclogged after a bend in the road, his dad maneuvered the truck around aimless drivers and sped for home. Ben stared out the window at the passing landscape, mile after mile after mile, stewing in shame and guilt. Silence, shrill as a scream, echoed inside the interior, inside his head. Ben reached for his phone and texted the only person who'd never cast blame.

> Ben: *You OK?*

A few minutes later, his phone vibrated against his leg. He checked the screen.

> Kayla: *I'm OK. You?*
>
> Ben: *Sorry my parents were rude. They're not handling this well.*
>
> Kayla: *I'm sorry for mine, too. This isn't easy for any of us.*

Ben: *Hardest on you, since you're carrying the baby. Did you eat?*

Kayla: *I had some crackers and broth. Nothing sounds good, and not much stays down. I'm ready for this phase to be over.*

Ben: *When does it end?*

Kayla: *Second trimester. Around 12 weeks.*

Ben: *How many weeks are you now?*

Kayla: *Eight.*

Eight weeks. He pulled up his calendar, counted back. The pulsing ache became a dagger. Oh, yeah. He was the dad.

Ben: *How do you know all this stuff?*

Kayla: *I looked it up online.*

Ben rolled his eyes. If he'd spent any time looking to the future instead of the past, he might know a thing or two himself. *Smart,* he texted back.

His dad braked, drawing his attention away from the phone.

"I've got to make a pit stop," his dad said. "If you need to use the bathroom, do it now."

Grateful to have a few moments alone in the truck, he watched his parents walk into the convenience store before picking up his phone. There was another message from Kayla.

Kayla: *I made a doctor's appointment.*

Ben: *When? Where?*

Kayla: *Next Tuesday. Here, in Atlanta. My mom's doctor. Not far from the clinic.*

He'd know the results by then. The official results. He typed *I want to come if I'm the father.* Using a conjunction felt wrong. He tried again.

Ben: *I want to come.*

Kayla: *One step at a time. Test results first. Doctor's*

appointment second.

She was being more than fair—and had been since the beginning. He liked that about her. She hadn't made him feel weird about asking for the test or the way his parents stared at her when they first got to the clinic. Cold. Condemning. Critical. Of course, her parents had done the same.

Her dad's gripping handshake was strong—too strong to miss the message: hands off my baby girl. Too late for that warning to do much good. Her mom was pretty. Petite, like Kayla. Looked youthful and fit. She checked him out casually with a tilt of her head, the sweep of her eyes, never lingering more than a second on any one feature, her expression polite but cool. Her parents wore class the way most women wear makeup—subtle with a hint of money. Jessica's designer shoes, handbag, and diamonds put his mom on the defensive. Anna Strickland, with her big hair and bright colors, hated subtle.

How would they proceed when the results came back? Would his parents soften? Would hers? Could they figure out what to do with the baby growing inside her belly without coming to blows? And if talking about the baby caused this much trouble, what fireworks would dealing with the actual baby ignite?

As his parents climbed back inside the truck, their faces pinched with worry, the only thing Ben could do was stop mourning and start doing. He'd dreamed of studying the law. Now was his chance. Before the results came back, he'd know Georgia's family law inside and out.

Chapter Seventeen

99.9% positive. I'll be at the doctor's appointment. Text me the address.

Kayla slumped against the pillow and read Ben's text over and over again. She'd spent the last three days in a constant state of worry. She knew Ben was the dad, but what if the test was wrong? What if they'd taken the test too early and paternity couldn't be determined? What if, after discovering the truth, Ben walked away and Kayla had to deal with the baby on her own?

Not only did his text confirm what she already knew, it eased her fears about Ben as a person. He wouldn't abandon her or the baby. Why else would he drive three hours to Atlanta for the doctor's appointment? Kayla wedged a bookmark into her paperback and set it on the window seat in her room before making her way downstairs to share the news with her mom.

She found her mom in the mudroom wrestling with Rambo, trying to wipe his muddy paws. "I swear this dog seeks out puddles just to tick me off."

"I told you a white couch was a mistake."

"It wouldn't have been a mistake if you didn't let him get on the couch." Rambo ran into the kitchen the second Jessica disengaged his leash. They both watched him make a beeline to the couch in the den, rubbing his body along the outer edge, explaining the slightly discolored stripe on the back. "Why do I bother?" Her mom tossed the towel into the laundry bin and sighed. "How are you feeling?"

"Okay. I heard from Ben." She lifted her hands. "He's the dad."

"Well." Mom marched past Kayla into the kitchen, giving her the side-eye. "I bet that was a bitter pill for the Strickland clan to swallow."

Kayla followed, ignoring the barb. "He's coming to the doctor's appointment."

"What?" Her mom retrieved an apple from the refrigerator and slammed the door. "Why?"

"Why do you think? I thought you'd be happy."

"I'm just … surprised." She rinsed the apple in the sink and dried it with a paper towel. "I didn't expect him to want to be at the doctor's appointment."

Kayla sat on a barstool and leaned her elbows on the counter. "He's a good guy, Mom. This shows he wants to be involved."

"He's involved whether he wants to be or not. He's the father."

"We've established that."

Mom cut the apple into chunks, the chunks into slices. "Are his parents coming?"

The thought of seeing his parents again burst Kayla's tiny

bubble of optimism. "I don't know. He didn't say."

"It's probably a good idea for him to come," her mom said. "The doctor's going to want a lot of information about your health history and his. You may want to give him a heads-up so he can write down any relevant information."

"What kind of information?"

Mom set the apple slices on a plate in front of Kayla and folded her hands together. "You know, if his family has a history of heart disease, cancer, diabetes, any babies born with congenital defects, Down syndrome. That kind of stuff."

"Oh."

"Look on the doctor's website. It's not a bad idea for us to write our medical history down, too."

Knowledge was power, but sometimes diving into the details made Kayla want to hide under her covers and never come out. There were whole stretches of time when she forgot she was pregnant—while reading a good book, watching a movie with her brother, when she was asleep. The more time she spent researching what was to come, the more she found she couldn't stop wondering and worrying about what life would be like in the days and months ahead.

"Now that we know Ben's the father—" her mother said.

"I already knew Ben was the father."

"Now he's been confirmed, you two have some decisions to make." Mom pulled a paper towel from the roll and squirted the counters with spray. "Have you done any research on adoption?"

"Mom, enough about research. Let me figure out what's going to happen at the doctor's appointment. It's not like the baby's going to be here tomorrow."

Jessica placed the spray bottle under the counter. Wiped with vengeance. "The baby's going to be here sometime next summer, and if you two don't have a plan …"

"We'll have a plan. I promise. Ben's going to talk to his grandmother. She was adopted."

Jessica stopped rubbing and stood up straight. "How is that going to help?"

"She'll provide some perspective on what it's like to grow up in an adoptive family. If she's always wondered about her birth parents, or if she ever felt abandoned."

"Honey." Mom moved around the island and sat next to Kayla, kicking her pulse into gear. "Do you really think you can carry this baby to term and give it away?"

Kayla swallowed. Looked at the apple slices. Picked one up. Tapped it on the plate. Dropped it. "I don't know." She snuck at look at her mother when the silence slithered between them like a serpent. Her expression—concern with a side of soberness—grabbed Kayla's attention. Held.

"This exhausted sick phase is going to pass." Her mom's voice was soft and careful. "When it does, your body is going to change. You'll have ultrasounds at your appointments—probably at your first—and at least one more after that. You'll be able to hear the heartbeat, see the baby grow, watch it wiggle its fingers and toes, eventually feel it kick and move. There's an amazing connection between a mother and her unborn child that happens long before the baby's born."

Kayla watched her mom's expression turn introspective, watched her own hand move over her stomach, watched her mom regard her with seeking eyes. "This isn't helping."

She placed a hand on Kayla's arm. "I know you. I know your soft and tender heart. As much as you'd love to wrap this baby up in a neat little bow and present it to a family who desperately wants a child of their own, I don't see you walking away. Since abortion is off the table—and Dad and I are proud of you for making that choice—his reaction the other night was shock—the only option left is to keep the baby."

"I know that."

"You know what?"

"I know I probably can't give the baby away. I love the idea of it. I've looked at some websites. I know there's a need."

"But?"

Kayla played with the hem of her shirt, rolling and unrolling it between her fingers. "I'm going to get attached. Even knowing it's the right thing to do, I don't think I can give it away and live with myself. I'd always wonder. I'd always miss it. I'd never recover."

Jessica's grip tightened. "Tell Ben. Stop pretending you've got options and start talking reality. You're going to have a baby. You live here. He lives hours away. You're going to be noticeably pregnant at school. You need to figure out how this is going to work for both of you. The sooner the better."

Kayla blinked back tears and tried to swallow the grimy grit of regret. "I'm sorry, Mom. I know you and Dad are so disappointed in me."

Her mother sighed and her shoulders drooped. "We're disappointed, sure, but we'll get over it. Right now, we're worried. Pregnant and unmarried at twenty-one isn't what we'd hoped for you, but it's not the end of the world. No matter the circumstance, a child is a blessing. We'll make do. We'll figure things out. You're not alone." She sat up straight and tilted her head, a sure sign she'd saved the best for last. "But honey, Dad and I are not going to step in and take over. You and Ben got yourselves into this mess, and you and Ben need to come up with a solution."

She was right. A baby would be born sooner than any of them were ready. Her baby. A baby that wasn't going to care how it happened or why, but a baby that needed a mom and a dad. Food and shelter. Stability. Her parents would never let her go homeless, but they weren't going to step in and make decisions for her. The small, selfish part of her wished they would, even though she knew it would lead to disaster. She and Ben had to talk honestly and plan for the future—not the future they'd dreamed of, but the one they'd been dealt.

"You're right. I know you're right."

"Your dad and I feel strongly you need to go back to school and finish your degree. We know you'll start showing during the semester. We know you're going to be embarrassed and maybe even shunned by your friends, but that's a deal-breaker for us. You can see the finish line. It's important to see that through, because you're going to need a job to support your baby."

"I agree. I never considered not going back."

"Good." Mom nodded and studied Kayla. "God's taking us all down a path we never saw coming. We need to tell your brother tonight."

Mom popped her with a left hook she never saw coming. "Tonight?" Kayla didn't want to tell Josh. She didn't want to let him down.

"He knows something is going on. He may not be around much, but he's a member of the family and this affects him, too. We're going to stop pretending nothing's wrong and get everything out in the open."

Kayla swallowed. "Okay."

Her mom sat, chewing her bottom lip, staring at Kayla through narrowed eyes. "Can I ask you something? You don't have to answer but it's been on my mind. If I don't ask you when

I'm calm, I know it may come out later as an accusation and I'll embarrass us both."

Kayla fingered the apple slices, assembled them into an apple shape before letting them fall back onto the plate, anything but lift her flaming face and look her mom in the eye. "Okay …"

"Was it a drunken hookup? A one-night fling with a cute stranger?"

She would have answered her mother if the fist around her ribs would have loosened just a fraction of an inch. As it stood, she slumped in her chair and tried to calm her racing heart. If she hadn't spent the entire time she'd been home trying to convince her parents she was a mature adult ready for the challenges of parenthood, she would have run to her room, locked the door, and never come out.

"It …" She cleared her throat when her voice cracked, picked the apples apart one piece at a time. "I had a class with him my freshman year and I liked him. I'd see him out occasionally and we'd talk, flirt. We kissed a few times, but we never exchanged numbers. The night we were together he sought me out, made me feel like I was the only person on the planet. He told me he liked me. I let things get too far because I liked him so much, and he seemed … I don't know how to describe it … a little lost. A little alone. I'm basically the stupidest, most gullible girl in the world."

"You're not stupid. But honey, sharing your body with someone is a sacred act intended for marriage. At the very least, it should only happen in a loving and respectful relationship."

"I know, and I know you won't believe me when I say this, but I don't sleep around."

Her mother sighed, folded her hands on the counter. "I

understand things can get out of hand when hormones are raging."

"Trust me when I say I've learned my lesson."

When her mom nodded and readied to stand, Kayla's heart took off like a sprinter at the starting block, adrenaline snowballing through her veins. Now was the time to admit the ugliest part. The part that kept her up at night. The part that made her feel as if her skin were on fire and submerged in ice at the same time.

"He has a girlfriend." She stared at her mom, watched her brows lift and her mouth open before everything collapsed onto itself like an accordion. It was time to be honest about everything. "She's from his hometown. He says they're on again-off again, but I saw them together the night I told him about the baby. They're a couple." She shrugged, tried to shake the envy, the guilt, the loathing. But it stuck. An anchor embedded in stone. "It complicates an already complicated situation."

Her mom sighed, a long, withering exhale. She stared unblinking across the kitchen to the window and beyond. For the first time in Kayla's life, her mom looked old. *I did that to her. I aged her overnight.*

The refrigerator hummed.

A distant airplane rumbled.

Rambo slurped water from his bowl in the laundry room.

"Or ..." Her mom pinched her lips, lifted mournful eyes to Kayla. "It un-complicates the situation."

"What do you mean?"

"Before we met Ben and his parents, I thought maybe you'd get married. But seeing how stiff you two were with each other and how harsh his parents are, I wondered if that was possible. Knowing he's with someone and not going to swoop in and propose, at least we know what we're dealing with." She scooched forward and hugged Kayla, resting her cheek on Kayla's head and rubbing her back. "That doesn't mean it doesn't hurt like a knife to the heart."

The hits kept on coming, like a top-forty countdown. Slicing her open. Making her bleed. She'd tried so hard to keep her emotions in check, to act as if she wasn't teetering on the brink of a breakdown every two seconds. All the heartache, all the fear, all the disappointment held back by a smokescreen now spewed forth in ugly, guttural groans. Exhausted, defeated, Kayla struggled for breath in her mother's arms.

"It's okay sweetie," her mother crooned, swaying her side to side like she used to do as a child. "It's all going to be okay. You're not the first girl to have a baby out of wedlock and you won't be the last."

Her throat raw, her breath erratic, her defenses scorched like a deep-fried donut, Kayla asked, "Who's going to … love me … now?"

Jessica pulled back, wiping Kayla's tearstained face with her palms. "What do you mean?"

"I'm … damaged goods … *and* a … package deal."

Jessica cupped Kayla's cheeks, her stormy eyes piercing. "Kayla Cummings. Don't you think for one second you're unlovable because you have a baby. Whoever God has planned for you is in for a double blessing. He'll be ready and willing to love you both."

"How can you … be so sure?"

"Because I believe our almighty God has taken you down this road for a reason. Don't give up hope because this isn't what you expected. Trust God has a plan for you and hold tight to his promise."

Kayla followed her mom's gaze to the ceramic plaque on a plate stand in the corner of the countertop where the words of Jeremiah 29:11 were fired for all to see. *"For I know the plans I have for you," declares the Lord, "plans to prosper you and not to harm you, plans to give you hope and a future."* She'd believed the words her whole life. She struggled to believe them now.

"God's got this, KayBear. Don't ever forget who's in control."

For now, Mom would have to believe enough for both of them. From the strength of her arms wrapped around her Kayla knew she could. "I love you, Mom."

"I love you, too." Her mom wiped the tears from Kayla's face, and straightened. "Now, how about I cut you up another apple since you destroyed that one."

Kayla wiped her nose with the back of her hand. "I never said I wanted an apple in the first place."

"I know. But you're eating for two."

Chapter Eighteen

Ben hit the brakes and swore under his breath. Fewer than ten miles out from Atlanta and he'd come to a dead stop on the highway at ten in the morning. He gritted his teeth and checked the GPS. Forty-five minutes to go eight miles. How did people do this every day?

He switched from streaming music to talk radio, and back again when he couldn't concentrate enough to follow the topic. Tapped his finger to mindless beats. Changed lanes. Changed back. When his phone rang, he welcomed the distraction.

He hit the button for hands-free. "Hey, Theo. How's it going?"

"Good," Theo said. "Good to be home for a while."

Ben pictured his roommate in his small clapboard house that smelled of fried chicken and lemons. Meeting Theo his freshman year had been one of the best things about college. Going home with him, meeting his extended family, fishing in the river than ran along his property, helping out in the general store his family had owned for three generations, eating so much homemade food his stomach ached for days. Visiting Theo's house was a highlight of most summers.

"You working at the store?"

"On and off. Ma's giving me a break for a few days to meet up with friends, hang out with family. I'll start working longer hours next week."

"They're proud of you." As the first in his family to go to college, Theo held superhero status with his family.

"Yeah, well." He cleared his throat. "I wanted to let you know Darcy's been calling and texting."

"Darcy? Why?"

"She wants to know the name of the girl you knocked up—her words, not mine."

Ben groaned. He hadn't seen or heard from Darcy since their day at the stables, a fact that both pleased and disturbed him. Silence from Darcy meant one of two things—she was plotting revenge or dealing with her mother. Neither option lessened his unease. Or his conscience.

"Sorry about that, bro. I should have known she'd go behind my back."

"I told her I had no idea—which is mostly true—but I figured I owed you a phone call. The girl's on the warpath."

"Thanks, man. I appreciate the warning."

"What's the latest?"

"Paternity test confirmed I'm the father. I'm heading up to Atlanta now for her first doctor's appointment."

Ben heard Theo's breath hiss, sizzling his already sensitized nerves. "You're going through with this?"

"Looks that way."

"How do you feel about being a dad? What's the plan?"

Ben felt nothing. Not fear. Not worry. Nothing. "All I know is she's carrying my kid. I'm not going to turn my back on either one of them."

"How are Wade and Anna handling the news?"

"About how you'd expect. Dad and I are in a bit of a standoff since the results came back. I figure he's going to have to talk to me some time before the kid's born."

"And Anna?"

"She's baking from sunup 'til sundown."

"Ouch. Give her my address if she wants to send me some of her cranberry bread."

"They'll be plenty to spare."

"Seriously, let me know if there's anything I can do to help. And don't worry—I'm not telling Darcy anything."

"I appreciate that, man. I really do."

"You hang tough. I'll see you next year."

Ben disconnected. For thirty-five minutes he maneuvered through highway and side street gridlock, speculating about next year. Next year he'd be a graduate. Next year he'd be a dad. Next year, he'd have a job and untold responsibilities.

Arriving at the doctor's building, Ben looped the parking garage, followed the signs to the elevator bay, and punched in the sixth floor. Next year he might call this contrary city home.

The elevator yawned, shuddered, and rose above the concrete spiral. It smelled of crushed cigarettes and stale air. When a jagged-toothed view of the Atlanta skyline came into view, his mom's long-ago voice echoed in his ears. "Boys, we're not in Swinville anymore."

She couldn't have been more prophetic.

This time he'd done his homework. Now that paternity

had been established, he and Kayla had to sign a voluntary acknowledgement of legitimation, but that couldn't be done until the baby was born. For now, all he could do was be there for Kayla and the baby.

He spotted Kayla and her mom in the waiting room the moment he entered the office, huddled together in a cluster of armless seats, whispering over paperwork. They sat next to a child-sized table covered with Lego pieces and building blocks. He felt too big, too masculine in the light green room that smelled of antiseptic and baby powder. Two other women filled the space, a very pregnant woman with dark hair, and a new mother with a tiny infant in a carry contraption with a big blue handle. When the baby kicked its legs against the light pink wrap, it may as well have kicked Ben in the head. He would have one of those next year. What in the world would he do with something so fragile?

Kayla glanced up from the clipboard in her lap. Her eyes brightened, and her lips slanted into a tentative smile that made her whole face come alive. Ben rubbed the sudden ache in his chest. Everyone in his life was either disappointed, mad, or concerned for him, but Kayla, with her honey-blonde hair and sunny smile, looked at him like a person, a man worth more than a scowl or a disparaging name muttered under their breath.

He should have expected to see Jessica with Kayla, expected her critical gaze, expected the distaste on her downturned lips as she watched him approach. Kayla clutched the clipboard to her chest while her mom uncrossed her legs but didn't stand.

"Hi, Ben," Kayla said. "I'm glad you made it."

"Me, too." He took the only seat available in their cluster on the other side of the kids' table, stretching out his legs. "How are you feeling?"

"I'm okay. Tired. Nervous." She lifted her brows. "Your

timing's perfect. I just got the to the part about your family history."

She passed him the clipboard and he scanned the papers. So much information. What did it matter that his grandfather had a heart condition or Ma had arthritis? Didn't kids come out like brand-new cars—shiny and new, with no wear and tear? He tried his best to fill in the information with what his ma had given him, her lips puckered, her hands caked in flour. She'd blamed the upcoming holiday, but he knew from experience she retreated to the kitchen whenever a crisis hit—Christmas or not.

He handed the clipboard back, and caught her mom staring. "How are you, Mrs. Cummings?"

"I'm fine, Ben. How are your parents?"

"They're …" He was going to give her the standard "fine" or passable "good," but the way she looked at him, her eyes steady and relaxed, made the trite answer futile. He was tired of pretending everything was okay. "They're angry, upset, disappointed in me. My ma's baking her fingers to the bone, which is what she does when she doesn't know how to handle a situation. My dad's not speaking to me at the moment. I guess you could say things are pretty tense around the house. Not the Christmas they expected."

Her lips quirked and she nodded her head. "They'll come around. Even when we try not to, we have expectations of our kids. It takes time to readjust when those expectations are shattered. I got arrested my sophomore year of college."

Kayla jerked her head, gawking at her mom. "You did?"

"Underage drinking. I wasn't drunk, but I was holding a beer at a party and got caught. Don't look at me like that."

"You never told me."

"Why would I? It's not something I'm proud of. My parents were angry, upset, and disappointed. We got past it."

For the first time since he entered the room, Ben took a full breath. The muscles in his jaw unhitched. No matter what happened from here on out, he knew Kayla's mom could see reason. He was grateful someone could. "I appreciate that, Mrs. Cummings. I appreciate you sharing something so personal."

"I appreciate your honesty, Ben. We're not going to get through this if we can't talk things through like adults. You two certainly won't."

And there it was, a call for civility, a challenge to engage, an example of just how easy it could be to talk about things even when they're uncomfortable or unflattering.

A nurse appeared in the passageway. "Kayla Cummings?"

Kayla sucked in a breath and stood.

Ben eased out of the chair, waited for her mom to rise.

Jessica squeezed Kayla's hand but made no move to stand. "You got this, baby. Remember what we talked about."

Kayla face was a study in panic. "You're not coming?"

"Ben's here." She speared him with a sharp, meaty stare. "You're the parents. I'll be here if you need me."

They followed the nurse into the hallway like two felons escorted from a courtroom. When the door clicked closed behind him, Ben swallowed around his impossibly dry mouth. Like it or not, there was no turning back. No matter what he wanted.

Chapter Nineteen

Kayla's mom backed out of the space, her tires squeaking around the hairpin turn at the parking garage's exit. Dazed, confused, and exhausted, Kayla sank into the soft leather seat and closed her eyes.

"You okay?" her mom asked for the third time since they'd left the office.

"Yeah. I'm just tired."

"We're alone now. You can tell me what happened."

Her mom had asked Ben to join them for lunch before he drove back to his hometown, but he'd politely refused, all but jogging to his car and peeling out of the lot. Kayla felt nothing but relief he'd bolted and left her alone to digest her feelings.

So. Many. Feelings.

Embarrassment at being semi-naked in front of him. Exposed on the table during the breast and pelvic exam. Mortified when the doctor sheathed the vaginal ultrasound wand and inserted it into her body. Mystified at the tiny blipping bean with the galloping heartbeat the doctor proudly proclaimed their baby.

"Looking good, Mom and Dad," Dr. Francis had said. Hearing the doctor refer to them as Mom and Dad made her stomach flutter with panic. *My mom's in the waiting room. My dad's at work. Do we look old enough—wise enough—to be someone's mom or dad?*

"Honey." Her mom rested a hand on Kayla's leg, soothing, prodding. "What happened?"

"We saw the baby. It looks like a bean or a … a gummy bear."

"They did an ultrasound?"

"And a pelvic exam. And a breast exam." Kayla covered her face with her hands. "Why did he have to come?"

"Kayla." Her mom stretched her name into two long syllables. "Don't be ashamed of your body. Ben's seen it before."

"Not in the daylight. Not on display. I'll never be able to look him in the eyes again."

"You're being a little dramatic."

Was she? Or was her mom enjoying her distress? "I'm sorry. I never expected to feel so … naked."

"It's your body that's giving life to that little gummy bear living inside you right now. I never felt anything but amazed at what my body could do when I was pregnant."

"I guess." She rubbed her belly, thought of the baby inside, felt nothing but the soft material of her sweater. "They calculated the due date at July twenty-eighth."

"That sounds about right."

"The doctor said we're at a great age for children. Said we mitigate a lot of problems by having kids in our twenties."

"She's right. I know a lot of women who didn't even try to get pregnant until their mid-thirties. Even an uneventful pregnancy is considered high risk after thirty-five."

"I guess we did one thing right." Kayla readjusted the seatbelt where it pushed against her sensitive breasts. "We made our next appointment for late January. On a Friday. Ben doesn't have class and I only have one that's over at nine."

Her mom glanced her way before signaling a right turn. "Sounds like Ben's coming to all the appointments."

"We'll see."

"What do you mean, 'we'll see'?"

"You should have seen him in there. He couldn't sit still. If he tried, his knee bobbed up and down and his fingers tapped against his thighs. As soon as the exam started and the flesh parade began, he turned his head away as if he couldn't bear to look. I wanted to die of embarrassment."

"Your dad felt like fish out of water at my appointments."

"Y'all were married."

"Yes, and it still embarrassed him. Look, it's a good thing Ben's coming to the appointments. You didn't make the baby alone. You can't raise the baby alone. The more invested he is now, the more invested he'll be later."

Kayla stared out the windshield at passing cars, watched a man on the sidewalk huddled beneath a puffy jacket, bobbing his head to a beat through his headphones. Studied the dark, low hanging clouds. Dread festered, coated her brain like fog in the mountains. "I'm scared, Mom. Seeing the doctor, hearing the heartbeat, watching it flicker on the screen made it real. I'm having a baby."

"Yes, Kayla, you are."

"I'm not ready to have a baby."

"Ready or not." Her mom turned right into a strip mall near

their house. "Do you remember when you were scared to go to middle school? The teachers had gotten you worked up over how hard it was going to be and how the teachers wouldn't coddle you the way they did in elementary school."

"Yeah," Kayla said. "Sort of."

"You made it through middle school just fine. Am I right?"

"This isn't about life science and Georgia history. It's about a living, breathing, human being."

"Honey, do you think Dad and I had any idea how to raise a baby when you came along?"

"Yes, I do."

"Newsflash." Jessica shoved the gear into park outside her favorite sandwich café. "We had no idea. I was a nervous wreck when we left the hospital and the nurse didn't come home with us."

"But you did fine. You had Dad and Grandma, right? Girlfriends who were moms."

"Your grandmother flew in for two days between European vacations and complained of jet lag the whole time."

"Oh."

"I was the first of my friends to have kids, so my girlfriends had zero advice. My point is, you can do this. You and Ben can raise this child just fine. All it needs is love, and I don't know anyone more qualified to love than you, my sweet girl."

Kayla clutched her jacket to her chest, folded her arms. "Ben doesn't know we're going to be raising the baby. I didn't say anything about adoption, and after today he's probably ready to sign the papers."

"He's probably as freaked out as you right now. Honestly, I'd be a little worried if you weren't freaked out. He'll be at the next appointment, but I suggest you say something soon."

"I will. I have to. But how can you be so sure he'll come again?"

"Instinct. He was here today even though his parents aren't ready to face what's coming. But he showed up. For you. For the baby. That says a lot."

"I suppose. But the naked …"

"Think of it this way." Jessica un-clicked the seatbelt and reached for her purse. "Naked is what got you in trouble in the first place. Do yourself a favor and get over the naked."

Just before ten, Kayla trudged up the stairs, changed into pajamas, and washed her face in the bathroom. She tossed aside the hand towel and studied her reflection. Still pale. Still drained. She lifted her pajama top and turned to the side, stared at her profile, stilled her hand over the tiny bump just above her pelvis. What was going on inside her body? How would that flickering blip turn into a human? She dropped her top and glanced at her phone when it vibrated on the counter, surprised and a little anxious to see Ben's name on the screen.

Ben: *You still up?*

Kayla: *Yes. Everything OK?*

Ben: *I want to apologize for bolting after the appointment. It's a lot to absorb.*

His brutal honesty relieved the knot of tension in her shoulders.

Kayla: *My mom had to talk me off a ledge. It's getting real.*

Ben: *Very real. I'm glad you've got your mom.*

Kayla: *She's been great. My dad's taking it harder.*

Your parents will come around. Telling my brother was weird ...

She set her phone down when she didn't see any scrolling dots, wondered if she'd gone too far. He probably only wanted to check on her, not have a full-blown conversation. She slathered on moisturizer and brushed her hair before setting her phone on the nightstand, crawling into bed, and picking up her romance novel. A text signaled a few pages in.

Ben: *How old is your brother?*

Kayla: *Josh is seventeen.* She hesitated, considered her next words. *Do you have any siblings?*

No dots. She stared at her phone. Waited. Frowned. Still no dots. She dropped the phone, picked up her book, tried not to obsess over the silence. Her phone quivered as she found her place in the story.

Ben: *No. Just me.*

No wonder his parents' disapproval seemed so intense. Without siblings to balance the blow and carry the burden, poor Ben was on his own to leave a legacy.

Kayla: *Maybe that's better. One less person to disappoint.*

Ben: *Maybe. Goodnight, Kayla.*

Kayla: *Goodnight, Ben. Sleep well.*

His smiley face response left her heart aching. How pathetic that a silly emoji left her feeling a little more cherished, a little less invisible? *He has a girlfriend. He's taken.* But kindness was kindness. She'd take whatever she could get.

Chapter Twenty

Ben set the phone aside and stared at the ceiling, listened to the stillness of the house, felt his blood heat, thicken. Between the occasional popping of the hardwood floors and the radiator chugging to life, he watched the moonlight slice through the blinds he'd left cracked. Ben wanted to sleep. He needed the rest after the long drive and the hours he'd spent chopping wood behind the garage when he couldn't think of another way to clear his mind.

Entering the doctor's office distracted—first by the news of Darcy pestering Theo, then by the sights and smells of babies—Ben tripped headfirst into temptation. Lured by the openness of Kayla's shy smile and her mother's kindness, he never saw it coming.

For the next forty-five minutes as Kayla lay bare on the table, her face turned from his while the doctor probed and prodded,

Ben's treacherous body stirred to life. Every time he closed his eyes, he saw her naked but for the thin paper gown. Her breasts, full and ripe. Her skin like mile after mile of undisturbed sand in the fading light of dusk. He'd had to look away, adjusting his pants like a prepubescent kid who gets hard at the slightest provocation.

You're a twisted jerk.

Kayla bravely faced the awkward exam, and he'd paid her back by becoming aroused. Until the swooshing sound of his baby's heartbeat made everything in his body go limp—posture, pulse, privates. Their kid in black and white, heart whoosh, whoosh, whooshing like a washing machine. They were having a baby. Until that moment it seemed like an alternate reality, a role he'd been assigned in a play, a cartoon piano falling on his head.

When Kayla showed up and announced her pregnancy, she'd slammed the door on law school. Hearing the baby's heartbeat nailed the door shut. He could no longer speculate about his future when the kid growing inside her belly needed a home, food, diapers, and a whole lot of other stuff he couldn't begin to comprehend.

His future meant a job—a real job with steady hours and insurance benefits—that would support a family. He'd call in a favor and so would his dad—once he started speaking to Ben again. It would give them something to focus on, something to control in a situation that felt as out of control as the path of a hurricane.

He rolled over, pounded his pillow, tried to force his mind to safer topics. Christmas was next week, and he hadn't bought a single gift. What could he buy his parents to make up for ruining their lives once again?

Ben woke to the sound of a banging door, the gruff tenor of his dad's voice grumbled from the other side. "You going to sleep the day away?"

Ben rubbed the sleep from his eyes, reached for his phone. His dad was ending the silent treatment at six thirty in the morning. "Be down in a minute."

The answering grunt came moments before Ben heard footsteps descend the stairs. He shucked the covers and sat up, stretched his tired muscles. The pre-dawn wake-up call was a calculated move. Deciding a shower was the best way to clear his head before caffeine took him over the finish line, Ben headed for the bathroom to relieve his bladder and arm himself for battle.

His father sat at the kitchen table, glasses perched on the end of his nose, coffee mug in hand, laptop open. He didn't make eye contact when Ben arrived and made a beeline for the coffee pot.

"Morning." Ben thought the silent treatment childish and refused to participate. His father's lack of response had Ben wondering if their standoff was over or if he'd been summoned to suffer another round. Ben filled his own mug, added a splash of creamer from the fridge, and took his regular seat at the farmhouse table nicked by age and use.

"I've got to be in court at eight." His dad stared at the laptop, captivated. After a few suffocating minutes of listening to the refrigerator hum and the wind rustling the leaves on the porch, Wade snapped the computer shut and lifted the glasses to the top of his head, piercing Ben with a lethal stare. "We need to talk about this baby."

It was past time to talk. "I agree."

"Your mama said you went to the doctor's appointment yesterday."

"Yes, sir. Baby's due late July."

Another grunt followed by a sip of the too-strong coffee. Wade set his cup down like a judge wielding a gavel. "I won't be paying for law school."

"I never expected you to."

"I was." His dad made a slashing motion with his hand. "Before you mucked everything up."

"I'm going to get a job, support the baby."

"And the mama?"

The way he said mama made Ben bite the inside of his cheek. "You mean Kayla?"

"What do you plan to do about her?"

"What do you mean?"

"What do you think I mean? She's going to want something from you."

"We made the baby together." Ben sucked in air, held it, forced himself to exhale and lower his shoulders from where they lodged near his earlobes. "I have a responsibility to her and the child."

"Your responsibility belongs to the child, not the mama." Wade ripped the glasses from his head, tucked them inside his shirt. "She opened her legs and got what she deserved."

Ben's hands tightened around his cup. The coffee in his stomach turned to boiling acid. "Is that what you said to Ma when she told you she was pregnant?"

Wade stilled, his nostrils flared, his lips firmed. "You watch your tongue, boy. You don't disrespect your ma in my house."

"But it's okay to disrespect a girl you don't even know?"

"I know her type. I see her type every day at work. Looking

for a man to knock her up, pave her way so she doesn't have to work."

When had his dad become so cynical? And why did it pinch every one of Ben's nerves? "Kayla's not that type."

"You see what you want to see. I see reality."

"Then maybe you need new glasses."

Wade snorted, shook his head. "Joke all you want, Benny Boy. That girl's motives are as clear as the paternity results." He stood up, his chair scraping against the wood floor, and flattened his palms on the table. He leaned into Ben's space, jabbing his finger in Ben's face. "I'm not the one who needs glasses."

"Then think like a lawyer. You can't convict without evidence."

Wade turned from the sink where he'd tossed the remains of his coffee. "I don't need evidence when there's precedent."

"Kayla's not looking for a husband."

"How do you know? Have you asked her?"

"She knows about Darcy."

"Oh." His dad nodded once, tilting his head, crossing his arms. Even his chin looked bored. "Now you remember your girlfriend."

"She's not my girlfriend."

"Every person in town knows you broke Darcy Keller's heart. Old man Keller's out for blood."

Darcy. It always came back to the Kellers.

"That man adored you, Ben. He would have done anything for you and this family."

"Like appoint you to his post when he gets promoted?"

"Well, that's off the table now, isn't it?"

"And that's what you're mad about. My little misstep is messing with your plans."

"Your misstep isn't so little and it's messing with everyone's plans. Maybe if you got your head out of that blonde girl's problems long enough to look around, you'd see where your misstep has landed this family. How do you think your mama feels walking into the grocery store knowing everybody's gossiping about her? About us? Again."

Even his mistakes were interchangeable. One cost a life, one created a life. "I never intended for this to happen."

"You know what they say about intentions." Wade glared at Ben as he plucked his coat from the peg by the door and shoved one arm inside, then the other. "All you owe that girl is to do right by the kid. You get tangled up with her, and you're on your own. If I were you, I'd stop hightailing it to the city every week and start working on your relations here at home."

The door closed at his dad's back, sucking all the air, all the promise of a new day, out of the room. Fix things with Darcy? Seriously? Ben dropped his head, clawed at the muscles of his neck. The caffeine curdled his stomach.

Faced with the same dilemma as the past, and nothing had changed. Ben had no options. No self-respect. No backbone. Ignore Kayla and kiss up to Darcy so his dad could climb the political rung and absolve the family their sins.

Sure thing, Dad. He'd get right on that.

Chapter Twenty-One

Kayla sat on the sofa in her pajamas, watching her brother open the present she'd bought him—a subscription movie service—and laughed at his reaction.

"What is it?" he asked.

"It's a movie streaming membership. The new releases are available when they're still in some theaters."

"Cool." Josh flashed a full-face smile. She hadn't seen that smile since she'd told him about her pregnancy. "Thanks."

"You're welcome."

Mom stuffed the wrapping paper into a trash bag and stood to stretch her back. "That's it," she said. "Sure is easier now that you two are older." She looked at Gary, her lips curling skyward. "Do you remember all the years we spent Christmas Eve putting toys together?"

"How can I forget?" Gary glanced at Kayla, his smile wistful.

"Guess next year we'll be at it again."

Kayla felt the blood drain from her face. She'd forgotten. Gathered in the den, fire blazing, Christmas music streaming through the sound system, she'd forgotten she was pregnant. She tried her best to force the grimace into a smile. "I guess we will."

Josh bolted from the floor and fled the room, taking the stairs two at a time.

"Where are you going?" his mother asked.

"To shower," he said over his shoulder.

Mom sighed and picked up a stray bow.

Kayla unfolded her legs from the couch. "I'll talk to him."

"He'll come around," Mom said. "Just give him some time."

"I'll talk to him," Kayla repeated, rounding the stairs. Her brother had been quiet—too quiet—since she'd told him she was pregnant. He'd looked at her like a stranger, his face drawn, and hadn't said another word about it since. He'd avoided her for days.

She knocked on his door when she didn't hear the shower running. "Josh?"

She heard movement behind his door. "I'll be out in a minute."

"Can I talk to you, please?"

"I'll be down in a minute, Kay. Just let me take a shower."

He sounded annoyed, like a petulant child. She went with instinct and opened the door.

He jerked around, still wearing his pajamas. "What the heck? I could have been undressed."

"Nothing I haven't seen before."

He looked her up and down, a sneer on his lips. "Guess that's true."

Her face flamed. "I'm going to let that slide because I know you remember I used to babysit you."

"Yeah," he said, ripping the shirt from his back and tossing it on the floor of his closet. "That's what I meant."

She closed the door and sat on his bed.

"Do you mind?" He placed his hands on his hips as if to shove his pants down. "I know you've seen this before, but I'd prefer a little privacy."

"Sit down, Josh. We need to talk."

"About what?"

"Please sit down."

Josh sighed, straddled his desk chair, crossed his arms along the top. "What?"

"You've been avoiding me since I told you about the baby."

"So?"

"If this makes you uncomfortable, we need to talk about it."

"I know how babies are made."

Now they were getting somewhere. She could tell by the way he spat the words his anger lay just beneath the surface. "Josh, come on. Talk to me. Tell me what you're thinking."

He snorted. "You don't want to know what I think."

She steeled her back and her backbone. "I do. It's okay. I want you to be honest."

He stared at her unblinking, running his tongue along his teeth. "Okay. Since you asked. I'm embarrassed. My sister—who I used to look up to—got pregnant by some guy she's not even dating and now she's having a kid. The same sister who lectures me all the time about saving sex for marriage."

Kayla felt each word blast through her, swirling, tossing debris, settling deep in her gut to steep. She nodded at Josh who sat shaking with adrenaline, ready for a fight. Ready for flight. She admired his bravado. If only their father would speak his mind instead of tiptoeing around her like a fragile doll.

"I screwed up, Josh. I liked him. I let things go too far, and now we're having a baby. I can't go back and change what happened. It's okay to be disappointed in me. I'm disappointed in myself. I just hope you can find it in your heart to forgive me."

He stared at her, his eyes in slits, his face a slab of stone. "Why didn't you use protection?"

She'd hoped to avoid specifics, realized that wasn't possible. Josh was seventeen, not seven. "We did. It didn't work. Let me be a lesson to you. Sex should be saved for marriage. Until then, the only way to avoid pregnancy is to not have sex."

"That's like saying the only way to stay skinny is to not eat. Easier said than done."

As the truth of his words hit home, so did the insinuation. "Are you … are you sexually active?"

"What? No. Don't turn this around on me."

"I'm not, I'm just … you made it sound like you were having sex."

"With who? I don't have a girlfriend."

"I didn't have a boyfriend and look what happened."

He scrubbed his fingers along his scalp as if scrubbing the image from his mind. "I don't want a lecture on sex. I took the class. I've sat through the talk with Mom and Dad. I don't need to hear it again."

"I'm not trying to lecture. I'm telling you like it is."

"I know what it is. You're pregnant. End of story."

"Beginning of story. I'm going to start showing when I'm at school next semester. Everyone will know I'm pregnant, whether I tell them or not. I'll be judged and talked about. People will wonder who the daddy is. They'll whisper behind my back. Whatever you're feeling about me, I promise I'm feeling a thousand times more about myself. I wish this hadn't happened,

Josh, but it did. I'm sorry you feel embarrassed. You have every right to feel that way. I love you and I'm sorry I disappointed you."

Josh chewed the inside of his cheek. "My friends are jerks, Kay. They're going to talk smack about you and I'm going to have to get in their face to shut them up. That ticks me off."

"You don't have to stick up for me. Whatever they say is probably true."

"True or not, you're my sister. I'm going to defend you. No matter what."

"Josh …" Her little brother, her protector. "Don't get in any fights over me. I can fight my own battles."

"Not when you're back at school you can't."

Plotting the pitfalls of one mistake was like trekking up a slippery slope in rubber shoes. The obstacles were endless. "Would it be easier if we told everyone now, before I go back, before I start showing? That way people can talk while I'm still in town, and it will die down before you go back to school."

"Kayla, I'm not going to tell you when or how to let people know you're pregnant. Like you said, it's going to come out eventually."

"I'll be back at the end of January for another doctor's appointment. Ben's coming with me and he's a big dude. If anyone's giving you trouble, let me know and I'll send him their way."

"Ben?"

"Ben Strickland. Baby daddy."

Josh's forehead fell onto his hands. "Don't say that."

Kayla shrugged. "It's the truth."

"Are y'all getting married?"

Kayla sucked in a deep breath at the soberness of his question.

"No, Josh. We're not getting married."

"Isn't that what you're supposed to do when you have a baby?"

"Sometimes. It's complicated. Ben and I aren't together."

Josh eyed her stomach.

"I got carried away with a guy I hardly knew. I'm a walking, talking billboard for the danger of casual hookups. Pay attention."

He rolled his eyes. "Whatever." He stood up, tucked his chair beneath his desk. "For what it's worth, I'm sorry this happened to you. I'll get over feeling embarrassed. But I'm not asking your baby daddy to fight my battles."

"I respect that. I'm sorry my bad decision put you in this position. I really, really am."

"Like you said, this will blow over and be no big deal. I just need to get used the idea of being an uncle."

Kayla stood, opened her arms, and waited for Josh to roll his eyes before stepping into her embrace. "You're going to be a great uncle, Josh. Young and hip. This baby's going to adore you."

"Yeah, well," he said, stepping back. "That's a given. Can you get out of here now so I can take a shower?"

"I'm going, I'm going."

Kayla shut Josh's door, a smile tugging her lips, and reached for her phone. She dropped it back into the pocket of her robe when common sense returned. She wanted to text Ben, tell him about her conversation with Josh. She stifled the impulse and returned to her parents. Ben wasn't interested in her family dynamics. They weren't a couple.

Wishes were as useless as a glove box full of condoms.

Chapter Twenty-Two

Ben exited the hardware store on Main Street two days after Christmas and walked toward his car, hitting the unlock button on his key fob. It wasn't until he rounded the front wheel that he spotted a pair of riding boots next to his driver's side door. He jerked his eyes up and stared at Darcy, leaning against his sedan, arms crossed, scowl on her face. He wondered why she'd gone to so much effort with her makeup when the sneer she wore voided her efforts.

"Darcy." Ben shook the bag in his hand, listened to the nails jingle inside. "Merry Christmas." He'd been surprised not to hear from her on Christmas Day, so surprised that her presence at his car now caught him off guard.

"Hello, Ben." Their meeting was no coincidence. Darcy had on full battle armor—silky hair he knew she'd spent hours taming, tight jeans showcasing her figure, a sweater with a plunging neckline, a gold chain nestled against her cleavage. "How was your Christmas?"

"Just fine," he lied. The day dragged on forever, from the opening of presents to the arrival of family—with very little conversation and an underlying tension that ratcheted everyone's nerves. The announcement of Ben's latest mistake had his grandmother, aunts, uncles, and cousins gasping, some from disgust, and some from delight in his misery. The silence turned to whispers faster than his grandmother's coconut pie disappeared. His dad walked outside under the guise of gathering firewood and didn't turn up until hours later, surly and withdrawn. "And yours?"

"Not bad. Mom asked about you. If anyone questions how you're feeling, it's because I told her you had the flu."

"Let me get this straight. You told your mom I have the flu and everyone else in town I got someone pregnant?"

She shrugged her shoulders, unable to mask the gleam in her eye. "Has your sordid secret hit the grapevine? I didn't know."

"You aiming for coal in your stocking next year, Darc? You know Santa's still watching."

"Coal would be an improvement over your gift." She snagged the bag in his hands, peered inside, pulled out the nails Nat had asked him to pick up on his way into town. "Let me guess. You're building a crib?" She delighted at his irritation. "No? A treehouse? Maybe a dollhouse?" She threw the box of nails at his chest.

Ben didn't flinch or try to catch the plastic container, but let it fall to the ground. He stared at the girl he'd known all his life and wondered how long she'd make him suffer. "You done?"

"Oh, Ben. I haven't even gotten started."

He bent to retrieve the nails, stood to his full height,

straightening his shoulders. "I'm not doing this here."

"Doing what here?" she asked. "You're not doing anything as far as I can tell."

"What is it I'm supposed to do?"

"Apologize, for starters."

"I did apologize. You slapped me and ran home to Daddy."

"What did you expect me to do? Hug you and tell you it's going to be okay? It's not okay, Ben. It's never going to be okay."

"Then I guess we have nothing to talk about." He stepped forward with the intention of getting into his car. She fisted her hands at her sides and refused to back out of his way.

"How can you be so cold?" she asked, changing tactics. "So unfeeling? After everything we've been through. I'm not the one who messed up. I'm not the one who's going to grovel."

"I'm not asking you to grovel. I'm not asking anything from you, except to leave Theo alone and stop bugging him about the girl. He doesn't know her, and neither do you."

"So I'm not allowed to be mad at you because you've apologized, and I'm not allowed to be mad at her because she's the innocent victim? Wake up and smell the coffee, Ben. The only innocent victim in this scenario is me. I'm the one hurting. I'm the one humiliated. I'm the one you were supposed to have kids with—not her."

Ben glanced around. Darcy's voice carried along the street where neighbors shuffled from the post office to the coffee shop to the corner store. Their paces slowed and their eyes turned in his direction. Darcy carried on and on. She'd gotten what she wanted—a scene in front of an audience—and he cursed himself for playing along. He was sick of going along to get along.

He grabbed her arm and walked her to the other side of the car, opening the passenger door and shoving her inside before slamming the door. The last thing he wanted was to close himself in a confined space with her, but his father's warning about town gossip had forced his hand. He didn't need to add fuel to the fire and make his mama any more ashamed.

He got in the driver's side, tossed the nails in the back, and started the engine. When he turned to check for oncoming traffic, he noted the satisfied smirk on Darcy's face and gritted his teeth. He'd given her exactly what she wanted.

"Shall I drop you at home?"

"That depends," she said.

He waited, refused to engage.

"Are you ready to face my father? He's out for blood—your blood. You've got a long break, and he's taking some time off. I'd watch your back if I was you."

Judge Keller wouldn't jeopardize his appointment by threatening Ben, not this late in the game. "I don't owe your father anything. I apologized for hurting you. If you refuse to accept, that's on you."

"I'm supposed to say it's okay and all is forgiven? That's not how this works."

"How does this work? This has nothing to do with you. You weren't there when we made the baby, and you can't be there when I try to figure out what to do next."

"It's always been the two of us. Why are you shutting me out now when you need me more than ever? I can handle this, Ben. I'm upset and embarrassed, but that'll pass, and we'll make it work. We always do."

"I'm starting to think that's the problem." He signaled left at the stoplight, and looked both ways before turning on the arrow. "I don't need you or anyone else to ride in and save the day. It's time I started taking responsibility for my own mistakes."

“What is this, Ben? Penance? Are you lashing out at me because you know I’m the only person you can’t chase away?”

He sucked in a breath, counted to ten. “You want to psychoanalyze this? Have at it. But ask yourself if this is what a normal, healthy relationship looks like. I don’t think it is, Darc. I really don’t.” He pushed the accelerator when the speed limit rose from thirty-five to fifty-five and glanced at her when she didn’t respond.

She licked her lips and threw her hands in the air. “See? You’re not thinking straight. You never do in a crisis. I’ve thought a lot about this, and I have a few ideas. If you can’t talk your little skank into an abortion, you can rescind your rights and let her deal with the bastard on her own. Or pay her off. You owe her child support and nothing more. Perhaps a generous lump sum will send her on her merry way. You need to stop thinking like a victim and start thinking like a problem solver.”

Ben braked, jerking the car onto the shoulder. It was past time to lay all his cards on the table. No matter what his dad demanded. No matter how much he didn’t want to hurt Darcy. He turned in his seat, calmed his voice. “Calling her and our kid names doesn’t change the facts. The sooner you get that through your head, the better.”

“She’ll change her mind if you press her. Trust me, no college girl wants to raise a baby on her own.”

Ben closed his eyes and let his head fall against the headrest. “I feel like we’re playing a game of tug of war. All we do is tug against each other. All. The. Time.” He opened his eyes and looked at her, tried to see the girl he’d once been so desperate to call his before life turned them into dissimilar and disinterested adults. “Maybe it’s time to cut the cord and see what happens.

We've never done that before. I don't think we ever would if this hadn't happened."

"Ben, you're overreacting. This is just a bump in the road."

For the first time in a long time he pitied her. His life was crap, but at least he saw things clearly. If she refused to see the end of their relationship, he would have to make her see. "Darcy, don't you want better? Don't you want someone who can put you first?"

"I want you, Ben. I've always wanted you."

"Well, I want better for you. As your friend, after everything we've been through together, I want someone better for you than me."

Tears sprang to her big brown eyes, knifing through him. "You don't mean that. You're just panicked and confused."

"I'm not. Darcy, I'm really not." He reached across the console and stilled her frantic hands. "I don't want to hurt you, but this is for the best."

She ripped her hands free. "You can't do this to me."

Color rose in her cheeks and Ben knew she wouldn't let him go without a fight.

"I won't let you to do this to us."

"It's done, Darcy. I'm done. I'm not a dog on your leash you can bend to your will. Aren't you tired of tugging me back when all I do is try to get away?"

"You're not the strong one in this relationship. If I have to carry you through like I've done before, so be it. You'll thank me in the end."

"This is the end. You need to accept it and move on."

"Move on to what? I've given you everything."

"And I'm giving you freedom. Take it, Darc. Figure out what you want for your life."

She wrung her hands like she couldn't figure out if she wanted to strangle him or wipe the angry tears from her cheeks. "You're making a mistake."

"Maybe. Maybe not. But I'm done playing along to make everyone happy."

"And you're going to be happy with some two-bit whore and a kid? Who are you?"

"I'm your ex-boyfriend and your friend. And the woman who's carrying my baby isn't a whore. She's got nothing to do with this."

"She has everything to do with this!" Her voice frayed with a frantic air of alarm. "She's the reason you're abandoning me."

"Darcy, I'm still your friend. I'll always be your friend. I just can't be your boyfriend."

"You're a coward, Ben Strickland. A lily-livered coward."

He'd take the insult if it helped her see he wasn't changing his mind. "Maybe so, but I'm stubborn and I've made up my mind."

Her eyes bored through him, demanding he bend to her will. When he simply stared at her, not smiling, not yielding, her eyes flared with something close to madness before she jerked her head away. "Take me home. I can't stand to look at you."

He'd done all he could to ease the sting, to help her understand. The rest was up to her. He put the car into gear, checked the mirrors, and accelerated onto the road. Two silent miles later he signaled and turned into her drive. An eerie sense of déjà vu settled deep in his bones.

Darcy reached for the door handle, turning to face him before she bolted. "I hate you, Ben Strickland. I'll never forgive you for this." She slammed the car door and stomped up her drive.

He watched her in the rearview mirror before turning back toward home. How long until her daddy grabbed his gun and came to find him? How long until his dad heard and went ballistic? Not long. Ben used hands-free to call his roommate and scheduled a getaway to one of his favorite places on earth.

Chapter Twenty-Three

Kayla pulled into the apartment complex, cut the engine, and reached for her phone. Her mom answered on the second ring.

"I'm here," Kayla said.

"Good. How was the drive?"

Kayla glanced at her apartment door, wondered who was home and what her reception would be when she entered. "Uneventful."

"How are you feeling?"

"I feel good. A little stiff and ready to stretch my legs."

"No nausea?" her mom asked.

"No. It's better every day. Thank goodness."

"All right, sweetie. I love you. Give your roommates a hug and remember what we talked about."

Tell or don't tell, that's up to you, but you don't owe anyone an explanation. Respect yourself, respect Ben, respect the life you're carrying. "I will. I love you, too, Mom. More every day."

"Keep your chin up, Kaybear. I'm praying for you."

She had a lot to be grateful for—a supportive family, a stronger stomach, a growing connection to the baby's father. She just needed to feel thankful and not wish for more. More acceptance. More stamina. More than friendship from Ben.

She'd started to look forward to his texts, his little check-ins every couple of days. She was an incubator and nothing more. If her fingers tingled when his name popped on her screen, she shook them out and chalked it up to her out-of-whack hormones.

Kayla shoved the phone into her purse and got out of the car, retrieving her suitcase from the trunk and lugging it up the stairs. She paused to catch her breath and gather her nerves before opening the door. She loved her roommates and cherished their time together—especially since this was their last semester—but she worried there'd be probing questions, lingering hugs, pitying glances. She couldn't stomach pity. Not from them.

Reagan hopped up from the couch when Kayla entered, yanking the suitcase from her hand and pulling her into a hug. Her serious roommate had been more demonstrative since falling in love. "Why are you carrying this heavy suitcase up the stairs? Why didn't you call me?"

"I'm pregnant, not lame."

Emily and Shelby appeared from the hallway. Emily wore yoga pants and a long-sleeved shirt, her hair pulled back with a headband. Shelby's long hair flowed over a threadbare sweatshirt. Seeing them all together, smiling natural smiles, acting normal, made Kayla feel like she'd stepped into a warm embrace. She couldn't have asked for a better homecoming.

"Welcome back," Emily said. "How was the drive?"

"The usual. How long have y'all been here?"

"I beat you by an hour." Reagan tugged Kayla's purse from her shoulder and set it on the suitcase.

"Dylan and I got back a few days ago," Emily said.

"I got in last night." Shelby wagged a thumb at Emily. "Walked in on the lovebirds playing house."

Emily rolled her eyes. "With all the family in town for Zach and Jenna's wedding, we hadn't been alone in weeks."

"How was it, watching your ex get married?" Kayla asked, grateful to have something other than her pregnancy to talk about.

"It was wonderful. It's nice to see Zach happy, and I adore Jenna."

"Y'all should be a reality show," Shelby said. "Like *The Bachelorette* except all the bachelors are brothers."

Emily ignored Shelby's dig and blinked at Kayla. "You look good. How are you feeling?"

And so it begins. May as well get comfortable. Kayla shed her coat and sat on the couch. "Good. The queasiness has subsided for the most part, and I'm getting my energy back."

"Your color's better." Shelby sat, folding her legs under her. "You looked like a dead fish the last time we saw you."

"Ouch."

Shelby shrugged. "Don't blame the messenger."

"Seriously," Kayla said. "I appreciative y'all more than I can say. Your calls and texts over break meant a lot."

"Don't be stupid." Reagan propped a pillow against the coffee table and sat on the floor in front of her. "We love you. And you'd have done the same for us."

"Did you tell anyone at home?" Emily sat next to Kayla. "I mean, other than your family?"

"I told a few friends from high school. I figured it was better to tell them now than wait until I ran into them looking like I swallowed a basketball."

"How hard was it to break the news?"

"Hard, and I'm sure everyone in my class knows by now, but it's over. I may as well get used to the shocked looks on everyone's faces and the phony excitement. I'll figure out who my real friends are in the next few months, that's for sure."

"We're your real friends." Emily squeezed Kayla's arm.

"I know." Kayla covered Emily's hand with her own. "And I love y'all. It's going to be a tough semester. I'm going to start showing. People are going to talk." She tucked the hair behind her ears and looked each roommate in the eye. "I'm probably going to complain a lot, so I'm apologizing in advance."

"Are you kidding me?" Reagan said. "After all the drama you had to deal with between me and Dash, I'd say you're due."

"Not to mention me and Dylan," Emily said.

Shelby lifted her hands in the air. "You're welcome. Not dating has its advantages. But I'm here for you, too. If anyone gives you a hard time, just let me know. I've mastered the cold stare."

Kayla chuckled. "I may need some lessons."

"Consider it done."

"What about Ben?" Emily asked. "Are y'all still talking?"

"He checks in." Kayla shrugged, picked her nail, heard her mom's chiding voice in her head, and sat on her hands. "He's been great."

Her roommates exchanged meaningful looks, one to the other, dripping with dread.

Kayla swallowed, trying in vain to tamp the heat scaling

her chest. "Just go ahead and say it," she said. "I know he has a girlfriend."

"We just don't want to see you get hurt," Emily said.

"It's your heart." Reagan sighed. "It's so big and soft."

Shelby crossed her arms. "What they're trying to say is you're a hopeless romantic. We're worried about you falling for him and getting your heart broken."

Kayla stared at the rug. When she spoke, her voice cracked. "I'm worried about that as well."

"Oh, no." Reagan's shoulders drooped. "Is it too late?"

"No. Like you said, I'm soft. And hormonal. And the only one who understands what I'm going through is Ben. He came to the first doctor's appointment, says he's coming to all of them, and he texts me regularly to see how I'm doing. It feels … intimate in a weird kind of way."

"Does he talk about her?" Emily asked. "The girlfriend?"

Kayla understood Emily's obsession with Darcy. If Dylan got someone pregnant—someone other than Emily—it would rock her world. And not in a good way. "No. That's part of the problem. It would help if he'd throw her name in once in a while to remind me he's taken. But all he does is ask about me, show concern for me and the baby, and I start to spin fantasies in my head." She dropped her face into her palms. "I'm pathetic."

"No, you're not," Shelby said. "You've always wanted to fall in love and he's acting like a boyfriend. It's only natural to feel confused."

"He's just so nice." Kayla let her hands fall, sighing like a lovesick teenager. "Why does he have to be so nice?"

"He did sleep with you and never call." Reagan yelped when Emily kicked her foot.

Emily shot Reagan a pointed stare. "That was a little harsh."

"She's right," Kayla said. Reagan's honesty sat like a splinter under her skin—a splinter Kayla needed to leave right where it jabbed. "He could have found me, and he didn't. Not once. And he never told me about his girlfriend." She nodded and glanced at her friends. "I needed this pep talk. More than you know."

"We love your soft heart," Reagan said. "It's one of your best qualities—the way you're open to loving everyone."

"It also leaves me vulnerable. I get it. I appreciate the reminder."

"It's our last semester together," Emily said. "And we're family. We're not going to let anyone hurt our family."

Tears sprang fast to Kayla's eyes, too fast to stop. "I love you guys."

Reagan got to her knees and hugged Kayla's shoulders as Emily leaned in from one side, Shelby from the other. Kayla spread her arms and welcomed the group hug. She needed them—their love and support—now more than ever.

She would do her best to feel grateful. For great friends. A supportive family. A dutiful father to her baby. She could do so much worse.

Chapter Twenty-Four

Ben walked to his car after class, his pace unhurried, his mind adrift. After he'd bombed the LSAT last semester, he'd been laser focused on getting into law school and starting the next phase of his education. This semester, he faced the end of his educational aspirations and didn't have a clue about his future. He'd graduate with a political science degree, but what then? Every day without a goal in mind felt like another day wasted.

A meeting with his counselor hadn't helped. He knew he needed to get a job, and her recommendation to apply widely didn't exactly set him on a career path. Whenever he explored his options—which were many—he kept coming back to something Theo's brother said over break. *You thought you'd spend your life in the law. Nothing says you still can't.*

The more Ben thought about it, the more his advice resonated.

There were many ways to work in law that didn't require law school. Did the world need another lawyer? But Ben needed a career—not just a job. He needed to support his child.

Ben cut through the staff lot, his attention drawn to an SUV with "Just Married" written on the back of the windshield, and tasted the sour sting of regret. He never thought he'd have a kid out of wedlock. Even now, weeks after coming to grips with reality, the idea didn't sit well. Shuffling his kid back and forth between Atlanta and wherever he settled sounded like torture. Dealing with the traffic. Missing milestones because he'd only see his kid every other weekend. It was a life he couldn't imagine. And he'd tried. A lot.

And then there was Kayla. Sweet Kayla, raising his kid on her own. Working. Carting the baby back and forth to daycare. Up all night with no one there to help. Nothing about that sat well with him either. He'd gotten to know her over the past few weeks and appreciated her optimistic attitude, her ability to find a silver lining. He found himself longing for that optimism when thoughts of the future got him down.

He paused at the crosswalk, looked both ways for on-coming traffic, and continued to his car. The only thing he felt confident about was ending things with Darcy. Her silence had him worried. He knew she'd cried on his mother's shoulder—the ensuing phone call and chewing out hadn't been fun. He wouldn't spend his life with someone who called his baby a bastard or the mother numerous colorful terms. After all that, did Darcy really think he'd ever trust her with his kid or his heart?

"Ben!"

He glanced up, saw his frat brother, Joel, jogging down the sidewalk in his direction. "Hey, man." They bumped knuckles. "What's up?"

"Haven't seen you around," Joel said. "How was your break?"

"Good," Ben lied. Calling his break "good" was like calling a nuclear war a disagreement. There wasn't anything good about it. "How was yours?"

"Great," Joel said. "Got a job with my uncle's accounting firm, so the pressure's off. Finally."

"Congrats, man. Good for you."

"You still shooting for law school?"

"Ah … no. I've had a … uh … change of plans." He should tell Joel about the baby. What would be the harm? He was having a kid. Everyone would find out eventually. But if he kept it under wraps until after graduation, then he wouldn't have to deal with the fallout from his friends. At least not right away.

But then he thought of Kayla. Sometime this semester her pregnancy would be impossible to disguise—especially as the temperatures increased and the amount of clothing she wore decreased. She wouldn't have the option of whether to tell people she was pregnant—they'd know.

"I, uh, I'm having a kid, so I need to find a job."

Joel jerked backward, his mouth opened, worked, closed. He blinked once. Twice. "Wow," he half chuckled, half choked. "That's … unexpected."

"You could say that."

Joel took a deep breath, shook his head, and slapped Ben on the shoulder. "Congrats, man. Darcy's a great girl. I wish you both the best." Joel turned and continued on his way.

Gobsmacked, Ben swayed as if glued to the concrete. Of course Joel assumed he was having a baby with Darcy. Of course he would. So would everyone else. Ben blinked against the bright winter day, his cheeks stinging from the cold, and walked to his car in a daze. He thought he'd done a good thing—owning up to the baby, voicing the turn his life had taken—but Joel took the news and threw a curve ball Ben never saw coming.

Ben stewed for a few days, replaying Joel's reaction in his head over and over, like a movie on repeat. *Darcy's a great girl. I wish you both the best.* He should have stopped him, reached out and grabbed his arm, told him it wasn't Darcy having his baby, but someone else. Someone better. Beyond that, he didn't know what he would say, how he would explain. It didn't seem a decision he could or should make on his own.

Kayla agreed to meet him at an off-campus coffee shop at ten on Saturday morning. He looked forward to seeing her. He didn't look forward to the topic they had to discuss. When she entered the café at ten on the nose, his pulse quickened, and his palms grew damp. She exuded warmth—from the top of her sunny blonde head to the soles of her pink canvas shoes. Everything about her oozed joy.

"Hey." Ben stood to greet her, gave her a hug, inhaling the fresh scent of raspberries. Even in the dead of winter, she made him think of hot summer days.

"Hi, Ben." She took the seat he offered, linked her hands on the table, and graced him with a shy smile. She was so pretty, so feminine without all the trappings Darcy used to lure a man. Wearing only a shimmery gloss on her lips and nothing else, she captivated his attention and had him returning her smile with one of his own.

"It's good to see you," he said. "You look good." She smelled good as well, but using the word "good" in another sentence seemed like overkill.

"Thanks. You do, too. I like your haircut."

He rubbed his hand over his trimmed locks, his lips curving into an embarrassed grin. Darcy never noticed or commented on his haircuts. He'd mocked her for it regularly. "Your hair always looks the same," she'd say. "How am I supposed to tell you got it cut?"

"Figured it was time for a trim."

"It suits you."

So do you. He shooed the thought away in favor of something more appropriate. More welcome. "Thanks. Thanks for meeting me."

"Of course." She brushed the hair from her eyes with pink painted fingers. "Is there … do you have—"

"Yes," he said. "There's something we need to discuss."

She took a deep breath, thrusting her chest in his direction, making him notice the way her shirt stretched across her bust. "Okay."

He shook his head, wrenched his eyes to hers, held. "I … uh …" He glanced down at the empty table to gather his courage and realized his mistake. "Where are my manners? What can I get you to drink?"

"Oh, um …" She shrugged her shoulders. "Water, I guess, but only if you're getting something for yourself. I'm fine with nothing."

He needed caffeine in his system about as much as he needed a shot of adrenaline, but he hopped up to place an order. They could hardly take a table at the popular shop without buying something, and it gave him a few minutes to organize his thoughts. He knew he was bungling an important conversation.

He returned with her cup of water and resumed his position across the table from her, cradling his mug in his hands. She thanked him and considered him with worried eyes.

"I ran into a friend the other day," Ben said. "I told him about the baby."

Her brows leaped into her hairline.

"He asked about law school, and I had to explain that my plans had changed."

"That makes sense." Her voice was soft, measured.

"He said something that made me ..." Ben stopped, struggled, decided there wasn't any way to sugarcoat the truth. "... he wished me and Darcy well."

She made a noise in her throat, something like a cross between a gag and a whimper.

"His comment caught me off guard." Ben fumbled for a way to explain, for a way to ease the horrified look on her face. "And I kinda froze. I ... I didn't correct him. I mean, I wanted to, but he walked away. Well, he jogged away as fast as he could. Nothing like an unplanned pregnancy to send people fleeing."

His joke didn't lessen the tension in her eyes. She cringed and tugged at the scarf around her neck. Color flooded her face.

"I'm going to set him straight—I am," he said at her disbelieving stare. "But I'm not sure how to do that. I mean, I don't know what you want me to say, if you want me to use your name or ... not." Ben felt like he'd kicked her when he noticed the way her hand trembled as she raised the cup to take a sip. "It's nobody's business, but I'm not sure ..."

"Um." Kayla cleared her throat, picked at the lip of the cup in her hands. "I don't know what I want you to say. I haven't told anyone at school yet—other than my roommates—and I haven't thought about what I'm going to say when I do. I'm sorry. I know that makes me sound immature."

"It doesn't."

"I'm not trying to be difficult."

"Kayla." He reached across the table, placed his hand over hers. "You're not being difficult. This is … uncharted territory. For both of us."

She stared at him, her eyes seeking, searching. "I guess what you tell them is up to you. You can use my name if you want. If you'd rather not, you don't have to. But you do need to correct him. Just because Darcy is hours away at another school doesn't mean a nasty rumor won't reach her or people she knows. I'd hate for this to come back on her any more than it already has."

Even at her lowest, she still thought of others. The depth of her empathy shocked him, left him humbled. "I will. I wanted to talk to you first."

"I appreciate that, Ben."

She wanted to leave. He could tell by the way she pulled her hand from his, fidgeted in her seat, and glanced around the café, not meeting his eyes. He needed her to stay, wanted to erase that haunted look on her face, make her smile. Make everything okay. "How are your classes going? How are you feeling?"

"They're good. The nausea is mostly gone, and I've got more energy. I can go whole stretches of time and forget I'm expecting."

"Yeah?" he asked. "Me, too. Kind of."

"But when I remember, it's like a hangover—not worth it in the end. It's better to face reality."

"True."

"I'm impressed you told someone. I'm scared to tell, but I'm going to have to eventually. Before too long, I won't have any choice."

"If I do mention your name," Ben said. "I mean, if it comes up because someone asks, I'll tell you. I won't let you get blindsided."

Kayla nodded. "I'll do the same. Girls will ask. I can protect you if you want. The truth is if you tell people you're having a child and I start walking around campus visibly pregnant and we're ever seen together, people will know. It's a big campus, but it's not that big. People aren't stupid."

She was right. People would figure it out whether they used names or not. "I guess the best we can do is not worry about other people."

"My mom told me to respect myself, respect you, and respect the baby. Nothing else matters."

"I like that. Your mom's right. At the end of the day, what others think doesn't matter." Ben pushed his cup aside, looked into Kayla's bright blue eyes. "I'm going to call Joel and set the record straight."

"Good."

"I'm glad we talked. I'm glad …" He stopped, felt his ears flame.

"What?" she asked, tilting her head to the side.

Ben swallowed, gathered the courage to be as honest with her as she'd been with him. "I'm glad it's you. I mean, if I'm having a baby, I'm glad it's with you."

Chapter Twenty-Five

"He said what?"

Kayla prayed Reagan could untangle Ben's parting shot. "He said, 'If I'm having a baby, I'm glad it's with you.'"

Reagan clicked a few keys and closed her laptop but not her mouth. It flapped while she stared wide eyed at Kayla. "I don't even know what to say."

"I know, right?" Kayla sat down at the kitchen table, let her palms fall open on the surface, and tried to sort through her swirling emotions. "He must have meant if he had to have a baby with someone other than his perfect, beautiful girlfriend, don't you think?"

"That must have been what he meant, but he had to know how that sounds."

"How does it sound?" Kayla knew how it felt. Sitting across

from him, fresh shaven, hair shorn, she'd gotten lost in bright, greenish-brown eyes, the woodsy scent of his barn jacket, the feel of his calloused fingers on her skin. It felt like he was happy to see her, trying his best to assuage her fears and put her at ease. Her imagination was on a crash course with heartbreak.

"It sounds like he's grateful you're making it easy for him. No pressure. No expectations."

"For them," Kayla said, as much to herself as to Reagan. "Ben and Darcy."

"Is that why he wanted to meet? To thank you for having his child?"

"He told someone about the baby, and his friend assumed Darcy was the mom. He didn't correct him—he's going to," she said when Reagan's eyes popped. "But he asked me what I wanted him to say. Whether or not to use my name."

"What'd you tell him?"

"I told him it didn't matter what he said. People will figure it out anyway."

Reagan tapped her fingers on the table in a move that reminded Kayla of Dash. They were mirroring each other's behaviors.

"You know, this whole thing is unfair. He could hypothetically fly under the radar this semester while you take all the heat."

"I know, and he knows it, too. But we're going to be seen together. It's inevitable. People will talk and put two and two together."

"How does that make you feel?"

Kayla scrubbed her hands over her face. "Like I'm a walking PSA about the dangers of unmarried sex."

Reagan glanced away, sucking her lips between her teeth.

"What?" Kayla asked. "Why do you have that look on your face?"

"What look?"

"Like you just ate the last cookie, and I'm having a craving."

Reagan sighed, considered Kayla. "It's just .... your situation, what you're facing, forced a serious conversation between me and Dash that was long overdue."

"A conversation about what?"

"About us. About our relationship. About the future. When you found out you were pregnant, Dash and I were inching closer and closer to intimacy. We even talked about not waiting like we promised."

Kayla sat back, let her shoulders sag. "But now you're not."

"What happened to you made us take a step back and examine our motives. We were being selfish and thinking with our bodies instead of listening to what God wants from us. We've decided to wait. We're more committed than ever to let God's will prevail."

"Wait for marriage?" Kayla asked.

"Yes."

"To each other?"

Reagan's cheeks turned a lovely shade of peach. "Yes, of course to each other. I know it sounds crazy. He just graduated and I've got another semester."

"Honey." Kayla placed a hand on Reagan's wrist, stilling her frantic movements. "That's wonderful. I'm so happy for you. But why do you look … angry?"

"I'm not angry. I'm … It's not like I planned this. Never in a million years did I think I'd be talking about marriage at my age, much less before I graduate college." She shook her head and scoffed. "All the times I bashed Emily for planning her future around a guy and here I am doing the same."

"You're following your heart—just like she is."

"I know, but it still makes me a little queasy. I mean, we're so young. Can it really last a lifetime?"

"Of course it can. My parents met in college and they're still married—happily married."

"That's encouraging."

"Let me ask you something. Are you willing to let Dash go just because your timeline isn't what you expected?"

"No. I love him. When I think about my future, he's there. We're there together. I may feel a little nervous but I'm not willing to screw up a good thing because I'm scared."

Her roommate had come a long way in a short period of time. "Sometimes the most amazing blessings are the ones we least expect."

Reagan's gaze traveled to Kayla's belly. "The same could be said for you."

Kayla snorted. "An out-of-wedlock pregnancy isn't what I'd call a blessing."

"Why can't you call it a blessing?"

"Reagan …"

"You can call it unplanned. You can call it a surprise. You can call it a mistake if you want. But it's a life. It's a life that's a part of you, Kay, and you're fantastic. So, why would you choose to look at that life as anything but a blessing?"

"Are you serious? Do I need to make a list?"

"Yes, I'm serious. And I know how ironic that sounds coming from a cynic like me. But one thing I've learned in the last year is that so much of life is how we choose to look at things. I'm so grateful that when my mom was in the same position as you, she chose the hard way because she knew my life counted."

"I'm having the baby. It's not like I haven't already chosen life."

"I know, and I'm proud of you."

Kayla watched her friend fiddle with her laptop cord, a crease between her brows. She could tell there was more Reagan wanted to say, something she wanted to get off her chest.

"You should know." Reagan cleared her throat. "You're a big part of the reason I opened myself up to love. A huge part. You showed me how to let go of the fear and let someone in. I never would have found this happiness without you."

Kayla's eyes filled with tears. "Oh, Reagan …"

"Don't cry, Kayla. I'm sorry."

"Oh, please." She swiped her cheeks. "What doesn't make me cry? Just because I'm knocked up and alone doesn't mean I can't be happy for you. I wish I'd learned from you and not let everyone in, not let my emotions rule every decision I make. Maybe then I wouldn't be in this position."

"Maybe so, but if anyone can handle what you're facing, it's you."

Kayla appreciated the vote of confidence, but she still felt like a fish swimming upstream. "I'm not exactly handling anything right now."

"Yes, you are. You're taking care of that baby and loving it like only you can." Reagan pulled her hair back and tied it into a knot on her head. "Would you … would you have any interest in talking to my mom?"

Kayla pinched her lips, considered the question. "I don't know, Reagan."

"I know your situation is different. You'll have a college degree and Ben is willing to be a part of the baby's life, but she's been there. She's raised a child on her own. Maybe talking to someone who's been through it will help."

Or completely freak her out. "I appreciate the offer. Can I think about it?"

"Of course. No pressure. I just thought it might help."

Kayla wrestled her face into a smile, determined to bury the ugly seed of envy threatening to sprout. "What helps is knowing two of my favorite people are planning their lives together. Reagan, I'm so happy for you and Dash. I mean it. You deserve to be happy."

Reagan reached across the table, squeezed Kayla's hand. "So do you, Kay. Don't lose faith. God has a plan for you. I know He does."

God definitely had a plan, and right now, more than anything, Kayla wished He'd clue her in. Because at this moment, His plan was as clear as mud.

Chapter Twenty-Six

Ben inhaled, savoring the raspberry and sunshine scent infusing his car, and exhaled before glancing at Kayla in the passenger seat. She'd drifted off to sleep not long after they'd started the four-hour drive to Atlanta, her head propped against the window, her arms limp in her lap.

Despite feeling like a pervert, Ben took advantage of her unconscious state to study her profile. Her nose was petite like the rest of her, her modest chest edging toward curvaceous beneath her thin down jacket, her dusty pink nails twitching against her leg as she dreamed. Her honey hair shone with health, her complexion was smooth and unblemished, and her jeans were snug in all the right places.

He'd thought of her more times in the last few weeks than he dared admit. He'd looked forward to seeing her again, spending time with her in the car, hearing the sweet sound of her voice.

Even if it was because they were on their way to see the doctor and spend the night with her family before heading back the next day.

Theo noticed the change in him. "You're a little chipper for a guy who's about to spend hours in the car with a hookup on his way to a prenatal doctor's appointment. What gives?"

Ben had shrugged him off. "What you call chipper I call resigned. May as well make the most of it."

Theo eyed him suspiciously, but he'd let it lie.

If Ben could understand his feelings, perhaps he'd know what to do with them. Considering he'd just gotten out of an unhealthy, unstable, unpredictable relationship, he should be reveling in the freedom. Instead, he'd developed a crush on the girl Theo coined his "baby mama."

But Kayla didn't make him feel trapped and cornered the way Darcy did. She made him feel comfortable. And that was the problem. Ever since Scott died, nothing felt comfortable. Every decision he made—no matter how big or how small—was viewed through the lens of keeping the peace with his family.

Going to Southeast State like he'd always dreamed? Out of the question. It was too far from home. Breaking up with Darcy? Not an option. Her family's loyalty was the only reason the Stricklands could hold their heads high in town. Pick his own college major? Impossible. His dad's dream of a family legal practice took precedence over Ben's dreams for his future. His sons were interchangeable, like matching puzzle pieces. One dies, the other takes his place. No fuss, no muss, and certainly no discussion.

Kayla stirred, bringing Ben back to the present and halting his trip down woe-is-me lane.

She stretched her neck and blinked her eyes against the sun. "Where are we?"

His blood stirred at the gravely sound of her sleepy voice. "About an hour out."

Kayla sat up in her seat. "I slept for almost three hours? I'm sorry, Ben."

"Nothing to be sorry for. You were tired." He glanced over, gave her one of his gentlemanly smiles. "Feel better?"

"I do. Thanks." She rubbed the back of her neck. "I was up late, writing a paper. It took more out of me than I thought."

"You're sleeping for two."

She gave him a don't-remind-me smile before staring out the front windshield, worrying her lip as they listened to Jason Aldean sing about the flyover states.

"Ben."

He grunted in response, lifting his chin and gripping the wheel tight. He didn't like the anxious sound of her voice.

"Did you … did you ever talk to your grandmother?"

His stomach shifted into low gear. Ever since he saw the baby on the ultrasound, he'd considered adoption out of the question, and he figured she did, too. He turned the volume down. "I went to see her. She spent most of the time reassuring me my dad would come around."

"Is he still upset with you?"

"For a variety of reasons, yes."

"Is she your dad's mom?"

"Yes."

"Did you ask her about …"

If she couldn't even say it, how did she think they could consider it? "Adoption?"

Kayla nodded.

"After her pep talk, it didn't feel right telling her we were considering giving the baby away. It felt …"

"Disloyal?" Kayla asked.

"Pretty much. She said she was proud of me." He saw Kayla wringing her hands out of the corner of his eye, decided to give her an out. "I don't know about you, but after the last appointment, I don't think I can give the baby away."

She whipped her head in his direction, her words coming out on a whoosh. "You don't?"

"The more time we spend going to and from the doctor, making sure we're doing what's right for the baby, watching it grow …" He shook his head. "I don't see us handing it over to strangers."

When she sighed, he turned his head to see her eyes shining, her palm over her heart. "I don't either. I'm glad we're on the same page."

He reached over the console, took her hand in his, linked their fingers. "It may not have been planned, but it's here, and it's ours. I know we won't be perfect parents, but we won't be the worst, ya know?"

Kayla chuckled. "Surely we can manage something between perfect and the worst."

Ben didn't let go of her hand, and Kayla didn't pull hers away, not until she needed to rummage through her purse for a tube of lip balm. They sat in companionable silence with the low hum of country radio playing softly in the background. The city came into view and Kayla fidgeted in her seat, her knee bobbing up and down.

"Do you need to use the bathroom?" Ben asked. "We probably have enough time for a quick stop."

"No," she said. "I mean, yes, but I can wait until we get there." She ran her hands back and forth against her jeans, back and forth.

Ben waited, curling his fingers around the steering wheel, applying the brake when traffic slowed.

She cleared her throat. "You can … you can talk about her, ya know."

"Talk about who?" When he glanced at her, she looked away.

"Darcy."

His head fell against the seat rest. "We—"

"She's going to be a part of the baby's life, and I'm okay with that. I mean, she's a part of your life, so you can talk about her. It's … it's kinda weird that you don't."

"Darcy and I broke up. For good this time."

Kayla blinked at him, her forehead ruffled. "Oh, Ben ..."

"It's okay. It was a long time coming."

"It's because of me." Kayla sighed and rubbed her belly. "Because of the baby."

"No. Listen, your pregnancy may have spurred it along, but it would have happened eventually."

"I'm sorry, Ben. I feel … I feel terrible."

"You shouldn't feel bad. I don't, so you shouldn't."

"She must hate me," Kayla said softly, so softly he barely heard.

He wouldn't let her beat herself up over something he should have done a long time ago, long before Kayla came into the picture. "Whatever Darcy thinks about you or anyone else is not important. I don't blame you, because I know the truth. I should have broken up with her years ago."

"Why didn't you?"

He inched along in Atlanta traffic, thinking of everything he'd have to explain to make her understand. If he told her everything, he'd sound weak and pathetic—two characteristics he tried his best not to display to the woman he wanted to impress. "A lot of reasons. It's—"

"Complicated," she said. "I get it. It's also none of my business."

Ben reached over, squeezed her hand. "It's over, and I'm not looking back. I'm looking forward. We have a lot to look forward to."

She looked at him, her big blue eyes, wary, guilty, her lips gliding into a grimace. "I'm sorry. Even if you're not, I am. I never meant to come between you."

"Kayla, you're not. It's okay. It's for the best. I promise."

He pulled into the parking garage, rolled his window down, and pressed the button for a ticket. He'd never get used to paying to park every time they had to see a doctor. He found a spot, wedged his sedan between a truck and a sports car, cut the engine, and looked over at Kayla. "Ready?"

She got out of the car and met him by the trunk, her shoulders hunched, her eyes downcast. He didn't grab her hand like he wanted as they walked inside the doctor's building, but he put his hand on her back as they entered the elevator. She was quiet—too quiet—and Ben knew why. He swallowed an oath and vowed never to let Darcy Keller come between him and Kayla ever again.

Chapter Twenty-Seven

Kayla showed Ben to the guest apartment over the garage and left him to get settled, then found her mom in the kitchen. Chicken sizzled in a sauté pan. Kayla sniffed. Her nausea had definitely subsided. She was starving.

"They broke up," Kayla said.

Her mom jerked around, spatula in hand. "What?"

"Ben told me in the car that he and his girlfriend broke up."

Her mom inhaled. Her brows arched. She blinked and let her breath out with a hiss. "Wow."

"I know, right?"

She turned back to the chicken. "What did he say? Is he upset?"

Kayla walked around the dog sprawled at her mom's feet and leaned against the counter. "That's the weird part. He's not. He said it should have happened a long time ago."

Mom shrugged. "Maybe that's true."

"But what if it's not? What if he's just trying to make me feel better?" Kayla pictured Darcy, face down on a bed in a fancy bedroom, surrounded by pictures of her and Ben, tears staining her pillow. "What if she's crying herself to sleep every night because of me?"

"Honey." Her mom cocked her head to the side and brushed Kayla's shoulder. "If that's the case, there's nothing you can do. You're pregnant with his baby. There was no way that wouldn't have affected their relationship—if not now, then in the future. Maybe it's for the best."

Kayla let her head drop into her hands, rubbed her tired eyes. "I feel like a homewrecker." Her mom stayed silent, adding to her distress. "And I gained three pounds."

"Good," her mom said. "I was worried when you hardly ate anything. What else happened at the appointment?"

"They did some kind of urine test. And we got to hear the heartbeat again. It's so fast. Other than that, not much."

"When's the next appointment?"

"Four weeks. They'll do another ultrasound. We can find out the sex of the baby if we want."

Her mom added mushrooms, chicken broth, and garlic to the pan before covering it and lowering the temperature. "Will you?"

"I don't know. We haven't talked about it yet. There was an accident on Peachtree we had to navigate around. Traffic seemed worse than usual."

"Friday starts early. You know that."

"It drives Ben crazy. He can't understand how we deal with traffic every day."

"We don't like it either, but that's why we live close to dad's office." Her mom gathered napkins and silverware. Can you set the table, please?"

"He doesn't want to give the baby away." Kayla placed knives, forks, and spoons on her mom's pretty pale-blue placemats. "We agreed adoption's not the answer."

"Well." Her mom sighed and turned on the rice cooker. "At least that's settled."

Kayla finished with the silverware and approached the island, propping her elbows on the granite surface. She appreciated her parents welcoming Ben into their home, but worried about their motive. "Is dinner going to be an interrogation?"

"No." Jessica pulled lettuce from a colander and shredded it into a bowl, eyeing her daughter. "Dinner is dinner, and Ben is our guest. We want to get to know him better, as should you."

Kayla walked around the island and washed a tomato and cucumber for the salad. "I do. I just don't want Dad asking weird questions and making him feel uncomfortable."

"Honey, your dad is breaking bread with the boy who got you pregnant. I'd say it's not your dad who should feel uncomfortable."

Ben rounded the corner from the mud room into the kitchen. Kayla inhaled sharply and averted her eyes. Ben would have heard Mom's comment. He had to have.

"Smells good in here." Ben flashed a smile at mother and daughter. "What can I do to help?"

Kayla couldn't make eye contact, could barely breathe. The knife in her hand wobbled whenever she attempted to slice.

"I think we're good, Ben," her mom said. "There are drinks in the refrigerator. Help yourself."

"Thank you, ma'am. I appreciate your hospitality. That apartment over the garage is really nice."

"It comes in handy when we have guests." Her mom stepped

up when Kayla remained tongue-tied. "My mother, in particular. It's best for everyone if she has her own space."

"With the kitchenette and bathroom, she wouldn't need to come out if she didn't want to."

"Exactly." Her mom graced Ben with a flirty smile.

How did she do it? How did she carry on as if nothing had happened when Kayla knew Ben had overheard her comment? Did the woman have ice in her veins?

Ben pulled out a stool and sat at the counter, watching Kayla and her mother prepare the salad. Kayla could feel his eyes one her, knew she should make conversation, but the words jammed in her throat.

Ben stood up, walked around the counter, and rested his hands on Kayla's shoulders, his touch as gentle as a mossy bed. Her muscles tensed. He smelled like a woodsy forest.

"You're going to cut off a finger." He took the knife from her grasp. "Sit down and relax. I can slice."

Kayla did as instructed, watching Ben wash and dry his hands before expertly slicing the cucumber and tomato. She admired his long, blunt-ended fingers as much as his knife-wielding skills. The guy knew his way around the kitchen.

"Do you like to cook?" her mom asked.

"The only way to have a home-cooked meal when I'm at school is to make it myself. I don't mind, and my ma taught me the basics."

Mom glanced at Kayla and quirked her lips. "I've tried my best to get Josh in the kitchen. He has no interest."

"Where is Josh?" Ben asked.

Her mother tilted her head at the grinding drone of the garage door. "Speak of the devil."

Kayla closed her eyes and said a silent prayer her brother

and father would be civil. She placed herself between the garage entrance and the kitchen, accosting her brother and father as soon as they walked inside. "Josh." She tilted her head, widened her eyes. "Meet Ben. Ben, my brother Josh."

Josh eyed Ben from his boot-covered feet to the top of his wavy brown hair. He jerked his chin, his face impassive. "Hey," Josh said.

Ben extended his hand. "Nice to meet you." Josh looked as eager to shake Ben's hand as he was to clean the toilets.

Her dad followed, gave Ben a salesman grin. "Ben, good to see you."

"Thank you, sir. I appreciate your generosity."

"It's no problem. How'd the appointment go?"

"Very well, sir." Ben slid his eyes to Kayla, quirked his mouth. "Your daughter's taking real good care of herself and the baby."

Her dad's smile could only be described as a grimace. He dropped his keys in the junk drawer and gave Mom a kiss.

"Long day?" she asked.

"Let's just say I'm glad it's the weekend." He unbuttoned his top button and loosened his tie. "I've got to fly to Miami on Monday."

"Miami?" her mom asked while giving Josh the stink eye. "Josh, go shower. Dinner's almost ready."

"I've got plans." Josh made his way to the stairs.

"You're eating at home." Jessica's tone left no room for argument. "Go shower."

Josh stopped, gripping the handrail. "But I'm meeting the guys at The Shack."

"You can meet the guys at The Shack after dinner. No buts."

To Kayla's surprise, Josh huffed up the stairs but didn't argue, sparing them an embarrassing scene. She turned her attention to her father, who poured himself a bourbon from the minibar in the den. He shocked her by offering Ben a drink.

"No, thank you, sir. I'm fine with water."

Her dad settled onto the couch. "Do you drink?"

Ben followed suit, took a seat in the opposite chair. He was brave to face her dad head on, not run and hide in the kitchen like she would have done. "Yes, sir. Socially."

Her dad swirled the amber liquid, watched it spin in the crystal glass. "Any plans for after graduation?"

Her parents were so predictable. He may as well have asked, *How do you plan to support my grandchild?*

"I've got some ideas."

"What's your major, son?"

"Political science. I'd planned to go to law school." Ben jerked a shoulder, shifted in his seat. "Before."

"I'm with Johnson and Boles, the international acquisitions firm. We've got a fantastic training program for new graduates." He lifted his brows and took a sip of his drink. "I could put in a good word."

Ben tugged his bottom lip before running his hands along his thighs. "I appreciate that, sir. My plans are pretty up in the air right now. I'm exploring my options, working with my counselor at school."

"Your counselor can get you a job, not a career. Connections get you a career. I've got them or know someone who does. When you're done considering, let me know and I'll make some calls."

"Thank you, sir."

Kayla joined her mom at the sink, her back to the den, and lowered her voice to a whisper. "Mom, please make Dad stop. He's embarrassing me. And Ben."

"They're just talking." Her mom transferred the rice to a serving bowl. "He's trying to help."

"He's not helping."

When Josh appeared with wet hair and a sour expression, Kayla wanted to hug him for providing cover.

"What's for dinner?" Josh asked.

"Mushroom chicken. Grab a drink and have a seat."

Josh scanned the kitchen. "We're eating in the dining room?" He rolled his eyes.

"We have a guest." Her mom's smile was as fake as a knock-off designer purse, plastic and stiff. "Dinner's ready."

Kayla sat at the table next to Ben, across from Josh, her parents like bookends at each end of the table. When Ben reached for her hand under the table while her dad said the blessing, her pulse spiked. She felt the callouses on his fingers and drew comfort from his warm skin. That simple touch made them feel like a team. She took a deep breath and prayed for a peaceful, uneventful dinner. For her sake and for Ben's.

Josh stabbed a piece of chicken and heaped food onto his plate, shoving food into his mouth before all the serving dishes had made their way around the table. Her mom admonished him to slow down—warnings he ignored.

"This looks delicious, Mrs. Cummings," Ben said. "Thank you for dinner."

"You're welcome, Ben. Does your mom like to cook?"

Ben placed his napkin on his lap and picked up his fork and knife, cutting into his chicken. "Yes, ma'am. She enjoys baking the most, but everything she makes tastes good." He placed a bite in his mouth. "Ummm. Tastes as good as it smells."

Josh somehow managed to snicker around a mouthful of

rice. Kayla stabbed him with a death stare he pretended not to see.

"I'd bake more if Gary and I had any self-control."

Her dad grunted, wiping his mouth with a napkin. "Speak for yourself."

"I am." Her mom winked at her dad. "But I'm also talking about you."

"I'd like more sweets," Josh said, pushing back from the table. "May I be excused?"

"If you leave, you're going to miss the cobbler I made."

Josh stood, gathered his plate and utensils. "Not a chance everyone eats the entire cobbler. And that comment proves you've never had ice cream from The Shack."

"What do you think I'm serving with the cobbler?" her mom asked.

"Save me some." Josh disappeared into the kitchen.

"Dishes in the dishwasher," Mom called. "And be home by eleven."

"Midnight," Josh called back.

"Eleven thirty," her dad said, ending all negotiations. Her dad had the final word.

In fewer than two minutes the security alarm beeped, alerting them to Josh's departure.

"Don't take it personal," Kayla said to Ben. "He never wants to be home."

Ben shrugged, buttered a roll, spared her a crooked grin. "He's seventeen and it's Friday night. I get it."

"Josh tells us he's going to The Shack," her dad said. "Which he will, for a while, until he and his friends try to sneak into a bar or go to a party at someone's house. Happens every weekend. What kind of Friday night antics go on in your hometown?"

The rice in Kayla's mouth to turned to paste. She guzzled water, setting her glass down hard. She glared at her dad. Was his question some kind of trap?

"We've only got two bars in town and everyone there knows our folks, so sneaking in is out of the question."

Her dad nodded, encouraged Ben to continue.

"Back when I was in high school, I played football in the fall and baseball in the spring. We'd go to basketball games in the winter or have field parties and the occasional house party. Our options were pretty limited."

"I'd love it if Josh had limited options," Mom said. "Up here, the opportunities for trouble are endless."

"Trouble's easy to find when you're looking." Ben took his last bite of chicken, stared at the table. "No matter where you live."

"True enough." Her dad tossed his napkin on the table and reclined in his seat. "Jessica, that was wonderful."

"Thank you, sweetie," Mom said. "Why don't you go change? I'll clean up and get dessert ready."

"I'll do the dishes, Mrs. Cummings." Ben stood, picked up his plate, and reached for Kayla's.

"We'll both do the dishes and I'll plate dessert. You go relax," Kayla said as her mom opened her mouth to refuse.

"Are you sure?" Mom asked.

"Absolutely. There's no need to wait on us. Let us wait on you for a change."

"Well." Her mom lifted a shoulder, gave a coy smile. "If you insist."

Alone in the kitchen after her parents walked hand in hand up the stairs, Kayla exhaled, scrubbing a plate with more force than necessary. She glanced at Ben where he stood next to the sink, dishtowel in hand. "I'm sorry about dinner."

"What are you sorry about? Your mom's a great cook."

"I mean my dad's questions about your job search and my brother's salty looks. They're usually a little more subtle."

"Kayla." Ben placed a plate in the dishwasher and reached for some silverware in the sink. "Your brother is looking out for you, and so is your dad. He has a vested interest in my gainful employment, and so do you."

"What you do for a job doesn't matter to me."

"It should." He continued loading the dishwasher, carefully placing the silverware in the same direction as her mom. "We've got a baby on the way, a baby that's going to need a lot of stuff. Stuff costs money. It's up to us—you and me—to provide for our baby. Not your parents. Not mine. Your dad wants to make sure I can live up to my responsibility. My parents would ask the same."

"My mom has already made it clear she and my dad aren't raising the baby for us."

"They shouldn't. If my dad and I were on speaking terms, he'd say the same."

Kayla rinsed a glass and handed it to Ben, tried not to squirm when his fingers touched hers. "What about your mom?"

"She'll do whatever my dad says. Don't get me wrong. They love me. This is how my dad communicates when things get tough. He'll come around. And my mom's a softie. A few months from now they'll have gotten over the disappointment."

"I hope so, for your sake at least. That can't be fun to be around."

He used the dishtowel to dry a serving dish. "I've got a fraternity brother who lives not far from here. He wants to meet for breakfast. Do you mind if I meet up with him before we head back?"

"Of course I don't mind." She shut off the tap and dried her hands on the towel he'd discarded. "You don't have to ask permission."

"I'm not. I just wanted to let you know in case you got up and my car was gone."

He was being nice again—too nice to avoid her gratitude—not only for handling her family so well but for coming to the doctor's appointment. And, if she were being honest with herself, for looking so handsome in his jeans and button down, for the way he reached for her hand at the table, for not taking her brother's rudeness personally. It would be easier to resist him if he showed her something—anything—she found objectionable.

"Now, where's that cobbler your mom was talking about?"

Chapter Twenty-Eight

Ben pulled up to his apartment, got out of the car, and stretched his back, relieved to be home. As far as overnight stays with the family of his baby mama, he thought it went pretty well. As well as it could have gone. Kayla may look at him with stars in her eyes—and he loved the way she looked at him—but her parents weren't so easily fooled.

Perhaps they noticed his interest in their daughter. It was hard to hide his appreciation. She was easy to be around, and he could talk to her about things he never could with Darcy—sports, his friends, fraternity life. She listened and asked questions. Unlike Darcy who used him as a sounding board for all her drama.

Constantly comparing Darcy and Kayla wasn't fair to either of them. One was his past. One was his future. If he could figure out Kayla's role in his life and his role in hers.

He lifted his overnight bag from the trunk and spied one of

Kayla's pink mittens under his bag. He picked it up and rubbed the soft fabric between his fingers. It was a good excuse to see her again. After all the comfortable conversation on the way home, dropping her off with no plans to see each other except for the next appointment had been awkward. He tucked the mitten into his bag and made his way inside.

Theo sprawled on the couch in a T-shirt and flannel pants, flicking channels on the television. He glanced up when Ben walked in.

"Hey," Theo said. "How'd it go?"

"Not bad." Ben dropped his bag on the floor by the hallway and joined Theo on the couch. "Her house looks like something out of a magazine. Even the garage apartment has a view of the Atlanta skyline."

"Well, if you're going to knock someone up, it may as well be someone rich." Theo settled on a basketball game and tossed the remote on the couch. "How were the parents?"

"About like you'd expect parents to act around the guy who got their baby girl pregnant. Nice but cautious." Ben toed off his shoes and crossed his feet atop the coffee table. "Her dad's pressing me to apply for a training program at his international acquisitions firm."

"Sounds lucrative."

"Sounds boring. What do I know about international acquisitions?"

"About as much as you know about fatherhood. You can learn."

"I know." Ben rubbed his neck, tried to dig at the nagging ache building at the base of his skull. "I'm sure it's a great opportunity."

"What's the problem?"

"I don't want to feel beholden to him for a job. That's like jumping from the frying pan of my dad into the fire with hers. What's the point?"

Theo pursed his lips, crossed his arms. "I don't know, but it seems stupid to look a gift horse in the mouth without at least checking it out."

"I guess." Ben admired a half-court shot and tried to follow the game. He couldn't focus on anything but the questions boomeranging through his head about the future. "It would mean living in Atlanta. The more I visit that place, the less I can imagine living there. The traffic is horrible—even on the weekends. It's Saturday, and it still took us ten minutes to go two miles."

"So find something else."

Easy for Theo to say. He already had a job with the company he interned with in Savannah. The game segued into a commercial. Maybe talking to Theo would help reduce his irritation with the decisions he had to make and his lack of direction. "I met with Gregg Anson this morning."

Theo stopped reaching for the remote at the mention of their fraternity brother. "How's he doing?"

"Good. He likes the Georgia Bureau of Investigation. Says the best way to get involved is to intern."

"How would you intern when you're about to graduate?"

"I could do it post-grad. It would put me in Atlanta for when the baby's born—which is preferable—and if I like it, I'd hopefully get assigned a field office."

Theo studied him, a crease between his brows. "What about the regular police route?"

"I'm still thinking about that. I'd need to get peace officer standards and training certified and the only classes that work start in the fall which would leave the summer open anyway."

“So, you could intern at the GBI in Atlanta while the baby’s born or do her dad’s training program, and then either get POST certified and get on with a small-town force or join the bureau?”

“That’s what I’m thinking. Summer in Atlanta, a bureau field office position or POST training, and then get a job somewhere I can set down roots.”

“It’s not a bad plan,” Theo said. “What does Kayla think?”

His stomach knotted at Theo’s question. He was still working everything out in his head—dates, locations, long-term employment—and didn’t want to bring it up to her until he had everything set. “We haven’t talked about it.”

Theo ignored the game, turned to face Ben. “Why not?”

“We’re not in a relationship. We’re having a baby.”

Theo shook his head slowly, as if watching a player miss an easy layup. “Come on, Ben. Use your head. You’re raising a baby together, which means you’re in a parenting relationship. No matter what you work out for employment, you’re going to shuffle the kid back and forth between you. Don’t you think she needs to know what you’re thinking? Don’t you want to know what she has in mind?”

The dull ache in Ben’s neck pulsed. “Yes. I know I do, but I don’t want to sound like a flake when we talk about it. If I have everything figured out when I bring it up, she won’t feel like I’m some kind of loser, and neither will her dad.”

“Let’s table the idea that you care what she thinks about you and concentrate on the obvious problem with your plan. It’s great if you’re in Atlanta when the baby’s born, but if you move out of the city and she stays, you’re not going to have much of a relationship with your kid. She’ll be raising the baby, and you’ll be the weekend dad. Is that what you want?”

Leave it to Theo to poke at the scab until it bled. "No. That's not what I want."

"What do you want? Leave out all the stuff you should do and tell me straight. What kind of relationship do you see for you and her and the baby?"

Ben stared at the wall, saw Kayla holding a blonde-headed toddler on her hip, the sun at her back, a tender smile on her face. "I see us raising the kid together. Not just weekends. I want to see her and the kid during the week. I want us to be a family." He had high school and college friends whose divorced parents hated each other, and the kids were collateral damage in the middle of a never-ending war. Even his friends whose parents managed to be civil had to juggle parents' weekends at school, holidays, and vacations. Managing their parents became a full-time job.

"Then the first thing you need to do is talk to Kayla. I don't think either one of you has thought much past the birth. In the scheme of things, that's the easy part. You go to the hospital, have the baby, and take it home. The way things stand now, you have no idea where you or the kid are heading once you leave the hospital."

Like a counter punch, Theo's words hit Ben square in the face. It wasn't up to him to come up with a plan for Kayla to follow. She had to be on board. Every time he imagined them leaving the hospital with the kid, he imagined them going to the same home. Together. He needed to adjust his thinking or stop being a coward and talk to her, tell her how he felt. If they were going to raise the kid together, then maybe he needed to ask her out on a date to see where things stood. "You're right. I need to talk to her."

"Yes, you do." Theo turned back to the TV.

Ben sat and stewed.

"Didn't you just share a four-hour car ride?" Theo asked.

"Yeah."

"What in the world did you talk about where this didn't come up?"

"Whether or not to find out the sex of the baby at the next appointment."

Theo shook his head. "And?"

"I think we're going to find out. Surprise now or surprise at delivery doesn't seem to make much difference."

"You know what will make a difference?" Theo asked.

Ben got up and headed for his bedroom. "I know, I know."

"Making plans for after the baby's born," Theo called from the den.

"Yeah, yeah, yeah." But Theo was right. Ben had avoided the topic for too long.

Chapter Twenty-Nine

Kayla walked down the steps of her sorority house, glanced over her shoulder at the stately columned building with window boxes full of pansies, and wiped a tear from her cheek. She'd always felt welcome at the house, surrounded by sisters and laughter and a bond she thought would last a lifetime. Sure, she'd expected disdain, expected they'd demand she quit as an active member, but their reaction still stung.

She stumbled on the sidewalk, displacing her backpack from her shoulder. She yanked it back in place and put her face to the wind, tried her best to stifle the tears she knew would come as soon as she was alone. As it stood, she only needed to make it to her car around the back of the building and pray she didn't run into anyone along the way.

Her prayers were wasted.

Two members of her pledge class came giggling around the

corner, huddled in down jackets, weighted down by bulging backpacks like the one she carried.

"Kayla, hey," Dru said, stopping Kayla in her tracks. "I haven't seen you in forever."

Kayla tried to blink away the tears, lifted her brows, and lifted her cheeks into something she hoped resembled a smile. "Hi, Dru. Melissa."

Kayla must have looked as bad as she felt because Dru grabbed her arm and said, "Honey, what's wrong?"

"Nothing." Kayla fought not to cry. "I'm just … I'm …" She couldn't do it. She couldn't paste on a smile and pretend everything in her life hadn't turned upside down.

Dru and Melissa gathered her between them and tried to usher her back to the house. Kayla stopped walking, tugging against them when they urged her forward. Dru turned to face her, a question in her eyes. "What's wrong?"

"I can't go to the house," Kayla said. "Please, I'm okay. I just have to go."

Drucilla stepped forward, squeezing Kayla's arm. "Kayla, it's okay. You can trust us. Tell us what's wrong."

She couldn't say the words, not after the way they'd looked at her inside the hallowed halls of her sorority. Sisterhood forever? What a joke. But she and Dru had been close freshman year, living on the hall together, sharing clothes and secrets. It wouldn't be long before everyone knew anyway. She may as well tell them herself. "I've been asked to go on alumni status."

Dru's face went slack and she dropped her arm. "What? Why?"

Kayla stared at the sidewalk, followed a crack where it meandered, desperately wanting to keep her eyes on the concrete and not witness the shock on her friends' faces when she told them about the baby. But she refused be a coward and act ashamed. She took a deep breath before lifting her eyes to stare at Dru then Melissa. "I'm pregnant."

The girls exchanged looks so loaded with questions their eyes bugged to exploding. "Oh," Dru said. "Wow. That's … wow."

"I've decided to keep the baby. I'm trying to get excited and make plans for the future. I understand it's a shock, but I'm happy and I hope you can find a way to be happy for me, too."

"We are," Melissa chimed in, her voice strangled and overly bright. "If you're happy, we're happy."

"Congratulations." Dru pulled Kayla into a hug. "You're going to be a great mom."

Kayla blew out a breath and sagged against her friend. It hadn't been so bad, telling her friends. She knew word would get out when she went to the house and told the president about her pregnancy. Telling her closest friends gave her the control she craved in an unpredictable situation that left her more vulnerable to gossip and censure than ever before.

"Thank you." Kayla pulled back, clasped Dru's hand. "I appreciate that." She wanted to leave, wave goodbye and tuck tail to her car, especially since her friends looked so uncomfortable standing on the sidewalk with no idea what to say. "Look, I know I'm going to be the talk of the house. I mean, I know I'd talk about someone in my situation, but I hope you'll be respectful of me and of the bonds of sisterhood."

"Of course," Melissa said. "Kayla, don't worry. We'll talk to the others, make sure the younger girls don't gossip."

Kayla nodded. "Thanks. I appreciate that. I'll see y'all later."

Kayla walked to her car, got in and drove home, tired, foggy, but not on the verge of tears like before. Taking control of the situation felt like a positive step.

As Kayla entered the apartment, Emily came out of the kitchen with a mug in her hand. "How'd it go?" she asked.

"It was hard to watch their faces when I told them, as if something like this couldn't have happened to any one of them. The worst part was watching the committee judge me with a shiny coat of glee. They love gossip, and this will feed the mill for ages. But at least it's over."

Emily set her tea on an end table and pulled her into a hug. "I'm proud of you for setting up the meeting and telling them yourself. Did they put you on alumni status?"

Kayla nodded. "I don't even care. It's not like I'm going to go to any date nights or to the formal."

Emily pouted. "I hate that you're missing senior formal. That stinks."

"Even if I wasn't pregnant, who would I take?"

"You could take Ben."

"Emily …"

"What? You two make a seriously cute couple." She picked up her mug and took a sip. "And he did just break up with his girlfriend."

Kayla collapsed onto the couch. "Don't remind me. I've ruined enough lives as it stands."

"You can't beat yourself up over their relationship. You didn't know he had a girlfriend."

"That doesn't make me feel any better."

Emily set the mug on the coffee table and folded her leg to sit at Kayla's side. "I didn't tell you this before, but I've got a friend at SE State who's in the same sorority as Ben's ex. She said she's not very nice."

Kayla glared at Emily. "That doesn't make any difference. I still ruined her relationship. Whether she's nice or not doesn't matter."

"It should ease your guilt that you didn't steal Ben from a great girl."

"I didn't steal Ben. He's not mine."

"Then what is he to you? I mean, you spent the weekend together and he texts you all the time."

"He doesn't text me all the time. He checks in to see how I'm feeling because we're friends, and someday soon we'll be parents to the child growing inside me."

"Are you sure about that?"

"Yes, Emily. He's not interested in me."

"How do you know?"

"Because I know." Kayla's phone dinged, so she got up from the couch to retrieve it from her backpack.

"Why are you scowling at your phone?" Emily asked.

"Ben texted. He wants to meet for coffee."

"You mean the Ben who's not interested in you?"

"Yes, I mean that Ben." She texted him back, telling him she was free. "Stop putting ideas in my head. I'm trying not to get attached."

"Why?"

"Why do you think?" She went into the kitchen, pulled a glass from the cupboard, and filled it with water. When she turned around, Emily stood behind her with her arms crossed over her chest. "He's gorgeous, he's nice, and we're having a kid together. Even without the kid part, I'd be caught, hook, line, and sinker. You know me, Emily. You know how I am."

"I know you're a romantic who'd love to have a relationship with the man who fathered your baby. I don't know why you think that's out of reach."

"He's not interested." Her phone dinged again, and she read his text.

"Really?"

"He wants to meet at McGill's," Kayla said. "Do you think that's a good idea?"

"Why? Is something wrong with McGill's?"

"No, but I just told the Deltas about the baby. If we're seen together, people will think he's the dad."

"He is the dad. And I thought he already told people about the baby."

"He did, but nobody knows it's with me."

"You're not exactly an ogre." Emily opened the pantry and pulled out a sleeve of cookies. "Who cares if people know he's the dad? Is it a secret?"

"I don't want to embarrass him." Kayla sat at the table. "Should I invite him over here?"

"If that makes you more comfortable, go ahead." Emily propped her hands along the back of a chair facing Kayla. "But seriously, you can't spend the rest of the semester hiding out in our apartment. You're pregnant, and you're keeping the baby. The decision you and Ben made is admirable. Like you said, it could have happened to any of us. You're not doing anyone any good by hiding."

"I'm going to ask him to come over here. I can warn him about the Deltas and give him time to prepare."

Emily threw her arms in the air. "Fine. Prepare the guy you're not attracted to."

"I never said I wasn't attracted."

"I knew it!"

"I said he's not attracted to me."

Emily cocked her head to the side. "We'll have to wait and see."

Chapter Thirty

Ben knocked on Kayla's door, shoving his hands into his pockets and swaying from side to side. He didn't know why he was nervous coming to her apartment. It wasn't like they hadn't spent time together, but he hadn't stepped foot inside her apartment other than right after she told him about the baby. And then her roommate had looked at him like something she picked off the bottom of her shoe. It seemed like an unwritten rule they kept their living spaces at school as an oasis from the drama of impending parenthood.

Her invitation broke another barrier and got him wondering. Did she want to be alone with him, or was she afraid for them to be seen together? He hoped it was the former and not the latter.

Kayla opened the door and stood back to invite him in. The scent of raspberries and the unmistakable smell of a girl's apartment lingered in the air, unlike the sweat and tennis shoe smell of his own. The first thing he noticed besides her guileless smile and the warmth in her eyes was the tiny bump beneath her thin yoga pants. He resisted the urge to touch it, run his fingers over her clothes and let the baby know he was there. The impulse surprised him almost as much as the way the low hum of desire sprang to life in her presence. Oh, yeah. He was asking her out for sure.

"Hi, Ben. Thanks for coming over."

"Thanks for seeing me. I hope it's not too much trouble for your roommates."

"They're out." She skirted the couch and took a seat, reached for a pillow, and hugged it to her lap. He hated the way she covered herself, as if she was ashamed of her condition. Didn't she know how pretty she looked with the glow of health in her cheeks and the way her hair shone in the light?

Ben sat on the end of the couch, leaving a cushion between them. Every time they saw each other it took a while for them to relax with the baby, the future, and their past between them. He hoped their impending conversation eased the tension in her shoulders and afforded her some peace.

"Can I get you something to drink? Water, coffee, tea?"

"I'm good." Ben stretched his legs beneath the coffee table and rested his arm along the back of the couch to try and ease the strain around Kayla's eyes. She reminded him of the hummingbirds that hovered gracefully around his mama's feeders every summer, a little shy and easily spooked. "How are you feeling?"

"I feel good. Still a little tired." She shook her head and chuckled. "I'm more ditzy than usual. I've lost my keys a hundred times in the last few weeks. It's driving my roommates crazy."

"Does that happen when you're pregnant?"

"According to the websites I'm reading, yes."

"What else do they say?"

"Well, the baby's the size of a pear right now. My appetite is back, but I get heartburn when I eat, which is also normal."

"That stinks." He scanned her body, felt the hard knock of yearning and tucked it away. "You still don't look like you're pregnant. Have you told anyone else?"

She tossed the pillow aside and clasped her hands in front of her belly. "That's why I wanted to meet here instead of McGill's. I told my sorority executive committee and a couple of my sisters."

Something about the way she said "sisters" let him know the conversations hadn't been easy. "How did that go?"

"They asked me to go on alumni status so I can't to any functions, which I wouldn't have anyway. But, more importantly, I wouldn't be surprised if everyone on campus knows by now."

She may have tossed her status aside as if it didn't matter, but she didn't meet his eyes and the way she fiddled with the sleeves of her shirt told him as much as the flush creeping up her neck. His brave girl had faced a firing squad and come out bruised.

He scooted next to her on the couch and reached for her hand. His other hand kneaded the knots in her shoulder. "I'm sorry about your sorority. That must have stung."

She gripped his hand and shrugged. "Walking around campus with my sorority letters and a pregnant belly makes the sorority look bad. If this had happened to someone else, I would totally support the decision."

"It didn't happen to someone else." He lifted their joined hands and brushed his lips against her knuckles, inhaled her sweet scent. "It happened to you. If you tell me you wanted to meet here so we wouldn't be seen together, I'm going to be mad at you."

She looked at him beneath lowered lashes, not coy like Darcy, but embarrassed. "Then I guess you're going to be mad at me."

"Kayla." He lifted his hand from her shoulder, pushed the hair from her face, let his fingers brush against the soft skin of her cheek. He lifted her chin. Her eyes, so blue, so innocent, met his and held. "You don't need to protect me. I can handle the gossip."

"There's no reason for everyone to talk about both of us. It's bad enough about me. It shouldn't be about us."

"It is about us. You didn't get pregnant on your own."

She let out a choking laugh. They sat so close that he felt her breath on his face. He watched her eyes widen before focusing his attention on her parted lips. Why did he fight his feelings when everything in him was drawn to her, to her goodness, her strength, her humility? Fighting seemed futile when sitting in the quiet room, hearing her shallow breaths over the incessant pounding of his heart.

He leaned in. He couldn't have stopped himself from kissing her if every one of her sorority sisters had come charging into the room. She made a sound in her throat, something between a gasp and a moan, before her lips moved against his. Asking. Answering. He ran his tongue along her lush bottom lip, and she opened for him. Giving. Taking.

The taste of her swamped him and he groaned. Her flavor carried him back to a starless fall evening and the pleasure she gave him on a night he felt desperate for peace. A night of longing and loss. A night, unbeknownst to them, of new beginnings.

She pulled back, gripping his shirt, blinking the lust and confusion from her eyes. When he went back for more, she straightened her arms. "Ben, wait."

He swallowed, inched away, tried to steady the punishing

thud of his heart. "I'm sorry," he said. "I didn't mean to assume—"

She shook her head. "No, no, it's okay. I liked it. Obviously."

She was cute when flustered. Flustered and aroused.

"We need to think about this."

"I have thought about this. A lot. I like you, Kayla. I always have."

"I like you. A little too much."

He jolted back. "What do you mean?"

"I mean, I liked you since that class we shared. It was totally out of character for me to sleep with you, but when you came up to me and we started talking and then you asked me to leave with you, I couldn't say no. I didn't want to say no. No one had ever made me feel the way you did, and I got caught up in the moment. The truth is …"—she covered her face with her hands and took a shaky breath—"… you were my first."

Everything inside of him went icebox cold, his heart, his face, his limbs as if flushed with frigid water. He couldn't have heard her right. He pulled her hands from her face. "You were a virgin?"

Kayla nodded. Even though her hair concealed her face, he saw the blush creeping up her neck. She wouldn't look him in the eye.

Stunned, shamed, speechless, Ben slumped against the couch. How could he have been so oblivious? How could he have taken advantage of her like that? He'd robbed her of her future and her innocence? "I'm … I'm sorry, Kayla." His tongue felt thick and worthless. "I never would have touched you."

"You didn't force yourself," she said in a low, tortured voice. "I could have said no."

"Why … why didn't you tell me?"

She jerked a shoulder, picked at her nails, didn't look up. Her neck flamed. "I didn't want to disappoint you or make you think I was a tease."

"Kayla." He wanted to touch her, wanted to comfort her the way she'd comforted him. But touching her felt as welcome as his useless apology. "I would have stopped. I never would have …" Climbed on top of her. Kissed her like his life hung in the balance. Taken. Taken. Taken. He pounded his fist into his thigh, wished he could pound his head for being so stupid. So careless. "I would have stopped."

She looked at him then, her eyes fierce. "It's not your fault. It was my choice, and you didn't know."

He ran his hand down his face. He should have known. Her innocence was what attracted him—then and now. He'd taken her precious gift and changed the trajectory of her life forever. She'd sacrificed more than he could ever repay.

"I wish you'd told me. I never would have … I would have stopped."

"Wishes don't change the outcome." She stared through him as she spoke, her eyes as limp as her voice. "I wish you'd told me about Darcy."

Wishes didn't change the outcome, but honesty would have. Kayla was too principled to sleep with man embroiled with someone else. And he'd been too selfish, too immature to come clean. He'd taken what she'd offered and stolen something he could never give back. "I should have told you. It's no excuse, but I'd liked you for a long time, too. I knew if I told you, you'd never speak to me again."

"I would have spoken to you, Ben. I wouldn't have slept with you."

He couldn't tell her how desperate he felt that night, how alone, how close he'd come to doing something stupid. He couldn't tell her how she'd saved him from himself and his demons. None of that mattered in the face of what she'd lost. "Sometimes doing the right thing isn't so easy."

She reached for him, wrapped her hand around his. He clung to her, craved her warmth, her forgiveness more than his next breath.

"I need to do the right thing now and explain." She licked her lips, took a deep breath.

Ben's stomach tensed, prepared for the aftershocks.

"I'm a hopeless romantic," Kayla said. "I always have been. I've dreamed of falling in love and getting married since I was old enough to know what that meant. I may have grown up, but those dreams never went away. And now I'm pregnant and really, really attracted to the father of my baby, which sounds like a good thing, but it's complicated. He had a girlfriend I think he's not over—"

"Kayla, I—"

"Let me finish, please, or I may never get this out." She took a deep breath and looked him in the eyes. "You just broke up, and I don't want to be your rebound. So that's one. And too embarrassing to admit, but I figure I've got nothing to lose by being honest at this point." She swallowed and looked down at their joined hands. "The dirty little secret they don't tell people is how … how amorous you get when you're pregnant."

"Amorous?"

The blush that had receded zoomed up her neck, along her cheeks, to the tips of her ears. "Food isn't the only thing I'm hungry for these days."

Ben choked as he realized the meaning behind her words. "Are you serious?"

"It's on all the websites. I'm a ticking time bomb. So starting this now isn't a good idea."

Images of them together flashed through Ben's mind. He swallowed. Tugged at his collar. Shifted. Her admissions left him staggered and longing for a do-over. He wanted more than memories. He wanted to take things slow and show her all the ways a man could cherish a woman. He wanted another chance. "I … I had no idea."

"So you understand my dilemma. I've liked you for a long time and now we're spending a lot of time together, going through something extraordinary that will bring us closer and bond us indefinitely."

He was too confused, too dumbstruck to follow her train of thought. "You say that like it's a bad thing."

She pulled her hand from his, linked her fingers. "I'm in serious danger of falling for you. If we take things to the next level again, I'm going to disappoint myself *and* get my heart broken when you're done."

Annoyance, swift and lethal, crawled along his spine like a centipede. "When I'm done? Kayla, who says I'm going to be done? We're having a baby. I get why you'd question my motives after the way I behaved, but I wish you'd give me a little credit." He drew a breath, gathered courage to say what he felt in his heart. "I want you to give me a chance—give us a chance."

She shot to her feet, stepped around the coffee table, turned to face him with her hands on her cheeks. "Ben, stop. I can't get my hopes up like this. I just can't."

He stood, deliberately leaving an arm's length between them. "Kayla, I have feelings for you, and it seems silly not to explore them—especially if you have feelings for me—just because you're scared it's going to end."

"I'm scared of being alone, of raising this baby alone. It scares me to death."

Ben placed his hands on her rigid shoulders, rubbed circles along her collarbone with his thumbs. "No matter what happens between us, you'll never have to raise the baby alone. I'm not going to abandon you or our baby."

"You say that now—"

"And I mean it—now and forever. No matter what." She bit her lip as if fretting over all the things that could go wrong when the one thing that felt right sizzled between them. He could feel it in the warmth of her skin beneath his fingers and the way her pupils dilated as her eyes pinged between his. "If you want to take it slow, we'll take it slow. But you're not a rebound. I want to be with you because I want to be with you, not because I miss Darcy. I don't miss anything about her."

"Maybe you miss being in a relationship."

"Our relationship was too dysfunctional to call a relationship." He shook his head, tightened his fingers on her shoulders, loosened them, and rubbed where he may have been too rough. "Darcy has nothing to do with the way I feel about you. I want you and only you. I wish you could believe that."

She blinked once. "I wish I could believe it, too," she said in a tiny, faraway voice.

"Believe this." He went with instinct, lowered his head, feathered his lips against hers. She melted against him, opened for him again.

Her words may have said to go slow, but her body had other ideas. He would have to draw on every ounce of restraint not take what she so clearly wanted.

He gentled the kiss and pulled back, dropping his forehead to hers. He struggled for composure. "I'm taking you out on a date this weekend. If you can't believe the way I feel about you, I'll show you. I'll show everyone whose baby is growing inside of you."

"Ben ..."

"Is that a no?"

"People will talk. People will know."

"I don't care what people think. I want to spend time with you."

"I want to spend time with you, too, but I think you're being foolish."

"And I think you're acting like a coward."

Her muscles tensed beneath his fingers, her head lurching back.

"You're not a coward, Kayla. I've watched you face everything we've had to deal with like a warrior. I'm asking you to be brave for me. For us."

She stared at the buttons on his shirt. When she lifted her eyes, he saw the fear, the confusion, the doubt, and witnessed the moment the courage broke through, the moment she decided to take what he wanted to give.

"Okay," she said. "I hope you don't regret this."

Chapter Thirty-One

Kayla lifted the dress over her head and flung it onto the bed where it joined a chorus of other clothes, tried on and discarded. She flipped through the hangers in her closet, dismissing outfit after outfit in a fluster of panic and doubt. She never should have agreed to go on a date with Ben. He wasn't thinking straight. He was only trying to make her feel better after she admitted her secret. He was being nice—again—to his own detriment.

Shelby walked by her room, glanced in, and did a double take. "Are you cleaning out your closet?"

Kayla sat atop the pile of clothes on her bed and dropped her head into her hands. "I have nothing to wear."

"Your bed says otherwise." Shelby stepped inside the room and crossed her arms over her chest. "What's the matter? I thought you'd be excited about your date."

"I was, until I tried to find something to wear. It's hopeless. My jeans are too tight, yoga pants aren't appropriate for a date, and all my dresses are sundresses. I have a thousand skirts, but they all have zippers. And the one maternity dress I ordered online looks ridiculous until the baby gets bigger."

"Kayla," Shelby stepped closer and put her hand on her shoulder. "Between the three of us, someone will have something you can wear."

"I didn't want to take the chance of stretching out someone's clothes."

"I don't think a couple of hours will permanently stretch someone's jeans or skirt. I may even have a dress that will work."

"We're not the same size," Kayla said, her voice a whiny tone that made her want to vomit. "You're bustier than I am."

"I was before your breasts grew two sizes."

Kayla looked down at her chest, then up at Shelby's. "Huh. You might be right."

"I am right. Follow me to my closet, and let's have a look."

Kayla hopped up and followed Shelby to her room. Shelby flicked on the light illuminating the unmade bed and the clothes littering the floor. "Don't be frightened by the mess. I'm cleaning up tonight before Reagan blows a gasket."

Their tidy roommate's OCD ways had gotten even worse since dating Dash the clean-freak. "You might want to keep your door shut until she leaves for Atlanta."

"She's visiting Dash this weekend?" Shelby asked.

"It's his first time as worship leader at his church and he's nervous. I told Reagan I'd go with her until Ben asked me out."

"Hallelujah." Shelby raised her hands in the air. "A reprieve. Now I have all weekend to clean." She stepped over a pile of shoes and flicked on the closet light.

Kayla did her best not to cringe. Shelby's closet looked like a wild animal had ransacked the tiny space. There were countless clothes bulging from hangers as well as shirts and shorts dangling out of half-open drawers. "How do you find anything?"

"It's organized chaos." Shelby's arm disappeared into the hangers, and she plucked a dress from the abyss. "Try this one. It has an empire waist and long sleeves."

"This is cute," Kayla said. "I've never seen you wear this."

"I've worn it. It would look great with your ankle boots."

"Keep looking while I try this on." Kayla slipped the dress over her head and walked into the bedroom to see how it looked in Shelby's full-length mirror. "It really is cute." She turned to the side and admired how the waistline and floral pattern hid her baby bump.

Shelby peeked her head out of the closet and wagged her brows. "Look what the neckline does for your chest."

Kayla looked down, admired her cleavage. "Impressive. Do you mind if I borrow this?"

"Don't be stupid. One look at you in that dress, and Ben will forget his name."

"I just want him to forget the name of his ex-girlfriend."

"Are you still worried about that?"

Kayla sat on Shelby's bed while her roommate dropped to the floor and picked up clothes. "How can I not be? They just broke up. Don't get me wrong—I'm thrilled he asked me out, but I'm trying not to get my hopes up."

"Kay, you're having his baby. I think you have the advantage in this situation."

"Maybe." She picked at a hangnail. "But I want him to like me for me, not because I'm his baby's incubator."

"Kayla." Shelby tossed a pair of jeans into a hamper, pulled

Kayla to her feet, and moved her in front of the mirror. "You are a beautiful woman—with or without his baby growing inside you. The fact that you're carrying his baby probably makes you more attractive. Don't guys get off on that kind of thing?"

"What kind of thing?"

"You know, that he planted his seed. That his boys couldn't be stopped. That kind of thing."

"Oh, my gosh, you are such a guy sometimes."

"I'm not a guy. I'm thinking like a guy. And as such, I think you look seriously hot. If I were Ben, I'd do you."

Kayla's heart wilted and her smile dissolved. "Do you think that's what this is about?"

"What do you mean?"

"I mean, he just got out of a long-term relationship that included regular sex. Do you think he's using me for sex?"

"Are you going to have sex with him? Because if you're trying not to get attached, that's not going to help."

"I know. I told him that, and he said we'd take it slow."

"Then no, I don't think he's using you for sex."

Kayla bit her lip, admired the dress. "Thanks for the dress, and the pep talk. I needed both—more than you know."

"Happy to help." Shelby sorted through more clothes. "At least one of us has a date."

"Shelby." Kayla gave her best you've-got-to-be-kidding-me stare. "You could have a date every night of the week if you wanted."

"Yeah, yeah, yeah."

"Why don't you ever let your guard down and give someone a chance?"

Shelby directed her eyes at Kayla's midsection, boosting her brows. "Look where that got you."

"I'm the worst example." She threw her arms in the air. "You know I let everyone in—and I don't mean that sexually."

"I know what you mean."

"Look at Reagan and Dash and how happy they are. And Emily and Dylan. They're two fabulous couples who prove how awesome it can turn out if you give someone a chance."

"I'm not looking for happily ever after. It was just a flippant comment."

"A flippant comment that speaks volumes. You could handpick your dates, yet you never go out with anyone. I may be a walking train wreck, but at least I'm trying. You have so much to offer, I hate that you're alone all the time."

"Kayla, you may hate that I'm alone, but I don't. I'm fine with it. Guys bring a whole slew of issues I don't need or want—especially so close to graduation. I mean, what if I did go out with someone and fall head over heels and he's from Alaska or someplace I'd never want to live? Can you see me in Alaska?"

Kayla placed her hands onto her hips. "Who do you know at ASU from Alaska?"

"No one, but that doesn't mean he's not here."

Kayla sighed and shook her head. "Reagan and Dash had different life plans, and they're figuring it out."

"I don't want to have to figure anything out other than what I want to do with my life." Shelby picked up a suede boot. "You know me. You know I want to start out in Atlanta. We even talked about living together before Ben came along. Now, where's the mate to this?"

"It's not like I'm going to be living with Ben, ya know. We haven't even talked about what happens after the baby's born."

Shelby stopped looking for her suede boot and narrowed her eyes at Kayla. "You haven't?"

Kayla stared at her toes as humiliating heat rose like steam. "Not exactly."

"Don't you think that's a conversation worth having? Soon?"

She stifled the urge to pick her nails. "I know we need to talk and make some plans."

"Isn't he from somewhere around here?"

"He's from Swinville."

Shelby sent her a blank stare.

"It's about an hour from here."

"Okay. You're from Atlanta. You're having the baby in Atlanta, I presume?"

"Yes."

"And Ben will be there for the birth?"

"Of course he will."

"Will he be living there?"

Kayla gave in and picked at the skin around her thumbnail. "I don't know. He hasn't said. I know he's talking to his counselor, looking at options. My dad offered to get him on at his company in some kind of training program."

"Is he considering it?"

"I'm not sure."

"Kayla." Shelby got to her feet and reached for her hand. "I'm not trying to bully you, but these are important questions you need to ask. You need to know what your life is going to be like after the baby's born. A lot of that depends on where Ben is and how often he's going to be around to be a father."

"He said he'd never abandon us." Her voice sounded as feeble as her excuse. "Me and the baby."

"Does that mean financially or physically? Because if he's living in South Georgia and you're in Atlanta, he's not going to be much help."

Shelby's comment wouldn't have stung so much if hadn't rang true. "I'm going to ask him." But not tonight. Tonight was about them—the two of them—and if she peppered Ben with questions about the baby and the future, their date would be nothing more than a grilling. "I will. I'm not a total masochist. I know we have decisions to make."

"Kayla ..."

"Trust me. It's on the agenda."

"For tonight?"

Kayla picked up the missing boot and handed it to Shelby. "Maybe. Maybe not. It depends on how it goes."

Shelby shook her head.

"Don't look at me like that," Kayla said. "I'm barely showing. We have time to figure things out."

"Think about it this way. If you and I were still planning on living together in Atlanta, we'd be looking for apartments right now. We'd be making plans. So don't act like you and Ben have all the time in the world."

Chapter Thirty-Two

Ben pulled up to the restaurant, put the car into park, and let his eyes linger on the girl beside him. Since her admission, he felt like a fool. Only a desperate fool would've missed the glaring signs of her inexperience—the vulnerability, the sincerity, the modesty—despite the sexy dress showcasing her curves. Even now, fully aware of her innocence, he was going to have a hard time keeping his eyes and his hands to himself.

He thought of Theo, the words of caution he'd offered before Ben left to pick up Kayla. "I'm glad you finally admitted you like her. But dude, do yourself a favor and take it slow. If you jump in and it doesn't work out, you'll have a scorned baby mama you'll have to deal with for the rest of your life."

Theo was right, and Ben had every intention of taking it slow. But it wasn't going to be easy, not with the way she looked at him. Now that he knew the way pregnancy amped her desire, he wanted her more with every second they spent together. It would take Herculean strength to abide by her wishes.

"Ready?" he asked.

Kayla wrung her hands and glanced out the windshield. "Are you sure you want to do this? It's not too late to change your mind."

"Kayla." He reached for her hand and squeezed. "You look fantastic. Any guy in his right mind would be proud to have you on his arm."

"That's the problem. I don't think you're in your right mind."

"Because I want to be with you?"

"Because you haven't thought through what this will do to your reputation."

"I don't have a reputation." And if he did, he wouldn't care. He'd spent too much of his life worrying about what other people thought. He leaned over, brushed his lips against hers, and felt her sigh. "No more excuses. Let's go have a nice dinner."

"It's your funeral," she mumbled before he got out of the car.

He opened the passenger door, reached for her hand, and helped her out. She gave him a half-smile—all lips and no teeth—and glanced over his shoulder. He wanted to tell a joke or tickle her or make her laugh, something to relax the high set of her shoulders, but he linked their fingers and escorted her inside the main street restaurant.

Ben blinked and glanced around the interior. Darcy never liked the place, said it was too dark, too much like a men's country club, with its leather banquet seating and the exposed brick walls. He loved the atmosphere created by the softly lit bulbs hanging from the tin ceiling, and enjoyed the smoky aroma of the wood-fired grill.

"This is nice," Kayla said. "I've never been here before."

"It's one of my favorites."

The hostess showed them to a table.

Ben helped Kayla into a seat before taking his own. "The pizza is amazing, and so are the entrées." He placed his napkin in his lap, straightened the cuffs of his button-down shirt, and glanced across the table at his date as she perused the menu. He licked his lips and stared at her.

She caught him ogling her cleavage. "Everything okay?" she asked.

Ben cleared the lust from his throat. "Yeah. I'm just … hungry."

"Me, too." She skimmed the menu a last time before setting it down on the table and lifting her eyes to his.

He felt the jolt the second she recognized the look in his eyes, and watched fascinated at the blush that crept up her cheeks. "Ben …"

"What?"

She tucked the hair behind her ear, glaring at her silverware. "Stop."

"Stop what?" he asked.

"Stop looking at me like I'm on the menu. Because I'm not."

Ben shrugged and tried to tamp down his attraction. "You look and smell better than anything they serve."

Her blush deepened. "We talked about this. I thought we were going to take it slow."

"We are. I haven't touched you, Kayla, and I won't until you're ready. I promise."

"I'm not trying to be difficult. I'm just being honest. Jumping into bed won't strengthen our bond. It'll test it."

Her honesty was meant to warn him, not fan the flames or

apply pressure. The last thing he wanted was to pressure her into anything. He wanted her to come to him, willing and ready. Then and only then would he show her how she made him feel. Show her what they could have together if she gave them a chance. Until then, he had to leash his emotions and his tongue and give her the reins.

First, he had to explain.

She fidgeted in her seat. Her eyes, so blue, so vivid in the muted setting, looked at everything but him.

"You have no idea," he said. "Do you?"

"No idea about what?"

"How beautiful you are. How special."

Her lips quirked. "Ben …"

"I'm serious. Kayla, look at me."

She took a deep breath and lifted her eyes to his. He tortured them both by reaching for her hand, caressing the soft skin of her palm. "You're stunning. You always have been. Being with you is like the first sunny day after a long, harsh winter. You make me feel alive."

"Okay." Her head angled adorably to the side. "That's not helping."

"It's the truth. I'm twelve times a fool for not doing this sooner, not taking a chance and asking you out."

Her fingers toyed with his. "We kinda skipped over the formalities."

"I'm sorry for making you feel used, discarded. It must have seemed as if I never cared, as if you were one of many."

She shrugged and looked away, but didn't withdraw her hand.

Ben's stomach dropped, his heart rate spiked, and the rustling of nearby patrons dulled to a drone. It was time to come clean about that night, confess his sin, and seek her forgiveness—or her understanding, at least. His leg bobbled, jostling the table. He steadied it with a damp palm. "I'm no saint, and this is no excuse but—"

"Welcome to Artello's," the waiter said in a bright tone. "Have you dined with us before?"

Go away! Ben abandoned Kayla's fingers and gave the perky waiter a death stare he politely ignored. "I've been here, but this is her first time."

"Lovely," he purred.

Ben imagined yanking the waiter's tie until he fled.

"Do you have any questions about the menu?"

Ben didn't know what irritated him more, the sing-song sound of the waiter's voice or the way Kayla stared at him, spellbound.

"How big are the pizzas?" Kayla asked.

The waiter/actor demonstrated with his hands. Ben slammed his teeth together, grinding them to paste.

Kayla ordered a pizza and a water. Ben did the same, willing the interloper to disappear. When he finally slipped away, Kayla smiled at him. "I'm sorry. What were you saying?"

The moment had passed, leaving Ben deflated. How could he explain now, with the faint smile on her lips from basking in the glow of the waiter's attention? "I was apologizing for making you uncomfortable. I want you to know how special you are, how much I enjoy spending time with you."

She swallowed, nodded, chewed the glistening pink from her lips. She wouldn't meet his eyes.

"What's wrong?" he asked. "Did I say something wrong?"

She cleared her throat. "I wasn't going to bring this up on our date because I wanted tonight to be about us and not about the baby." She lifted her shoulders, let them fall. "But I don't think this can wait."

Ben sat up, ran his hands against the soft denim of his jeans. Whatever she had to say couldn't be good, not with the way she pulled herself away from him and tucked her hands beneath the table. "What is it?"

"I was talking to Shelby earlier, and she reminded me that we'd planned to move in together after graduation."

"Oh." His chest tightened. His hands clenched into fists. "Is that … is that still your plan?"

She chortled. "Shelby has no intention of sharing space with a newborn."

The vise on his ribcage lessened, his fingers relaxed. "Okay."

"She said if things were different, if I weren't expecting, we'd be looking for an apartment now. We'd be making plans."

"That's true." He knew where she was going. His cheeks stung from the sharp pinpricks of shame. If Theo was here, he'd shake his head at Ben over Kayla's shoulder with that I-told-you-so grin on his face.

"We don't have any plans," Kayla continued. "You and me. For after the baby's born. We've talked about the birth and I know you're going to be there, but I don't know where you're going to be before or after. I don't know where *I'm* going to be before or after, and that makes me nervous. If things were different, I'd know. Or at least I'd be working on it by now."

"Kayla, you're right. We need to talk about this. I've been chewing on a few ideas, trying to figure out the logistics of everything."

"You have?"

"I didn't bring it up because I wanted to have everything squared away so you wouldn't think I'm unreliable. I guess that was the wrong approach. I never meant to make you doubt me or make you nervous about the future. I'm going to be there. With you. No matter what, I'm going to be in Atlanta after graduation. I'm going to talk to your dad about the training position, and I'm also applying for a paid internship at the GBI."

Like a tide on its way out to sea, the color fled from her face. "The Georgia Bureau of Investigation?"

Ben nodded. "I'm thinking about going into law enforcement."

"The police?" Her voice pitched skyward.

"Or the bureau, if I like the internship. If I get the internship."

"Oh." She nodded and fiddled with the bracelet on her wrist, twisting it around and around. "I had no idea you were interested in being a cop."

"It surprised me, too, but I think I'd like it. I think I'd be good. I wanted a career in the law—or at least I thought I did. There's a shortage, so finding a job shouldn't be a problem."

She flattened her palms on the table. "Ben, there's a shortage because people hate cops. People target cops. It's … it's not my decision to make, but, wow, that's not what I was expecting."

He reached for her hands, tucked them into his. "I know this is unexpected, but I've given it a lot of thought. I've done tons of research and talked to some of my friends who are cops. Theo—my roommate—his brother's a cop, and when we were in Atlanta the last time, I met with a fraternity brother who's in the bureau."

He wished she would say something, do something other than look at him with wide eyes and a worried expression.

"I appreciate your dad's offer and I'm happy to talk to him and find out more about international acquisitions if you think it'll make him more comfortable with me. But I also don't want to give him false hope when I want to give law enforcement a try."

"Okay …" She shook her head as if coming out of a trance

or waking up from a bad dream. “Tell me what you’re thinking. Help me understand.”

He laid it out for her, piece by piece, only stopping when the waiter delivered their drinks and later their food. She asked questions, thoughtful, insightful questions that made him think, gave him hope she felt as invested in his career and their future as he did.

“Okay,” she said, picking at the pizza on her plate. “I get it. You’ve put a lot of thought into this and I see you have a plan. That’s good.”

“But?”

“No buts. I just wonder …” She shrugged, stared at the table.

Ben reached across the table, rested his hand by her plate. “Kayla, talk to me. You’ve been honest with me about everything from the beginning. I don’t want you to stop now.” He stared at her, willing her to look at him and give him her hand. If he could just touch her, he knew she’d understand how important she was, how much he needed her blessing in order to proceed.

“So you’ll be in Atlanta over the summer and when the baby’s born. That’s great. That relieves a lot of stress. But where will you live?”

“I can live with my friend Gregg.” The pizza in his belly turned to yeast, a doughy ball of denial. “Or, if you think it’s okay, I could ask your parents if I could stay in the guest house.”

His entire body relaxed when she bobbed her head up and down.

“I think that would be fine—preferable since we’ll have a newborn and my parents would appreciate all the help you could offer.”

He hadn’t realized how much he was counting on being near her and the baby, how much he didn’t want there to be space between them before or after the baby was born.

"What will you do when the internship is over?" she asked. "If you decide to get POST certified?"

"Honestly, Kayla, it depends on us. I won't make a decision without talking to you first. And we'll decide what comes next." A sheen of tears appeared in her eyes so quickly he nearly fell out of his chair in surprise. "What's wrong? What did I say?"

"You make it sound like you're planning for our future—mine and yours and the baby's. Together."

"I don't want to be a part-time dad. I want us to be a family."

"Ben …"

"I know. I know I'm supposed to go slow, but we don't have time to beat around the bush. I'm making plans that put me in Atlanta for the summer. We'll wait and see what that leads to after, but if you're asking me what I think right now, I think whatever I decide depends on you and me more than anything. If I decide to go for POST certification, I want you and the baby to come with me. Wherever I get a job, I want you there. That may sound selfish, but it's the truth. That's what I want and it's what I'm planning unless and until something happens to change my mind."

Chapter Thirty-Three

Kayla blinked against the bright overhead lights. Nerves and anticipation tangled in her stomach.

"Nervous about seeing our little pear?" Ben gripped her hand. She and Ben had started calling the baby their little pear.

"Excited. This makes it more real."

Kayla's mom rubbed her arm from the other side of the exam table. "It's real. Boy or girl just helps you plan."

The tech came in and shut the door behind her, dimming the lights. "Good afternoon, folks. My name is Molly, and I'll be doing your ultrasound today. Have you had an ultrasound before?"

Kayla nodded. "At the eight-week appointment. But it was different."

"Eight weeks was probably vaginal. For this ultrasound, I'm

going to squirt some jelly over your uterus and run a wand over the jelly to have a look at the baby. I'll take some measurements, make sure things are progressing as they should. Before we begin, do you want to know the sex of the baby or would you like me to note it in the file for a baby reveal?"

"We want to know now," Ben said. "If that's possible."

"Should be. We never guarantee one hundred percent because of the way the baby may or may not be presenting, but we've not been wrong before."

"So, ninety-nine percent?" Kayla asked.

The tech chuckled, easing Kayla's nerves. "Let's get the show on the road, and I'll let you know if there's any question. I do the measurements first, because growth and health are most important."

Kayla nodded, looked at Ben. He leaned over the table and kissed her forehead. Kayla closed her eyes at the feel of his lips on her skin, letting her joy show on her face. She never would have guessed how much she would come to rely on him. She'd fallen and fallen hard, although she'd yet to admit the depth of her feelings to anyone.

When she opened her eyes and glanced at her mom, her mother looked like she'd just swallowed something sour, the same look she gave Kayla in the waiting room when Ben held her hand until their names were called. She hadn't told Mom she and Ben were dating, hadn't given her any hint they'd met nearly every day since their first official date. Anyone with a pulse on campus had probably figured out Ben was the father of her baby, especially now that she'd started showing, but he didn't seem to care. She'd given up trying to shield him.

She'd also given up trying to hold him at arm's length. They spent most days together when not in class, studying and laughing, Ben's hand on her belly waiting for the baby to move so he could feel the flutter of life they created growing inside her body. Touching her stomach usually led to more touching and make-out sessions that left them both aching. Despite feeling like a tease, something made her stop while every cell in her body screamed at her to give in and give up the fight. She'd blown it the first time around and she vowed to do it right this time. Even if it killed her.

Molly warned her before squirting gel on her tummy and smearing it around with the wand. Kayla ignored her mom and focused on the black and white screen. She couldn't tell what she was looking at until Molly walked them through the lines she drew on the screen with the roller ball on her keyboard. The tech focused on her job. Kayla focused on her face, noted her concentration, tried to pick up on any frowns or signs of trouble. Molly appeared focused but relaxed, and Kayla glanced back at the screen.

"Your baby looks good." Molly froze the screen, measured some part of the baby's anatomy, and unfroze the screen. "Do you know what you're looking at?"

"No," Ben said, glaring at the screen. "It looks like an alien."

Molly chuckled. "The flashing dot there is the heartbeat." She used the ball on her keypad to circle the beeping dot. "And this is the head."

"Oh," Kayla said. "I see it now."

"Is that railroad-looking thing the spine?" Ben asked.

"Yes," Molly answered.

"There's a foot," her mom said. "How cute."

"The profile." Kayla peeked at Ben. "Look at our baby."

"Look at our baby," he repeated, his voice soft with wonder. He wasn't the only one blown away by the images on the screen. Their little pear had grown real baby parts and looked like a living, breathing, human being. Amazement and awe dueled with fear and trepidation. How could something like that be living inside her right this moment?

"How does everything look?" her mom asked the tech.

"Everything looks good so far. I just need to take a few more measurements to note in the file before we try to assess the gender." Molly ran the wand over her belly in random patterns, sometimes wiggling the wand in order to make the baby move one way or the other, rolling the ball and drawing lines on the screen.

"Are those legs?" Ben asked.

"Those are legs." Molly froze the screen and glanced at Kayla and Ben. "Your baby cooperated. Are you ready to know what you're having?"

"I think I know." Ben waved an arm at the screen. "Unless that's a kickstand I'm looking at between his legs."

"That's one way to put it." Molly looked at Kayla. "You're having a boy."

Kayla's fingers tingled and her heart performed a backflip in her chest. A boy! She and Ben had made a son to carry on his name and make a mark on the world. She shifted her eyes to Ben.

He met her stare with a dumbstruck look on his face. "We're having a boy."

Kayla imagined baseball games and football uniforms and matching camouflage outfits for father and son.

"A grandson!" Her mom clapped her hands against her cheeks. "Wait until I tell Gary."

Ben leaned down and kissed Kayla full on the mouth, lingering long enough to leave no doubt in anyone's mind about the nature of their relationship. Kayla tried to focus on the good news—a healthy baby boy—and ignore the look of shock and dismay written all over her mother's face.

The tech wiped Kayla's belly clean and pushed the machine away from the exam table. The temperature in the room dropped—and it had nothing to do with the absence of warm jelly.

"Congratulations Mom, Dad, and Grandma." Molly seemed oblivious to the shift in the room. "I'll let Dr. Francis know we're done." She slipped out of the room.

Kayla sat up.

"Well." Her mom lifted her brows, stared at Kayla. "I guess we've got a lot to celebrate."

Kayla nodded, tried her best to gauge her mother's reaction. Kayla knew she'd be upset about being kept in the dark, but she couldn't read her mother's cool-but-polite reaction.

"Yes, we do." Ben helped Kayla off the table and wrapped his arms around her shoulders, folding her into a hug and kissing her forehead. Either Ben didn't notice the change in her mother, or he'd decided to ignore her misgivings and out them as a couple. "A boy." He shook his head. "Wow."

Jessica looped her purse over her shoulder and stepped around the couple. "I'm meeting dad for lunch. Is it okay to share the good news?"

"Of course," Kayla said.

Jessica nodded and pecked Kayla on the cheek. "I'll see you at home. Love you."

"Love you, too." Kayla watched her mom leave and turned to face Ben. "Well, you certainly know how to make an announcement."

"Why didn't you didn't tell her?" Ben's tone was sharp and accusing.

Kayla's throat closed and she lowered her gaze, unable to see the hurt in his eyes.

Ben lifted her chin with his finger. "Kayla, we're having a baby. Us being a couple isn't something to feel ashamed about."

"I know. I just … I wasn't sure she'd approve."

"From her reaction, I'd say she doesn't. But why are you ashamed?"

"I'm not ashamed." She reached for him, sandwiched his hand between hers, squeezed. "I promise, Ben, I'm not ashamed. Not at all."

"Then why the big secret?"

Kayla shrugged. She wished she could explain her hesitation, the gut-deep feeling her mother would assume the worst—a short-term relationship until the baby came and things got real. Things got hard. Or maybe it was Kayla's own gut-deep fear she saw reflected on her mother's face. "It's been so great being together that I didn't want any negativity. I didn't want to hear her warning me not to get attached."

Ben threw his hands in the air and paced the small room before pivoting around to face her, his hands on his hips. "Why does everyone think I'm going to bail? What have I done to give you that impression?"

"Ben …" Kayla bit her lip, tried to come up with something that would assuage his anger and her guilt. But the truth was the truth. He'd slept with her and never tried to contact her. Whatever they were building now was built on that shaky foundation. No matter how hard she tried, no matter how much he did, the past mattered as much as the future. "You've been great since I told you about the baby. Better than great."

"But?"

"But before …"

He closed his eyes and dropped his head to his chest, swaying it back and forth. His shoulders slumped and his hands slipped to hang at his side.

"I'm not trying to throw salt in a wound," Kayla said.

Ben looked up at her, crossed his arms against his chest.

"I was embarrassed after we slept together, but that didn't stop me from spinning fantasies in my head. When you dropped off the planet, I felt like a fool. Finding out about the baby and having to face you—especially after I realized you had a girlfriend—was the most humiliating moment of my life."

With two steps, he stood before her, clasping her hands and holding them against her stomach where their baby thrived. "Kayla, you'll never know how sorry I am for making you feel that way, for letting you down. I'm going to spend every day making it up to you. I hope—I pray—one day you'll forgive me. One day you'll believe me. I had no right to lose my temper with you just now. I get it. I have to earn your trust and pushing you too far, too fast doesn't help."

"Ben." She shook her head. "I don't expect you to grovel."

"You also don't expect me to stay. And that's on me."

Kayla couldn't stand the way he stared at her with pitying eyes. He'd seduced her, yes, but she'd gone willingly. He'd made no promises, but she'd never asked. How was he to know their night together meant more to her than it ever could to him? If they hadn't made their son, that night would be nothing more than a bittersweet memory.

"Stop," she said. "I forgive you. I believe you're not going anywhere. I'm sorry I keep doubting you. That's not fair to either one of us."

"I would never make a promise to you I wasn't willing to keep. I didn't make promises back then because I couldn't. But things are different now. Things are better."

She rubbed her belly, gazed at the man she loved. "Yes, they are. Our little pear is a boy."

He looked so relieved at the change in subject, at her forgiveness. A slow smile inched across Ben's face amplifying his appeal. "He'd probably appreciate a manlier nickname."

"Or a name," she said. "We need to name our son."

Chapter Thirty-Four

"Give me another name. A proper name, not one of your silly new age ideas," Ben said. He and Kayla were on their way to Ben's house for Easter break. His mom had pestered him into the invite, using guilt as only a mother could, and Ben talked Kayla into joining him for Easter. The fact that she relented spoke volumes about her not wanting him to face his parents alone and her desire to mend the rift with his family. He and his dad had exchanged a few words in the last few months, mostly because Kayla prodded him to reach out.

"You're going to need your parents when the baby's born—we both are. He's your dad. One of you has to make the first move." He'd made the first move and while they had talked, they hadn't had an actual conversation. Still, a few terse words were better than none.

"How about Maverick?" Kayla asked.

"Maverick Strickland? You've got to be kidding."

"Nobody's going to mess with Maverick."

Ben chuckled. Despite her nerves over spending time with his parents, she was doing her best to help them both relax. "You know what Maverick means, don't you?"

"Stud?"

"Rebel, among other things. Not a great idea, besides the fact that it's hideous."

Kayla giggled. The sound both eased his stress and ratcheted it up a few notches. Their visit home would either bring them closer or tear them apart. Chicken that he was, he couldn't bring himself to change the subject and douse her playful mood.

"What about Seth?" she asked.

"Does he come with a trust fund?"

"Seth's not bad. I like Seth."

"You like the double S, but every S name you've suggested is horrible."

"You haven't changed your mind about Simon?"

"Nope," he said. "Never."

"It's biblical."

"So is Solomon, but they're both a hard no."

While she stewed in the passenger seat, searching for names on her phone, Ben's gut twisted with every passing mile. He still hadn't told her about Scott, despite Theo's near-daily reminders. "What are you waiting for?" his roommate had asked. "She's going to find out eventually."

He'd never found the right time, never knew how to start the conversation, never wanted to jeopardize their newfound peace since she'd forgiven him, and they'd grown closer than ever. Like a flower slow to bloom, Kayla had finally relaxed around him and volunteered information about her life instead of him having to prod her with questions. Things between them were going too well to admit he'd kept the death of his brother a secret.

But buried secrets grew roots and wormed their way to the surface. This one had a lit fuse to clear the path, incinerating inch by inch as Ben's car ate up the road.

He meant to tell Kayla as soon as she got in the car, but she'd entertained him with a story about a dating show she watched with her roommates. He couldn't bring himself to interrupt with a story of death and gloom.

So he'd waited.

When he stopped to fill up with gas, he intended to tell her when she got back to the car after using the bathroom, but she'd been drawn into a conversation about pregnancy with the checkout girl. She chattered on and on about tidbits she'd read in her books about what to expect, which evolved into the name exchange. He hadn't wanted to cut her off.

He was delaying the inevitable.

As they passed the county line into Swinville, she resumed her search for baby names on her phone.

The ticking timebomb slammed against his chest, creating a cacophony of chaos in his head. The fuse hissed and crackled as it seared through his veins.

Tell her. Tell her. Tell her now.

It was time to come clean.

He reached over and grasped her hand. "Speaking of S names ..."

She lowered the phone and looked at him with excitement in her sparkling blue eyes. He hoped what he told her didn't change the way she looked at him. The way she felt about him. Baby or no baby, he wanted to be with her.

"Do you have a suggestion? I thought you hated the double S."

"The thing is ..." Fear gripped his torso, wrapped its fat fingers around his ribcage and squeezed—squeezed hard. His pulse sputtered. "There was a double S."

Kayla's stare looked past him, over his shoulder and out the window at the stores along Main Street. "Is this your hometown? Are we here?"

Ben punched his foot on the gas. Irritation and dread swirled in his belly, creating a nasty brew of desperation. He'd finally started to tell her, and the quaintness of downtown Swinville stole her attention. "Yeah. Listen—"

"Oh, my gosh, Ben, it's so cute." She twisted to get a better look as he whizzed past the courthouse. "Can we walk around down there sometime this weekend?"

Two miles from home. The fist around his chest clenched.

"Kayla." Her name came out louder and with more exasperation than he'd intended. The red light switched to green, he turned onto the highway that led home, and softened his tone. "I need to tell you something before we get to my house."

She twisted back to him. "I'm sorry." She folded her hands in her lap and gave him her full attention.

He could see his mailbox looming like a guillotine in the distance. He swallowed and eased his foot off the gas, slowing their progress. Now it was time—now he was out of time—he couldn't catch his breath or find the words. "I ... uh ... when I was in high school ..." He pulled into his drive and the plantation colonial he called home appeared ahead.

"Whoa," Kayla said. "Talk about a trust fund. Ben, this is beautiful."

He eased around the curve in the drive. His hands fisted on

the steering wheel when he spotted a car parked in the gravel lot. A sporty little car he knew well. A sporty little car reeking of perfume and privilege. Rage churned along his spine, blasting his skull into tiny shards of shattered glass. Blind with fury, he shoved the car into park. "What the …"

"What?" Kayla needn't have asked. The color drained from her face when Darcy stood up from the porch swing where she sat with his ma, a glass of tea in her hand. "Oh."

Every muscle in Ben's body coiled, wrung tight by confusion and madness. It took titanic restraint not to storm up the porch steps and chase her off the property. But he wouldn't do that to Kayla, wouldn't show her how much he despised his ex and her games.

He slammed his door, gave Darcy a death stare, and marched around the hood of the car to help Kayla stand. She looked pretty in her yellow dress, innocent and full of goodness as she speared him with a questioning gaze. "Why is she here?"

Ben shrugged his stiff shoulders, tried to smother the desire to flee. "I have no idea, but she's not staying."

Kayla gripped his arm. "Please don't make a scene. I can handle this. It's okay."

"It's not okay." Nothing between them would ever be okay as long as Darcy refused to leave his house, his life, his future alone. He'd driven all this way to start fresh, not to drag Kayla into the middle of their feud. Cornered, Ben had no choice but to lead his precious Kayla into a house tainted by lies and deceit. A house where he no longer felt safe.

Ben reached for Kayla's hand, linked their fingers, let her goodness ground him in the surreal moment. He needed her more than ever. He stepped in front of her, determined to protect her and the baby from whatever Darcy had planned. They walked to the porch and mounted the stairs. Kayla wiggled her fingers. Ben lightened his hold but didn't let go.

"What are you doing here?" Ben asked Darcy. At the harshness of his tone, Kayla squeezed his hand.

Darcy's jaw jutted to the side—her tell when she got mad—as her frigid gaze bounced from Kayla's belly to their linked hands. "Your mother invited me." She shifted, resting her tea on the bannister. "You must be Kayla." Darcy flipped her hair over her shoulder in a practiced move and shoved the other hand in Kayla's face. "I'm Darcy Keller."

Kayla had to disengage from Ben's grip to shake hands. He slipped his arm around Kayla's waist and secured her to his side. Darcy's nostrils flared at his countermove.

"Hi," Kayla said, her voice frail. "It's nice to meet you."

Darcy gave her the up-down with a half-smile in response, a mix of cool indifference and boiling disgust. Ben squashed the urge to lunge for her throat.

When his ma got to her feet, Kayla stepped forward and gave his ma a tentative hug. "It's good to see you, Mrs. Strickland. Your home is gorgeous."

His ma appeared dumbstruck at Kayla's protruding belly, as if she'd been in denial about the pregnancy until faced with proof. "Thank you. How's my grandson doing?"

"He's currently sitting on my bladder. Do you mind if I use the bathroom?"

"Of course," his ma said. "It's just inside. I'll show you."

"Thank you."

Ben stepped in front of Kayla and placed his hands on her shoulders, looked into her eyes. *I'll take care of her*, he tried to convey with his stare. *Don't worry about a thing.* "I'll be right in."

"Okay."

He bent down and placed a kiss on her forehead, lingering, savoring, trying to soak up a fraction of her integrity before he lost his temper with his devious ex. Kayla and his ma walked past him into the house. Ben turned and sneered at Darcy. "What are you doing here?"

"I never turn down an invitation from your mom."

Ben cringed at the nasally sound of Darcy's voice.

"Besides, if we're going to coexist, I figured the first step was to meet your little mistake." She picked up her tea and took a sip. "She's cute. Never figured you for the short blonde type, but what do I know."

"Absolutely nothing, if you think she's a mistake."

She laughed, as if to brush away his comment, but the way the muscle ticked in her jaw told him she cared more than she let on. She ran a hand down his chest, and he flicked it away. "You keep telling yourself that, Benny Boy, but we both know this won't last. You're going to get tired of playing the white knight to her damsel in distress."

"And you're going to get tired of playing the scorned ex when nobody cares."

His ma reappeared on the porch. "Benjamin Patrick. You will treat all our guests with respect."

"I'm sorry." Ben turned to face his ma.

"It's Easter weekend," Ma said. "Everyone's welcome."

Darcy dumped her ice cubes into the bushes along the porch. "It's okay, Mama Strick. I know when I'm not welcome."

His ma shot him a nasty look. "Darcy …"

"I'll drop this in the sink and be on my way. Happy Easter, Ben. It was good to see you."

Ben glared at her. She disappeared inside the house, her heels clicking on the hardwood floors. Ben turned on his ma. "How could you? Today of all days? You had to know how awkward that would be for Kayla."

"That girl practically grew up in this house. She's been through a lot in the last few months—which you'd know if you'd kept in touch."

"She's not the only one who's been through a lot the last few months." He needed to calm down and get a hold of his temper before he said something he couldn't take back. "You asked me to bring Kayla home so you could get to know her better, and the moment we arrive you're sitting on the porch with Darcy. Do you think that made her feel welcome?"

"I have no idea how that made her feel, but if you expect me to toss Darcy out of our house because it might be a little uncomfortable, you're not the son I raised."

And Ben had thought his dad was going to be the one he fought with this weekend. "If you can't show a little compassion for the girl I'm dating, you're not the ma I thought you were."

His ma's ears turned an angry shade of pink. "You need to stop right there before you say something you regret."

"Fine," Ben said. "I don't have anything else to say anyway." He turned his back on his ma and went in search of Kayla.

Chapter Thirty-Five

The interior of Ben's house reminded Kayla of a paint wheel explosion, a stark contrast to her mother's understated style. Every wall was either painted or wallpapered a different color. Between the vertigo-inducing colors and the confrontation taking place on the porch, Kayla found it difficult to focus.

She dried her hands on the monogrammed towel and stared at her reflection in the gilded mirror. She looked pale against the striped coral wallpaper, queasy and a little afraid. She ran trembling fingers through her hair, fluffed the ends, pinched her cheeks to bring some color—anything to enhance her appearance and boost her mood.

Or maybe it was the aftereffects of facing Ben's ex up close and personal. She was coldly stunning. Darcy's head-to-toe appraisal and scornful gaze made it clear she found Kayla lacking. Why wouldn't she? In her white jeans and off-the-shoulder denim top, Darcy looked like she'd stepped off the pages of a glossy fashion magazine. She could have worn a paper bag and looked better than Kayla in her pale-yellow sundress and growing belly.

Even the way Ben's muscles coiled when he found Darcy lounging on his porch didn't ease Kayla's anxiety at facing her rival. His feelings for Darcy were anything but neutral, and Kayla feared his passionate response could easily reignite into love as Kayla exploded with pregnancy weight.

She shook her thoughts clear and lifted her chin. Time to give herself a pep talk. She told Ben she believed him when he said he cared about her, when he said he'd be there. Just because the girl he'd grown up loving was as beautiful as she was intimidating didn't diminish Ben's words or her faith in him. They'd come too far to let someone from his past influence their future.

No matter how guilty she felt for driving them apart.

No matter how much she deserved the girl's derision.

No matter how practiced and cunning the girl appeared.

As many times as Ben had stood by her side in the face of her parents' and brother's distrust, he deserved the same in return. With a deep breath intended to fortify herself, she opened the door, determined to stay calm for Ben.

"Oh." Kayla clutched her gold necklace when she found Darcy leaning against the turquoise wall opposite the bathroom, the hard lines of her face highlighted in the glow of the wall sconce. "You scared me."

Darcy stood to her full height and folded her arms under her chest, her deep-set eyes narrowing into a haughty glare. She'd perfected the scornful look. "I meant to."

Kayla shifted until her heels bumped the wall. Were they really going to do this here? Now? With Ben and his mother steps away and his father who knew where? "Excuse me?"

"You took what's mine, and I want him back."

Okay, maybe they were. Kayla took a shaky breath. "Darcy, listen—"

"No." Darcy poked her finger at Kayla's face before sliding her hands to her hips. "You listen. He's going to come back to me. Maybe not now with his kid growing inside you …" Her lips thinned and her eyes traveled south to Kayla's belly before shooting back to hers, hard, angry, disgusted. "… But he will. When you're struggling to lose those last ten pounds, exhausted from being up all night with a screaming kid, and haven't run a brush through your hair in days, he'll come back to me. And I'll be waiting with open arms because Ben and I are meant to be together. You're just a blip on our story, a bad memory I intend to make disappear."

Kayla's heart rate clamored like a dryer with a lopsided load as Darcy spelled out every fear lurking in the dark recesses of her mind. Ben's scorned ex wouldn't slink away and lick her wounds until she found someone else. Darcy would wait. She'd enact her revenge when Kayla was least prepared and least equipped to fight. "We didn't mean to hurt you."

"We?" Darcy laughed, a high-pitched cackle that made Kayla's scalp itch. "There is no 'we.' There's only me and Ben. You'd better cut him loose and start looking for someone else to raise your little bastard, because Ben's mine. He always has been, and he always will be."

Kayla tried to quell the sickening tide of sorrow swelling inside her chest. She tried to think of something to say, something to silence Darcy's rant, but her heart pounded so loudly between her ears she couldn't think at all. She tried to focus on the facts. *It was only one night. I didn't know he had a girlfriend.* But her mind refused to cooperate.

Her gaze shifted away from Darcy's angry glare to the row of pictures along the wall behind her head, the smiling faces of Ben's family through the years. Young, adorable Ben and his parents stared back at her alongside another boy—an older boy—the spitting image of Ben. Her vision went hazy.

Kayla fought to stand when the hot hands of hysteria pressed her down and a maniacal sense of denial threatened to cut her off at the knees. The annoying sound of Darcy's voice vaporized. She squinted at each framed shot and stared at the familiar stranger, a little bit taller, his hair a little bit darker, the same dimpled smile, the same floppy hair as Ben.

"Who … who is that?"

Darcy stopped mid-sentence, an angry slant between her brows as she followed Kayla's gaze to the pictures. Her toothpaste commercial smile morphed into a brittle smirk of satisfaction. Darcy straightened and sucked in a breath, and Kayla recognized something in the set of Darcy's mouth she hadn't seen before. Leverage.

"He never told you about Scott?"

The baby drop-kicked Kayla's heart directly into her lungs lodging it there to clog her breath. *There was a double S.* She swayed and leaned against the wall as her muscles threatened to give up the fight.

Darcy leaned into Kayla's space with a mocking sneer.

"I knew this wasn't a real relationship." Darcy's low voice cackled with electricity. "I knew it. If he never told you about Scott, you mean nothing to him. Less than nothing." She poked her under the collarbone.

Kayla didn't stop Darcy's rant, didn't halt her outstretched finger, didn't slap her hand away from her face like she should have. Like she would have if she'd been able to muster an ounce of strength and move her limbs. Ridiculously, she thought of her roommates, how disappointed they would be in her for standing there and taking Darcy's abuse. Kayla needed something, anything to penetrate the drumming in her head and the tingling, out-of-body experience that left her floating.

"Darcy." Ben stood in the hallway behind Darcy, his feet spread, his hands fisted at his sides, his eyes like flint.

The ominous edge in Ben's voice penetrated Kayla's fog and whisked her back to the present. He had a look on his face Kayla had never seen before, like he'd taken a bite of something foul and wanted to spit it out.

He looks guilty. He's choking on the foul taste of guilt.

"You touch her again, and your name will never be spoken in this house."

Darcy's eyes fluttered and she lifted her chin. For a moment her mask slipped, and Kayla watched the ground she'd gained be ripped away by the menacing tone of Ben's voice. After searing Kayla with a withering stare, she straightened, schooled her face into the look of a petulant child and turned around, slapping a hand on her hip. "You're all talk, Ben." She yanked her head in Kayla's direction. "Or maybe not enough talk."

"Don't tempt me," Ben growled, grim and nasty.

Ben's mom appeared behind him, her face ashen. "Darcy, honey, I think it's time you went home."

Kayla watched with a weird sense of detachment as Darcy's shoulders sagged before she straightened and eased past Ben in the hallway, shimmying her body against his as she passed. "You know where to find me," she whispered loud enough for Kayla to hear.

He grimaced and turned his head away. "Don't hold your breath."

Ben's mom walked Darcy out of earshot, leaving Ben and Kayla alone in the neon hallway. He must have swallowed that foul bite because he looked nauseated, his face drawn, his eyes hollow and lifeless. "Kayla. I'm sorry. I tried to tell you in the car. I should have told you sooner."

She didn't ask about his brother because she already knew. She saw the truth in his slack posture, in his dull stare. "When did he die?"

"In high school. Don't listen to Darcy. She's just trying to cause trouble."

She wanted to ignore Darcy, would have ignored her if she hadn't pulled the rug out from under Kayla's feet and sent her spinning like dyed sugar against the cotton-candy walls. "We talked about your family, Ben. So many times."

"It's not a happy story." His impossibly sad gaze flicked to a portrait of the four of them dressed in jeans and navy shirts, smiling at the camera. "I try not to think about it, try not to talk about it."

Kayla's bubble of happiness burst as Cupid tucked his arrow into the quiver and fled the building. Even she—the eternal optimist—couldn't make lemonade out of the lemons Ben had dumped at her feet.

Despite his promises, he never shared the darkest moment of his life—a moment that scarred and shaped him into the man who stood before her today. He didn't trust her.

"Talk to me, Kayla. Tell me how you're feeling."

Would it help to know every word out of his mouth felt like a thousand woodchucks chipping away at her heart? "I feel sad. Sad for you. Sad for your family."

"That's not all you're feeling."

"No, but it's not about me. It's about you."

"Maybe." Ben scrubbed his hands over his face. "But right now, it's about us."

She heard her mom's voice in her head. After her last doctor's appointment, after her mom realized Kayla and Ben were dating, she'd warned Kayla. "I'm not discouraging you from exploring your feelings, but I urge you to take it slow. You may be looking at this as forever, Kay, and he may be invested until he thinks the kid is old enough to claim his freedom. Talk to Ben. Make sure you're on the same page."

But she hadn't talked to Ben because he'd asked her to trust him. She *had* trusted him, but he'd never trusted her. He never had to talk about his brother's life or death, because Kayla was a temporary visitor in his life and not a permanent fixture. His own actions made that clear. The best thing she could do for both of them was to be strong and voice the truth before this charade went any further.

"There is no us, Ben. I don't think there ever has been."

Chapter Thirty-Six

Ben stumbled as Kayla blew past him, left him standing in the hallway, dazed and dumbstruck. The frozen portraits of his family mocked him with awkward smiles and dated outfits.

He should have told her the first time she asked about his family. He didn't have to go into the gory details, he didn't have to relay the pain and heartache right away, but a simple acknowledgment of his brother's existence would have given him time to get to know her and trust her with the ugly truth of Scott's passing and what it did to their family. Would have given him the gift of her compassion. A gift he'd never received before.

He'd robbed them both of that experience.

Determined to make her understand, Ben started down the hall in her wake. His father stepped into his path, drink in hand.

"Looks like you blew this one all on your own." Wade shook

the ice in his glass. "Such a shame. I was looking forward to getting to know her." He smirked before strolling into the den.

Torn between going after Kayla and defending himself, Ben followed his father, spurred by self-loathing and years of pent up frustration. Yeah, he'd blown it with Kayla, but it was time—past time—to have the last word.

"What is your problem with Kayla?"

His dad had taken his usual position in the recliner and set his drink on the end table. He sighed as if he couldn't be bothered to explain. "I don't have a problem with her, son, but you sure do."

"Why do you have to stick your nose where it doesn't belong?"

"Is it my imagination or are you standing in my living room?" He steepled his fingers. "Seems to me you brought your problem home to us. Don't you dare stand there and lecture me on keeping my opinions to myself."

"I'm in love with her." The words were out into the world before he even knew what happened. Love for her wrapped around him like a warm blanket, a comforting hug, a bedrock foundation. How ironic he realized the depth of his feelings at the exact moment she'd given up on him. "When you disrespect her, you disrespect me."

"Good lord, son. Quit thinking with your pants for just a minute. That girl is using you and everyone knows it. Everyone but you."

"She doesn't have it in her to use anyone. If you took the time to get to know her, you'd realize she's as genuine a person as they come."

"I don't have to get to know her. Seems to me I won't be seeing her at all anymore. Good thing since that little hussy is nothing more than a dirt road to nowhere. If you had half a brain in your head, you'd be hightailing it over to Darcy's right now to make amends."

Ben's hands fisted. What was it about Darcy Keller that made his dad think their union would answer all his prayers? It wouldn't bring Scott back. It couldn't change the past. "Darcy and I are over. You need to accept that and move on."

His dad placed his hands on his thighs and stood up, the weight of the world on his shoulders. He took two steps in Ben's direction, using his physical stature and lethal stare as weapons of intimidation. Little did he know Ben was no longer intimidated. "I won't abide you bringing that little whore into our family."

It wouldn't do any good to unleash his temper and let his fists do the talking. But Lord help him, he'd never wanted to punch someone more. "I won't abide you talking about Kayla that way. I plan to marry her, if she'll have me."

"Don't compound one mistake with another. You marry her and it doesn't work out, you're on the hook for alimony in addition to child support."

"I'm not going into this looking for an exit ramp. If Kayla agrees to marry me, we're in it for the long haul."

His dad dropped his hands from his hips and shook his head. "You marry that girl and you're dishonoring your family."

He didn't understand. He would never understand. "Kayla and the baby are my family."

"Darcy's family." His dad chopped a hand into his palm. "Your mama and I are family. We can't support this."

They stood toe to toe, stare to stare, the breath puffing between them. "Tell me what's dishonorable about being a father to my baby, a husband to my wife."

"Darcy should be your wife. You made promises …"

"I never promised her anything. She may have thought

things, you definitely assumed things, but I never promised her forever. I have a child to think of. I won't turn my back on them to please you and Ma, or to stand by someone else's idea of what's expected."

Wade snorted. "You're a quitter and a fool. You're throwing law school and all your dreams away for some city girl who was probably trying to get pregnant in the first place."

Ben's fists were clenched so tight he couldn't feel his fingers. "Law school was your dream. The simple truth is we came together, we used protection, and God had other plans. I may not have seen this coming and I sure as heck don't feel prepared for what's next, but I'm going to be there for them. They deserve my best, and I'm going to give them everything I have."

"You're going to spend your life chasing after everything you're throwing away, everything that could be yours if you'd just take a step back and think about what you're doing."

"I have thought about it. I haven't thought about much else since I found out about the baby."

"Think harder. If you do this, if you marry that girl, you won't get a dime. I mean it, Ben. Not one dime from your mama and me."

"I don't want your money."

His dad chuckled. "You say that now."

"It's not about money. It's about being a man and owning up to my responsibilities."

"You're getting trapped into marriage with a gold digger."

"I swear, if you disparage her one more time I—"

"You'll what? Punch me? Curse my name?" Wade let out a heavy sigh. "Go right ahead. Just don't marry that girl."

"What is your problem with her?"

"I know her type. She's using you. She sees a vulnerable man with a well-off family, and she wants it to be hers. Just trust me on this, son. I've lived a lot longer than you. I've seen the worst in people, even those you'd least expect."

For the first time in his life, Ben pitied his father. He understood his cynicism. He'd lived through the moment when reality and illusion collided, burning them all to the ground. Now, years later, it was Wade's choice to wallow. Ben chose to crawl his way out. God had given him a roadmap with sunny blonde hair and an infectious zest for life. "That's funny. Kayla sees the best in people. She looks at everyone—even the meanest person—and finds a way to be nice to them. To pray for them. That's one of the things I love most about her."

"It's all an act." His father shook his head. "You're being taken in by a clever actress."

Pressure built in his chest. Ben stood with his hands on his hips. How many times had he shoved down all the criticisms and insults disguised as wisdom? How many times had he stalked away instead of standing up for himself or his friends? "You think she's a gold digger?"

"I know she is."

"I guess you don't know her house costs more than twice this one."

"Is that what she told you?"

"No. I looked it up online. You know how much they pay in property taxes each year?"

His dad stared, his eyes narrowing and his nostrils flexing.

"About as much as you paid for that fancy car you're so proud of."

"You can cover a con in money and they're still a con."

"Her family's loaded, and not one of them has accused me of knocking her up to get my hands on their money. But they could.

It kinda looks that way to anyone paying attention." Ben leaned forward. A large breath would have their chests bumping. "That's the problem, Dad. You're not paying attention. You never have."

"Fine. You want to screw up your life. Go right ahead. But know when you come crawling back the first words out of my mouth are going be 'I told you so.'"

"I'd expect nothing less." Ben's head buzzed and his lips struggled to function. The words that would alter their relationship forever lay heavy on his tongue. "I plan to marry Kayla, and we're going to raise our baby in a house filled with love. I'm sorry your stubborn pride means you and Mama won't be a part of your grandson's life."

The rush to escape made his stomach twist with dread. He turned to leave, propelled by the freedom of telling his dad off and desperate to make things right with Kayla, but stopped at the doorway and dropped his head. He wanted the last word, he craved it, but knew his last words should be better than the hateful anger he'd just spewed.

"If you ever come back, the last thing I'd say to you is 'I told you so' because that would upset Kayla. She's showing me a better way to live. For once, I'm going to do what I want, and grab hold of it and never let go. If you want to be a part of my life, of your grandson's life, all you have to do is say the word. But don't bother coming around if you can't be civil to Kayla. That's the one thing I won't abide."

"You're making a mistake," his dad said.

Ben shook his head, absolved. "We'll have to agree to disagree. I'll see you around."

Chapter Thirty-Seven

Kayla stopped at the end of the dock, her breath hitching painfully in her chest. When she swiped the tears from her cheeks, they came away dirty with makeup and dust. She toed off her sandals, collapsed onto the worn wood, and dangled her feet into the pond. Hyperventilating in the woods where no one could find her wasn't a good idea for her or the baby.

She tried to imagine how she'd feel if the child she carried and loved and raised died at the prime of his life. She palmed the spot where her son lay. How would she feel if Josh died? She'd feel the way Ben and his mom looked in the hallway, gutted by grief and doing their best to carry on in a world that kept on living despite their loss. She cried for Ben, for his family, for his brother. She cried for the life she and Ben could have made together if he'd let her share his pain.

But that was selfish. Ben and his family dealt with real grief and pain every second of every day. She mourned a fantasy—a happy-ever-after mirage she'd created in her head—while they mourned a loved one.

A son.

A brother.

A friend.

Just because it stung that Ben hadn't trusted her with his past didn't mean he couldn't be a loving father to their baby. He would be there. He would keep his promises. She simply had to face reality.

There would be no fairy-tale ending for Ben and Kayla. No other children for them to birth. No life for them to share. The sooner she accepted the truth, the better for all concerned.

She startled at the noise behind her, the sound of footsteps and heavy breathing. Ben, his hair mussed and his shoes muddy, leaned over with his hands on his knees, gulping air. "You scared the life out of me," he said, panting. "I couldn't find you anywhere."

She turned back to the water, to the trees mirrored on the glassy surface, still and serene except for the waves her toes created. So like her life—pretty on the outside but murky underneath, where creatures crawled and danger lurked. "I'm fine. I'm sorry if I scared you."

"Do you know how many snakes we have around here? Venomous ones?"

Kayla blanched. "No."

"They're everywhere, especially near the water."

She yanked her feet out of the dark green pool and crossed her ankles. She couldn't look at him, couldn't wipe the sympathy and disappointment from her face. She knew Ben well enough to know that was the last thing he wanted. Especially from her.

Ben plopped down beside her and let out a sigh. She inhaled his woodsy cologne under the faint scent of sweat. She craved him—his touch, his smile—even knowing her feelings weren't returned. She would get over it. Over him. She had to.

"I'm sorry I never told you about Scott."

"Ben, it's okay. You don't have to tell me. Whatever happened to your brother has nothing to do with me."

"It has everything to do with you."

Kayla jerked her head to glare at him. The color had returned to his face with his jog through the woods to find her, but his eyes, those bold expressive eyes, held sadness the way a child holds a firefly, firm and close. "I don't understand."

He brushed her hand with his finger, slowly, tenderly. The feather-light touch burned, sent goose bumps up her arm. Ben watched his finger glide across her skin. "The night we were together, the night we made our son, was the five-year anniversary of Scott's death."

Kayla gasped and clutched at her belly. The night they shared flashed before her, his tortured eyes, the desperate way he clung to her. "Oh, Ben."

"Everyone wanted me to come home, wanted us all to be together to mourn his passing, to wallow in our grief together." He shook his head, stared out at the water's edge, seeing horrible images she dared not imagine. "I couldn't do it. I couldn't stand the thought of gathering and multiplying the sorrow. I left my phone at home and went out to get drunk, to try and forget. But I couldn't get drunk enough to forget. Or forgive." He shifted his gaze to her. "And then I saw you."

Kayla closed her eyes. She remembered the way he stood up and approached her, offered to buy her a drink as if he'd been waiting for her to arrive.

"You smiled at me," Ben continued, his voice as soft as a caress. Or a confession. "So innocent and shy, and I wanted to be close to you, to feel your sunshine, to taste your goodness. I never thought about what I was doing, I just came up to you and started talking, hoped you'd let me into your orbit for a while so I could forget."

She swallowed past the emotion in her throat, blinked away tears, tried to muster a smile. "Well, I certainly let you into my orbit."

The serious look on his face said her humor fell flat.

"You changed me, Kayla, that night and every day since."

She wanted to believe him, wanted it more than she wanted her next breath, but there were too many puzzle pieces that didn't fit into the picture he painted. She dropped her head, stared at his finger making circles on her hand. "I let you into my orbit, but you never let me into yours." He shifted away. She flipped her hand over and grabbed his wrist in her palm. "That's not criticism. It's a fact."

"I want to explain. All of it, if you'll give me a chance."

Kayla looked over his shoulder to the woods at his back, heard the low hum of insects in the tall grasses along the pond's edge. "Ben, we're at your house and I have no way to leave. I checked. There isn't an Uber for fifty miles."

"Coming here was a mistake." He rubbed his forehead as if he could scrape their homecoming from his mind. "My parents aren't ready to accept you, or us together. Or anything. I know I promised you church and Easter lunch, but would you mind heading back to campus?"

She wanted to kiss him for giving her an out. "Where you go, I go." At least for now.

His mom waved goodbye from the front porch, but his dad

was nowhere in sight. Kayla sat quietly as they backtracked through town. Ben wrung his hands on the steering wheel, his eyes forward, his brows pinched. He said he wanted to explain, but she wouldn't force him. He could tell her now or wait until later. No matter when he explained, it seemed too little and much too late to make a difference.

He turned onto the highway, exhaled a breath, and started talking.

"Scott was two years older than me, larger than life and good at everything. He could charm his way into or out of any situation. He was smart, athletic, a natural salesman. A natural lawyer. I worshiped him. We all did." He signaled for a lane change, checked the mirrors, and accelerated past a truck carrying a load of wood.

"I figured out he was using a few months before he died."

"Using?" Kayla asked.

"I knew he smoked pot with his friends. Practically everyone did. But when I saw him snort a line of coke in his car, I was shocked. He didn't know I saw him, and I didn't know how to ask. So I kept quiet, kept a closer eye on him. He noticed. Told me to back off and mind my own business. Darcy and I were dating then, and even though it was pretty new, we fought all the time. She sucked me into her drama."

He cleared his throat and glanced at Kayla.

She nodded for him to continue.

"I hadn't seen any more drug use, so I did as he asked. Chalked it up to a one-time thing and moved on."

He swiveled the volume dial and the music she could barely hear disappeared.

"Scott had a girlfriend. They'd dated for a couple of years. They went out the night he died, supposedly to see a movie at the old drive-in just outside of town. Darcy and I went to a party at a friend's farm. We heard sirens and thought the police were coming to bust up the party. Everyone scattered, headed for home or back to town. Just away.

"But the sirens weren't coming for us. They passed right in front of the farm where we'd partied, a long line of police cars and ambulances and fire trucks. When something happens in a small town, there's no doubt you know someone involved. So we followed."

His voice changed, went a little quiet, a little harsh. Kayla squelched the urge to touch him, to squeeze his leg. She wasn't sure if he'd accept her gesture or push her hand away.

"When I got to the scene, I didn't even recognize Scott's car. It was that banged up. They'd rolled before smashing head-on into a tree. The force knocked a couple of trees down and left the wheels off the ground. The flashing lights were so bright it was hard to make heads or tails of anything. The cops told us to turn around, but I pulled onto the shoulder so I could see past the fire trucks blocking the road. Leaves and branches were scattered everywhere, like there'd been a bad storm. In between, there were sheets draped over bodies."

"Oh, Ben."

"Darcy shrieked and started pointing into the woods. That's when I noticed Scott's license plate, 'STRICK,' upside down."

In the pause that followed, Kayla tried to imagine teenage Ben stumbling upon the accident that took his brother's life. He could probably smell the scent of tires on the roadway and hear the radio blaring. She wanted to stop him from reliving the moment, but she knew he needed to get it all out.

"They wouldn't let us go past the fire trucks, so we had to watch and wait. I called my parents. My mama made a sound I'll never forget. It wasn't even human. They arrived shortly after. My dad sprinted out of the car, barking orders, trying to get to Scott, but the police held him back. Everybody was shouting and crying."

He went quiet, staring out the windshield, his eyes tortured.

"In the end, five kids died. Scott and Emma, plus three of his friends. It was like watching a movie. It didn't seem real. The days after are kind of a blur. The grief was like being trapped under a frozen pond with no escape, like banging your head against the ice and gasping for air. I didn't think it could get any worse. Until it did."

He shook his head, but he couldn't shake the weight of the memories from his empty gaze.

"Scott wasn't just using drugs. He was dealing. Using and dealing. We had no idea."

He stared out the windshield, the muscles in his jaw popping.

Kayla's vision blurred. The asphalt morphed into a think black line in the silence.

"If I'd told someone or not backed off when he told me, I would have known. I could have stopped him, but I was stupid and distracted by my pretty new girlfriend."

"You can't blame yourself," Kayla said around the slab of mercy lodged in her windpipe. "Ben, it wasn't your fault. He was your brother. You trusted him. You believed him."

"And look what happened. He's dead because of me. And Emma and Chase and Randy and Donny. All dead, because of me."

"Ben ..." Kayla couldn't stop from reaching for him, from placing her hand on his leg. He grabbed hold and squeezed. Hard.

"There was another kid —a year below me in school—he

OD'd the year before. The police took Scott's phone, and we found out Scott was his dealer. It was all in the phone. Every meeting. Every location. He killed himself, four of his best friends, a kid who'd just reached puberty, and took our whole family down in the process."

"*He* did," Kayla said. "Not you."

"The parade of casseroles turned into a parade of poop bags on the porch. And worse. Everyone turned on us." He looked at her and squeezed her hand. "Everyone but the Kellers."

Darcy. Of course. Darcy.

"Judge Keller and my dad were friends—good friends—but he'd do anything for his princess, and he proved it by standing by us through it all. Without him, we'd have been run out of town. Sometimes I think that would have been better. Just leave town and start over where no one knew us, where no one knew about Scott."

"But you stayed."

"We stayed, but small towns don't forget. When you kill the mayor's daughter and a handful of good kids, they certainly don't forgive. Judge Keller kept us in the club, kept us getting out of the house every day, kept my dad's job. We owed him—them—everything.

"If not for Scott dying, if not for Judge Keller and his unwavering support, I would've dated Darcy for a couple of months and moved on. Instead, it turned into a contract with no out-clause. Every time I tried to break up with her, she'd pull me back using guilt and manipulation."

He wrinkled his nose and changed his voice into a spot-on impression of his ex. "'Do you know how many friends I've lost? Do you know how much you've cost me?' I never had a comeback. She did lose friends. I did cost her everything. I eventually stopped fighting."

Kayla sank into her seat and watched the trees zip past. She'd been wrong when she said he'd not let her into his orbit. He'd plopped her right in the middle. She didn't know whether to apologize or sympathize. No wonder Darcy was territorial. She'd paid in blood, sweat, and tears.

"Say something," Ben said.

"You were right about one thing. Your relationship with Darcy is definitely complicated."

"My relationship with Darcy is over," Ben said, his voice rough and resolute. He linked his fingers with Kayla and looked her in the eyes. "It's been five and a half years. Haven't I paid enough?"

Chapter Thirty-Eight

Kayla entered her apartment and stopped short when she saw Shelby sitting on the couch, watching a reality show. "What are you doing here?" Kayla asked. "I thought you went home for Easter."

"Parental blunder." Shelby twisted to face Kayla, lifting her mane of dark hair from her face. "What are you doing here? I thought you went home with Ben."

"Relationship blunder." Kayla dropped her overnight bag and joined Shelby on the couch, more than a little relieved to find someone home. She'd planned to sort her feelings out over a good cry and a cup of ice cream, then debate whom to call and tell. Shelby's presence made the debate unnecessary. "You go first."

Shelby sighed, lowering the volume on a bleach-blonde's tirade. "My mom thought I was spending Easter with my dad, so she accepted a last-minute invitation for a cruise with her girlfriends. My dad thought I was spending Easter with my mom, so he jetted out of town for the weekend with his flavor of the month."

"That's awful. Didn't they check with you first?"

"That would have involved communicating with me or each other, and that's simply too much to ask." She shrugged, her face a mask of indifference. "No biggie. I've been binge-watching crap TV and eating candy, so it's just like being at home."

No matter what Shelby said, being forgotten at Easter—or at any time—had to sting. Kayla reached over and patted Shelby's hand, grabbed a few stalks of licorice from the bag on the coffee table. Cherry licorice would ease the sting of a blunder as well as ice cream. "It is a biggie. I'm sorry for leaving you alone. You should have told me, and I would have stayed here. It would have saved me some serious drama. Although it would have kept me in the dark, but I'm not sure which is worse at this point."

Shelby lobbed Kayla her trademark stare. "Explain, please. You're talking gibberish."

Kayla tried to recount the events of the last few hours with the same dispassion Shelby displayed, but the pressure in her chest made stoic flippancy impossible. She broke it down into simple terms. "Ben took me home, Darcy was there with his mom, and the walls were lined with family pictures of him and the dead brother he never told me about." Her voice cracked on the last word.

"His brother died?"

Kayla nodded. "It was horrible."

They sat quietly absorbing the gravity of Ben's home life before Shelby broke the silence with a whispered question. "Why didn't he tell you?"

Shelby's query—the same thought that had been boomeranging through Kayla's brain all day—looped back and crashed against her skull. Why? Even after hearing the details of Scott's death and the repercussions, his not telling her still smarted. It would have explained so much. "It's a long story."

Shelby lifted her hands, glanced around. "It's Easter weekend and everyone's gone. We've got nothing but time, and I'm bored with crap TV. I think your reality is going to be way more interesting than this made-up nonsense."

"Fine." Kayla toed off her sandals and lifted her feet onto the coffee table. "Hand me some more licorice, and I'll tell you. It'll probably help to bounce this off someone who's not so invested."

Thirty minutes later, Shelby sat with a creased brow and a gaping mouth. "Wow. Just wow. Darcy's had him by the balls all this time."

"Pretty much." Leave it to Shelby to grasp the heart of the matter.

"It's almost medieval, like Ben's family accepted her dowry and now he's got to marry her."

"That's exactly what it's like." She narrowed her eyes at her roommate. "Are you sure you don't read romance?"

"No, but I've taken history. I feel bad for him." Shelby stretched her legs along the couch. "But he also could have said enough is enough. I mean, it's two thousand twenty and this is America. Arranged marriages aren't really a thing."

Kayla replayed the day's events in her mind. Every time she tried to get upset with Ben for not telling her, she'd stumble over the same obstacle again and again. "You should have seen his face when he told me about finding Scott. He feels responsible."

"Why? Because he saw him snort a line of coke?" Shelby rolled her eyes. "I've seen my dad do a line of coke. Does that mean if he goes out and kills someone, I'm responsible?"

Kayla nearly choked. Between Ben and Shelby, Kayla's upbringing seemed as blissful as an '80s sitcom. "It's a wonder you're so normal. Sort of."

"Very funny."

Kayla could only handle one dysfunctional family at a time, so she tucked Shelby's bombshell into a vault and focused on her current crisis. "I told Ben he's not responsible. He thinks he should have done more. Should have said something to someone. But siblings have a bond. We don't rat on each other. If I found out Josh was using drugs, I'd try to talk to him before I went to my parents."

"Exactly. And Ben was the younger brother, so his hands were tied." Shelby shook her head, sighed. "So where does this leave you and Ben?"

The million-dollar question. "It feels like we're right back where we started. He says he and Darcy are over, and he was really angry and abrupt with her, but there's so much history. I would have understood if he'd told me, but all he ever said was, 'It's complicated.'"

"Well, he wasn't lying about that." Shelby crossed her arms behind her head. "What are you going to do?"

"I don't know. I thought we were building something real, but now that I know what he was hiding, it makes me doubt him. I want to trust him when he says he and Darcy are over, I want to believe him when he tells me he cares about me and wants a future with me, but a part of me wonders if there's another shoe that's going to drop."

"What's the alternative?" Shelby asked. "If you decide you can't get past this, that he's too big a risk, what happens next?"

Kayla stared at the oil painting on the wall—a riot of purple, orange, and yellow flowers waving in the wind—and tried to predict her life without Ben. "I'm trying to envision graduating from college, finding a job while visibly pregnant, and earning enough to support myself and my newborn son."

"And?" Shelby asked.

"I can't see it. Every time I think about the future, Ben is there. With me. With us. He wants to be—at least, that's what he says."

"But?"

"I don't know if I believe him anymore. Even if he's done with Darcy, was I just a way out? Is being with me and the baby an excuse to get away from Darcy and out from under his family's expectations?"

"All good questions," Shelby said. "And you know who has the answers?"

The one person she wasn't sure she could trust. "Ben."

"Ding, ding, ding. Give the girl a baby."

"You're such a comedian."

"And you're too good a person to be anyone's escape hatch. Talk to Ben, tell him how you feel, and feel him out. If he's lying, you'll know." Shelby shook her head. "But, Kay, if he's been trapped for the last five years, I think the last thing he'd do is hitch himself to someone else the minute he got free. He's tasted freedom, but he's still with you. That has to count for something."

"I've never asked him for anything except to be a father to our baby—which he is anyway."

"You're making my point. He can be there for the baby and not get involved with you. Guys do it all the time."

"I know." Kayla stared at the stalks of licorice in her palm. She couldn't eat her way out of this funk. She couldn't analyze her way out. All she could do was pray and let things play out. She wasn't going to pressure Ben. He didn't owe her a relationship.

Shelby started to sit up and paused. Kayla felt her eyes on her, watching, waiting. "Why are you frowning?" Shelby asked.

"I thought I was past feeling sorry for myself. I hate feeling sorry for myself, but this puts me right back where I was at the beginning."

"How do you figure?"

"I wanted the whole package. The romance, falling in love, the over-the-top proposal, and the fairy-tale wedding. I'd gotten over not having all that until he ripped the rug out from under me."

"So, you want the social media love story?" Shelby's tone reeked of sarcasm.

"No." Yes. She did want the proposal and wedding she saw on social media. She wanted it bad. "I wanted a traditional love story. One I could tell my kids about without having to embellish the details."

"So you're doing things a little out of order. So what? In the end, if you two are together and stronger than before, who cares?"

"I do. I've dreamed about falling in love my whole life."

"Okay. Let me bring you back down to reality. My parents met and married in the span of a month. They had a whirlwind romance that would have made them internet sensations. Their love affair lasted a little over a year and their marriage less than two. Now they despise each other. Don't believe everything you see on social media. I bet half the couples you envy will be divorced as soon as the likes disappear."

"You're so cynical."

"I'm right and you know it. Look, here's the thing. A lot of girls have unplanned pregnancies. A lot more than we know, because most of them take the easy way out. Despite my initial reaction, I'm proud of you for choosing the hard path. I really am. But you're also lucky because the guy who knocked you up is still in the picture. Not only is he still in the picture, but he's planning a future with you. Do you have any idea how rare that is—especially considering you weren't in a relationship when you got pregnant?"

Shame sat like a red-hot brand on Kayla's face. "I know."

"There's no formula for happy ever after in real life. It's not like all those books you read. I'm not going to tell you what to do, but I'm also not going to sit by and let you walk away from a good thing because it doesn't resemble your fantasy."

Kayla sighed. Shelby could lecture with the best of them. "I didn't even think you liked Ben much."

"I don't know Ben, but I know you and I know when you're happy. You've been happy the last few months even after getting kicked out of your sorority and people talking behind your back."

"Ignorantly happy. I didn't know the whole story."

"Now you do. You know what else I know?"

The girl was on a roll. "I'm almost afraid to ask."

"Do you remember when you first found out about Darcy and you described the way they were together by using Emily and Dylan as an example?"

"Yeah."

"Do you remember how you contrasted them with the way Reagan and Dash are with each other. What did you say—something about starry-eyed and careful?"

"Yeah," she said. "What's your point?"

"That's how Ben looks at you—starry-eyed and careful—the same way Dash looks at Reagan. Remember, that's how we knew he liked her, because he looked at her like she was the only person in the room."

A spark of hope ignited in Kayla's chest, threatened to burst. "If you're just saying that to make me feel better …"

"I wouldn't say it if it weren't true. You know me. You know I'm no romantic. But I've noticed how he looks at you. It's changed."

"Changed how?"

"He used to be afraid of you and the baby. That sounds harsh, but if you look at it from his perspective—even before you knew about his brother and all the crap Darcy's pulled—it's a natural reaction. Now, now he looks at you like you're his. Like you're the only one in the room. I think you're too cautious to see it, but I do."

"I wish I could believe that."

"Let me put it this way. If I hadn't seen him looking at you differently, if I didn't think he cared about you, I wouldn't have let you get attached and I wouldn't have encouraged you to go home with him, and I certainly wouldn't be sitting here defending him. I would have been in your ear, spewing my 'love stinks' mantra all over your hearts and rainbows." She looked at Kayla with her brows raised. "You know me."

Shelby's tough love had lifted her spirits and given her a lot to ponder. "You are a world-class pessimist when it comes to matters of the heart."

Shelby flashed a choirgirl smile. "Truer words were never spoken."

Chapter Thirty-Nine

"Benjamin."

Ben leaned his head back into the soft leather of the couch and cringed at the sound of his grandmother's gravelly voice over the phone. Taking off before he'd even said hello to her wasn't his smartest move, but he'd been desperate to get away from home, desperate to get Kayla alone so they could talk. So he could try and explain. "Grandma. I'm sorry about missing Easter."

"When your mama picked me up and told me you'd come and gone, I nearly fell out of the car. What in the world happened? I was looking forward to meeting Kayla and getting a sneak peek at my great-grandson."

He'd let everyone down. His apartment had never felt so lonely, and he'd never felt more alone. "I know you were, and I'm sorry. Did she tell you what happened?"

"She told me her version. I'd like to hear yours."

Greta Strickland was the only family member who ever gave him the benefit of the doubt. He loved her endlessly because of that and so much more. "Darcy was at the house when we pulled up, I got angry with Ma, had a confrontation with Dad, and Kayla found out about Scott."

His grandmother gasped, then there was a pause on the end of the line. "You never told her? Why in the devil not?"

"Because I'm an idiot. Because I've never had to work at a relationship with someone who hasn't known me since birth. Because I'm a coward."

"Ben. You are many things, but an idiot and a coward are not two of my top choices."

Top choices? She knew how to cut him to the quick. "Telling her about Scott meant telling her about everything, and I didn't want to see the disappointment in her eyes. She looks at me like I'm a good guy—or at least she did."

"How does she look at you now?"

"Like she doesn't know if she can trust me."

"Do you blame her?"

Ben sighed. "No." He didn't blame her at all.

"Ben, honey, I've never been one to stick my nose where it doesn't belong …"

That was debatable, but usually her nose sticking led him in the right direction.

"… but it seems to me you've flubbed this up royally. Now, if I were you, I'd figure out what you want and do everything in your power to make it happen."

"I know what I want. I've known all along, but I didn't realize how much I wanted it until I flubbed up. Royally."

"Are you talking about Kayla?"

"Yes, Grandma, I'm talking about Kayla." He rubbed at the throb in his temple. "I'm in love with her. Baby or no baby, I want to be with her."

"Did you tell her?"

"Not in so many words, but since I never told her about Scott, she doesn't believe much of what I say."

"Do you know what happens when people lose trust? When they damage a relationship?"

"It ends." Ben rammed his knuckle into the nailhead on the arm of the couch. "Badly."

"Sometimes. Sometimes not. It depends on how you handle it."

He'd handled it so poorly that Kayla had asked him—begged him—to give her some time. He'd backed himself into a corner where he had to agree. "Tell me what to do, Grandma. Tell me what to do, and I'll do it."

"You have to earn her trust back, and it's going to take some time. First of all, you need to give your troubles to God. I know you stopped going to church after Scott died, but God's still got you, Ben. He's the only one who can help, no matter what happens."

Ben had felt the pull of the Lord, tugging him back to the word. He'd prayed more in the last few months than he had in the last five years. "I know."

"Next, you need to live by the three P's."

"The three P's?"

"If you want Kayla back, you need to be patient, be persistent, and be present."

Patient, persistent, and present. That was her big advice? "What else?" Ben asked.

"That's it. That's the secret to earning her trust back. You thought I had a magic cure?"

Thought. Hoped. Same difference. "You were married for fifty-four years, so I figured you had something up your sleeve."

"Benny Boy, the only thing up my sleeve is saggy skin. And the only thing that's going to get you what you want is relying on God and patience, persistence, and your presence. Got it?"

Ben blew out a breath. "I got it."

"It's not going to be easy."

"Yeah, I know."

"She doesn't know your heart, Ben. You have to show her. To do that you have to let her in. All the way in. When you didn't tell her about Scott, you showed her some parts of your life are off-limits. That's no way to start a life together."

"She knows everything now." Ben sank into the couch and stared at the water stain on the ceiling. It looked like an elephant. It felt like that elephant was sitting on his chest. "I pray she can forgive me."

"I'll send some prayers your way and maybe something else—something that might help."

"I thought you said there wasn't anything else."

"Oh, it's no cure, but it might be just what you need—what you both need. If you can find the time to swing by and see your old granny, it's yours."

"I'll make the time and take whatever you can give me." Love potions, aphrodisiacs, herbs—he'd take anything. "I love you, Grandma."

"I love you too, Benny. Now be a good boy, and do what I say."

"Yes, ma'am."

Kayla wasn't going to make it through class without stopping at the restroom. Like her mom's gas-guzzling SUV, her bladder needed lots of fill-ups and frequent stops. But Kayla didn't radiate sporty sleekness like her mom's souped-up crossover.

With the warming spring temperatures, her growing belly had become impossible to hide. Being visibly pregnant on a college campus was like having leprosy in Biblical times. People cleared a wide berth when they saw her approach or flinched and retreated when she caught them by surprise.

Their reaction bothered her at first, but since Ben's duplicity, she barely noticed. Pregnancy fog, ditzy air-headedness, or whatever others termed the condition, she knew the cause. She'd given her heart to someone she couldn't trust.

She veered into the student center and the closest bathroom, lunging for the door as the boy ahead of her let it close in her face. Ben couldn't trust her, but at least he knew how to make a girl feel valued. She tucked the errant thought away and made a beeline for the ladies' room. With clean hands and an empty bladder, Kayla backtracked, determined to make it to class on time.

If she hadn't glanced at her phone to check the time, she would have seen him coming, would have avoided stepping into his path, would have evaded an unwelcome encounter. But her luck was like a shooting star, fateful and fleeting.

"Kayla."

She jerked her head up, tried to muster a smile. "Hey, Theo."

The look on his face, that placating grimace, made her want to turn around and hide in the bathroom.

"How ya holding up?"

Oh, no. Not here. Not now. "I'm late for class."

He reached his hand out, gave her shoulder a gentle squeeze. "It's okay. He told me."

"Theo, I …" Someone banged her backpack, jostled her, and she stumbled. Theo steered her out of the line of students coming and going between classes to a row of couches where students with headphones and time to kill slumped over laptops and listened to music.

Exasperated, exhausted, she gave up the fight. "I'm glad he told someone, because he certainly didn't tell me."

"If it makes you feel any better, I knew him for almost two years before I found out about Scott."

"Two years?"

"He doesn't talk about it. Ever."

"Well, he told you. Even if it did take two years."

Theo shook his head. "He never told me. I had a classmate from his hometown. When I asked if he knew Ben, he gave me the highlights. Ben filled in the gaps, but only after I prodded."

Compassion grappled with humiliation in Kayla's heart, ripping it down the center. Each half arm-wrestled for control, muscles twitching with exertion. "That's so stupid. You're his best friend."

"I am, and it stung that he never told me, but when I stepped back and looked at the big picture, I got it. He feels responsible."

"How could he be? He was just a kid."

"Have you ever lost someone you love?" Theo asked, his quiet tone in contrast to her escalating volume.

"No."

"Neither have I. My oldest brother's wife lost her sister when she was ten. When I told her about Ben, she told me to respect his wishes. If he didn't want to talk about it, that was his choice. Knowing explained a lot—with Darcy, with his parents—but I didn't need to understand. I just needed to be there for Ben."

"I want to be there for Ben, but he doesn't trust me. It feels ... it feels like a betrayal. We were planning a future, yet he never said a word."

"He didn't keep it from you on purpose. He knew he needed to tell you—he wanted to tell you—but he didn't know how."

"Did he think I wouldn't understand?"

"He thought you'd judge him, and he couldn't stand the thought of you thinking less of him."

"That's ridiculous. After everything I've put him through—bulldozing his life—he thinks I'd judge him? Does he think I'm that shallow?"

"Honestly, Kayla, he thinks you're too good for him. And he's an absolute mess without you."

Compassion slammed humiliation into her ribs, lifted his arms in the air, giddy with success. Humiliation lay dazed and immobile. "I'm not doing so great myself."

"Listen." Theo adjusted his backpack, schooling his lips into sympathetic smile. "Do me a favor. Try to take your emotions out of the equation and look at it from Ben's point of view. The brother he worshiped is dead, and he feels like he could have saved him if he'd said something. He can't go back and change what happened, so he does whatever his grieving parents ask of him. That's why Darcy's still around after all these years. They're like oil and water. He doesn't love her. I don't think he ever has."

"How can you be so sure?"

"Because I've seen Ben in love, and it wasn't with Darcy."

Theo's admission knifed into her heart, sharp and lethal.

"It was with you."

Chapter Forty

Ben did as his grandmother instructed. Kayla needed time. So despite wanting to see her every day and tell her over and over how much he cared about her, he gave her the space she needed. Every moment without her felt like a day, every day a week.

He used his time wisely. His dad's threats played over and over in his mind. Ben didn't need their money, but he'd made good use of it up until now. No wonder his dad thought he'd come crawling back, begging for a handout. It was time to cut the cord—past time, for him and for his parents. But that left him with little extra to spend on Kayla when she finally agreed to see him.

Ben picked Kayla up at her apartment in his new set of wheels. She greeted him the guarded way she used to, back when they were still getting to know one another, and gave him a suspicious look when he handed her a white rose. His grandmother had pre-approved the gesture. He'd lost Kayla's trust and he was determined to win it back. One small step at a time.

When he walked her to his car, she stopped short. "Whose car is this?" she asked.

"It's mine."

"You have two cars?"

"No, I had a car I bought with my parents' help. I paid them their half and then traded it in on something a little more affordable. It's got plenty of room and better safety features for the baby."

She frowned at him but let him lead her to the passenger seat and tuck her into the car. She didn't ask where they were going when he pulled out of her complex. When he turned in to his apartment complex a minute later and parked, he looked her in the eyes.

"I hope you don't mind a home-cooked meal."

"You're cooking?" Kayla asked.

Tonight she wore a striped maternity dress that tied in the front with a peekaboo neckline. All he could think when he looked at her was what would happen if he pulled the strings. He squelched his inner twelve-year-old and focused on her eyes. "I hope you don't mind."

"Of course I don't mind. You don't have to cook for me or take me out if you want to hang out."

"I do want to hang out and I'm hungry. I figured you were, too."

"I'm always hungry."

The shy way she smiled, her lips lifting and her eyes downcast, made his heart ache. She had no idea how much he wanted her. Wanted her to like him again. Wanted her to touch him again.

Just wanted to be with her. "Good. Keep your expectations low, and you won't be disappointed."

Her noncommittal grunt told him everything he needed to know. A battle stretched before him, long and uphill. He got out of the car and met her at her door, helping her out with a tug on her hand.

"Ugh. I'm starting to feel like a beached whale."

"You look beautiful, Kayla. You've got that glow everyone talks about."

She shooed his comment away with the flick of her hand and made her way to his door. She'd been there before—they'd studied with Theo, watched TV, gotten to know one another. She settled at the small kitchen bar when he refused her offer of help. "It smells good." She rubbed the rose petals against her cheek.

"My grandmother's spaghetti recipe. Her sauce is legendary."

"You made sauce?" Kayla asked. "Wow. I just open a jar and heat it up. I've never—"

Ben spun around when she stopped mid-sentence. When he saw her slumped over the counter he rushed to her side. "Kayla, are you okay?"

She looked up at him, her eyes wide with wonder. "The baby moved. Like, *really* moved. Here." She reached for his hand and drew it to her stomach. "He was right here, doing a little karate kick. Keep your hand there and see if he does it again."

Ben held still, slumped over Kayla's growing belly, grateful to their son for bringing him closer to her than he'd been in over a week. Their hair brushed as they stared at her belly. He inhaled her raspberry scent and savored, gasped when he felt her skin buckle and a body part glided under his palm. "Oh, my gosh. That's amazing. So much stronger than before."

She looked at him and smiled a real smile with teeth and

little parentheses bracketing her lips. Their faces were so close their noses almost touched. The starburst pattern of color in her sky-blue eyes reminded him of fireworks on the Fourth of July.

Their proximity set off a whole finale of fireworks in his heart. He yearned to kiss her—he would have before he'd made such a mess of things—but he knew rushing her wouldn't help his cause, so he straightened but left his hand on her belly.

"He's moving a lot more these days," Kayla said, her voice soft.

"I miss holding him like this." His grandmother told him to show her his heart. He would show her, and he would tell her. "I miss you."

"Ben …"

"I'm sorry. I don't mean to pressure you, but it's the truth. This has been the longest week. I'm grateful you're here."

She glanced away so he backed off and headed for the stove. His patience seemed at war with persistence in his vow to live by his grandmother's three P's, but presence was alive and kicking. Like their baby growing strong inside of her, he vowed to fight, one word, one moment at a time.

Kayla sighed. Ben was wearing her down, little by little. He'd given her the space she requested, then asked her out for a date, showing up on her doorstep with a single rose and his trademark jeans and button-down shirt. Gone was his fancy sedan with the leather seats and concert-quality sound system. In its place was a practical family car, a little worn and a little dated, but a statement nonetheless. The surprises kept on coming when he rolled up his sleeves and cooked a meal from scratch.

Theo's proclamation kept Kayla on edge, seeking proof of the love he'd claimed to witness. She scrutinized every look, typecast every touch, contrasted and compared every smile. Exhausted by playing detective and frustrated at her inability to read the man she loved, she gave up and tried her best to enjoy his company.

After the initial nervousness of seeing him again and the awkward moment when he almost kissed her then told her he missed her, they settled into safer, more mundane topics. They still hadn't decided on a name for the baby, and that seemed the safest topic of all.

"I've made a list of baby names," Kayla said.

She caught Ben's smile as he poured noodles into a colander.

"I separated them by names I thought you'd hate and names I thought you might consider."

"Oh, brother." Ben snorted, the steam from the noodles pinking his cheeks. "Let's hear them. Give me the good ones first."

Kayla pulled the sheet of paper from her purse and unfolded it onto the counter. "Don't laugh."

"I'll do my best."

"Beck?"

He glanced at her over his shoulder, his brows scrunched together like two kissing caterpillars. "You thought I'd like that?"

"Fine." She grabbed a pencil from his counter and marked it off the list, relieved at his playful tone. "How about Dillon?"

He piled plates with noodles and wrinkled his nose.

"Gavin?"

"Gavin Strickland." He set the plate down and shrugged. "Maybe."

"Maybe?" Kayla sat up and starred the name. "That's encouraging. What about Asher?"

"Asher?" The caterpillars leaped. "Are you serious?"

"It's biblical," she said. "Ash Strickland. I like the way it sounds."

"You'd be the only one."

"Fine." She marked it off. "Adam?"

Ben shook his head. "Sounds like that nerdy kid from the TV show."

She knew which Adam and which TV show—they'd talked about it and the '80s references they didn't understand—and had wondered if he'd object. "How about Gabriel? We could call him Gabe."

He ladled sauce onto one plate. "That's not terrible."

"Okay." Kayla starred the name. So he liked G names. "Joseph?"

He turned to face her, a grin tugging his lips. "You'd shorten it to Joey and that sounds like a New York construction worker."

Kayla chuckled. "Your logic is mystifying."

He topped the second plate of noodles with sauce. "Next."

"Joel?"

"Umm … maybe."

"Okay." She starred Joel. "Matthew?"

"Classic. Not bad."

"Daniel?"

He shook his head. "I was friends with a Danny in middle school who turned into a druggie in high school. Although so did my brother, so who am I to judge?"

Kayla's ears buzzed at the mention of his brother. She'd wondered if he'd talk about him or if he'd said all he planned to say on the subject. "Is that a yes or a no?"

"That's a no."

She moved on when he said nothing more. "Thaddeus, shortened to Thad."

While sprinkling both plates with parmesan, he shook his head. "Biblical, but no."

"Well, that's all the names on my good list. Do you want to hear the questionable?"

"Probably not." He leaned against the counter, gave her his full attention. "Say them all at once and I'll let you know if I like them."

"Baker, Booth, Cade, Cooper, Heath, Reid, Toby, and Webb."

He picked up the plates and carried them to the table, his lips pursed. "Say them again."

A bubble of hope sprung in her chest. She repeated the list. "Are there any you like?"

He grinned in the way that made his eyes twinkle and sent her heart fluttering. "My grandfather's name was Webb."

"It was?"

"Yeah. He was a good guy, quiet and strong. He loved my grandmother with everything he had."

"Aww. That's so sweet." Kayla tucked the list inside her purse. "Does that mean you like Webb?"

"Yeah. I do."

"As much as the others?"

"What were the others?"

She pulled the list out and read them again. "Joel, Matthew, Gabe, and Gavin."

He looked over her shoulder. "So we're down to five." He placed his hands on her shoulders and rubbed. Kayla closed her eyes, did her best to enjoy the casual touch. She'd missed him. More than she'd ever admit—to him or herself.

"That's progress." Ben plucked the rose from where she'd set it on the counter and put it in a mason jar he filled with water. He set it on the table next to the placemats he'd arranged. "Dinner is served."

Dinner would be served with a side of awkward with the name conversation over. Her "safe" topics evaporated like the steam from their plates. Kayla took a deep breath and faced her fears. She was done playing it safe. If they had a future, it was time to ask questions.

She got down from the stool. "How did you leave things with your parents when we left? You didn't even go inside and tell them we were leaving."

Ben pulled her chair out and helped her settle. He sat across from her at the small table and stared at her with solemn eyes. "I had it out with my dad before I came and found you. My ma and I had words on the porch when you went inside to use the bathroom."

The vague answer had Kayla fidgeting in her seat. "What does that mean?" She placed the napkin on her lap. "'Had it out?' 'Had words?' Are they mad at you?"

"My dad wants what he's always wanted—to support the baby financially but nothing more. Shall I bless the meal?"

Kayla's stomach twisted like the noodles on her plate. They needed more than grace, but that seemed a good place to start. "Okay."

"Heavenly Father,"—Ben bowed his head—"thank you for this meal, thank you for the time Kayla and I have together, thank you for her grace. We pray for those who need you, Father, for those less fortunate. Please bless this food to the nourishment of our bodies. Amen."

"Amen," Kayla mumbled. He may have used the Lord's blessing as a way to change the subject, but she plodded on like a farmer ahead of a storm. "And your mom?"

Ben passed her a basket of warm bread. "She's torn between her loyalty to my father, Darcy, and me."

Kayla set the basket down without touching the bread. "They want you to choose—the baby or your family."

Ben spun his fork around and around his plate but never lifted it to his mouth. He seemed to struggle with what to say, how to explain what was written so clearly on his face—instead of supporting him, they'd demanded he submit. "Yes, they do."

"What do you want?"

He rested his fork on the side of his plate and looked her dead in the eyes. "You and the baby are my family. There is no choice." His eyes flicked to her untouched plate. "Eat your spaghetti. It's getting cold."

She couldn't dodge Cupid's arrow. Her chest exploded with candy hearts and confetti. But what should have been a joyous announcement—He chose me! He loves me!—was doused with a bucket of sand. Losing his family because of her was one more thing he'd resent her for later.

"I know they don't like me," Kayla said. "I know they're upset about the baby, but you don't have to walk away from them if they can't support your choices. Can't you compromise to salvage your relationship?"

"Everything in my family is black and white. I'm either with them or against them. There are no shades of gray."

Kayla picked up her fork and held it in her hand. "I can't believe they'd sacrifice their relationship with you over something like this. They already lost one son. Are they willing to walk away from another—and their grandson—because you won't cooperate?"

Ben lifted the fork, stopped before taking a bite. "I bucked the system. They think I'll fold."

"This isn't a game, Ben. You're talking about severing your relationship with your parents."

"*I'm* not talking about severing the relationship—they are. The last thing I said to my dad was that we'd agree to disagree because I didn't want to draw a line in the sand."

The line was turning into a canyon. "This doesn't feel right."

"Welcome to the dysfunctional Strickland family." Ben stuffed a bite into his mouth, chewing as he watched her. "You don't like it?" he asked when Kayla set her fork down.

She couldn't let him ruin his relationship without at least trying to make him see reason. If that meant baring her soul, then she'd expose her feelings. "Look, I'm still upset with you for not telling me about your brother, but I'm here. I'm willing to try because you're the father of my baby, and it's in both of our interests to work this out."

She wouldn't talk about her feelings. She couldn't, not without getting emotional. But she could reason with him. "Life is messy and complicated, but when you care, you stick it out. You don't walk when things get hard or you get disappointed."

"I'm not walking out on them, Kayla. They won't accept you in my life, so I made a choice. It was either walk out on them or walk out on you." He looked at her, his brow furrowed. "What is it? I thought …" He huffed and shook his head. "I thought you'd be happy."

"I can't be happy about ruining your relationship with your parents."

"You didn't ruin it. They backed me into a corner. I didn't have a choice."

Not having a choice wouldn't ease the sting of regret when it finally hit. It would hit eventually, and hit hard. "You're going to regret this, Ben. They're your parents. You need them."

"I left the door open for when they change their minds. But Kayla …" Ben reached across the table and gripped her hand. "I'm done trying to please everyone. The truth is I do need them, but I need you more."

His expression changed. As much as Kayla vowed to stop analyzing his actions, a well of hope sprang in her chest, threatening to erode her walls. His eyes, so expressive, so exposed, surveyed her face as if memorizing her features.

"I know you're probably not ready to hear this," he said. "And I know I'm not being patient, but I have to be honest. After everything I kept from you, after what it did to us, I won't keep secrets again."

Her stomach smashed against the baby, prepared to protect.

He swallowed and his grip turned painful. "I love you."

Panic, swift and lethal, grabbed Kayla by the throat and squeezed. Her limbs tingled, and her mouth fell open. "What?"

"I'm in love with you. I have been for a while."

"Ben … I …" It was one thing for Theo to say Ben loved her, but something altogether different to hear the words from his mouth. To see the vulnerability in his gaze. To taste the fear on her lips. "You can't say that."

He jerked back as if she'd struck him. "Yes, I can. It's the truth. I love you, Kayla."

"Stop." She pushed away from the table, stood, and placed her hands over her ears. She'd waited so long to hear him say those words. Now he had, and her fear screeched in her ears. "Just stop."

Ben skirted the table and gripped her around the waist so she couldn't flee. "I love you."

"Stop it, Ben." She held her hands tight to her ears, but she could still hear the words, could still feel them in the deep timbre of his voice against her back. "Don't say that."

He turned her around and pulled her hands from her ears. "Why not?"

"You can't say that and expect me not to love you back. I already do, and I'm trying so hard to be careful and not get ahead of myself."

Ben's eyes glistened. "You don't have to be careful with me, honey."

She couldn't stop the tears from stinging her eyes and clouding her vision the way his whispered endearment clouded her mind. "There's so much you don't know."

"Tell me." He kissed her palms, linked their fingers. "Tell me what I don't know."

She couldn't think, couldn't put all the things she'd hid from him on display in any sort of order, so she blurted out the first thing that bubbled to the surface. "I'm grumpy in the morning."

He sucked his lips between his teeth.

Kayla stared at his trembling Adam's apple.

"I know you are," he said.

"How?"

"How many times have you fallen asleep over here, studying or watching TV? I've woken you up. I've faced your wrath." He shrugged. "I'm a morning person. We'll work it out."

If his smile were any indication, her "wrath" wasn't all that intimidating. She aimed higher. Her mother constantly berated her for this disgusting habit. "I pick my nails when I get nervous."

"I know that, too." He kissed the tip of her nose. "It's a good excuse to hold your hands."

How could he smile? She was being as honest as she could about her faults. She dug deeper. "I'm naïve. I believe the best in people, and I get hurt because I never expect people to be mean."

"You're optimistic. It's one of your best qualities."

Seriously? Would nothing irritate him? It was time to get real. "I talk too much."

"I like the sound of your voice."

He wouldn't slow down and let her think. He just stood there and stared at her with a goofy grin on his face—a grin that looked a lot like love. If he wouldn't take his foot off the gas and pump the brake, she was forced to reveal her greatest fear and live with the fallout. She had to—for herself and her baby. "Ben?"

"Kayla?"

"I'm head over heels in love with our son. I love him enough to ask you not to say you love me unless you mean it. I love you, but I can survive a heartbreak. I don't want that for him. He deserves our best, so if you don't love me enough to last through sleepless nights and crying jags and days at a time without brushing my hair, please don't love me at all."

"Kayla." Ben brought her hands to his lips, kissed her knuckles. "I love you enough to last through anything. I love you enough to last a lifetime. A million lifetimes." He let go of her hands and stepped back. "And I can prove it. Wait right here." He jogged down the hall.

Kayla swayed at his departure, his declaration shredding her defenses the way a tornado shredded shingles from a roof. "Where are you going?" She placed a steadying hand on the wall behind her and eased into its strength, afraid her knees would buckle. What had she done? Had she really demanded all or nothing? She was no better than his parents, putting conditions on him like he owed her forever.

Ben emerged from his room, his hands fisted at his sides, his expression serious—too serious for the joyous way he'd jogged to his room. He'd seen reason. He'd processed her ultimatum and hit the brakes with both feet. Her heart oozed like the inside of a burnt marshmallow, coating her insides with sorrow and dismay. She deserved whatever outrage he spewed in return. But first she would explain. "Ben, I—"

Her jaw fell open when he stopped in front of her and lowered himself to one knee.

Kayla covered her mouth with a shaking hand. "What are you doing?"

"Kayla, I know we've done this all backwards. I know I've mucked up a thousand things in the process and I'm bound to muck up more, but the only thing that matters is us. You and me and our baby. I love you, and I want to spend the rest of my life with you." He opened the box in his hand to reveal a beautiful antique diamond. "Will you marry me?"

His question cut her off at the knees. She dropped in front of him, gripping his arms for balance. "Are you … are you sure? I don't want you to feel trapped."

"Who's holding a gun to my head? Marrying you is the only thing I'm sure about. Everything else …" He shrugged and shook his head. "It'll work its way out. But only if you say yes."

Oh, how she wanted to bundle her arms around his neck and say yes, shout yes, scream yes. But she was done wanting a fantasy. If she said yes, she had to know what it meant.

"If I say yes, you can't take it back."

"The ask or the ring?"

The ring was beautiful, and at his question she glanced at the large cushion-cut diamond. Despite its brilliance, the ring—any ring—meant nothing if the sentiment wasn't true and abiding. "The marriage. I only want to do this once."

"I'll never take it back."

"No more secrets. No more saying or doing what the other

wants to hear. If we do this, we're going to be honest with each other. We'll argue and make up, but I'm never going to look for a way out. When I say yes it's forever—even when the baby's grown and in college and it's just us—I don't want you to take it back."

Ben cupped her cheek, his eyes steady and sober. "I'll still love you then, but I hope he'll have some brothers and sisters to keep us company when he heads off on his own."

Shelby was right—there was no formula for a happy ending. They were making it up as they went along. "Are you sure?"

"I'm a thousand percent sure. Time's up. What's your answer?"

The answer rolled off her tongue, sweet as molasses, true as the aim of Cupid's arrow. "My answer is yes. I'll marry you, Ben."

Chapter Forty-One

"Hold still." Emily tugged on the tie at the back of Kayla's dress. "I can't tie this if you don't hold still."

Kayla took a calming inhale and blew it out through her mouth. Graduation had come and gone, and her wedding day had finally arrived. She was wound tighter than Reagan on exam day. "Sorry. I'm just so nervous."

"You look gorgeous, Kay," Shelby said from beside the full-length mirror in Kayla's room. "Ben's going to swallow his tongue."

"I hope not." Kayla ran her hands along the plunging neckline of her A-line dress, admired the flattering cut. Despite doing everything backwards, despite shopping with a visible baby on board, she and her mom and her roommates had made the most of the experience. The floor-length empire waist was the unanimous choice. "His parents would accuse him of marrying me under duress."

"They're still not coming?" Reagan asked.

Kayla shook her head. "I held out hope they'd make an appearance at the rehearsal dinner, but they never showed. I don't think either one of us expects to see them today."

"That's so sad," Reagan said. "Last night was so fun. If they'd come, they wouldn't have any doubts about you and Ben."

"It's their loss." Shelby shrugged. "You did all you could to include them. Trust someone who's been there and done that. Expect nothing, and you won't be disappointed."

Emily finished tying the sash and stepped away. Kayla peeked over her shoulder. "I'm going to keep trying. Ben needs his parents in his life, and so does Webb."

"I love how you can call him by name now," Emily said. "It feels like he's here."

Kayla rubbed the baby perched under the dress's ruching. "Oh, he's here all right. Front and center."

They gathered around the mirror, linking hands over Webb while the photographer stepped in front of them and snapped pictures. "I never thought I'd be the first of our group to get married."

"Me neither," Reagan said. "But it feels right. You are the most romantic. Only you could've turned an unplanned pregnancy into a magical celebration of love."

"It does feel magical, doesn't it?" Kayla asked. "I never could have pulled this off without you girls. I love you all—more than you know."

The bedroom door opened, and Kayla's mom appeared. In her beige, beaded jumpsuit, she looked more like the bride's sister than the mother of the bride. "Chop-chop, girls." She stopped mid-stride. "Oh, Kayla." She cupped her mouth. "You look stunning."

"So do you, Mrs. C," Shelby said. "Love the jumpsuit. Sassy."

Jessica twirled and struck a pose. "Thank you, girls. You all look gorgeous. That blush pink is so flattering." She walked to Kayla and gripped her hands. "I hate to break up the party, but it's time to head to the church."

Her friends exited the bedroom. "Okay." Kayla hugged her mom. "Thank you, Mom. You and Dad have been great." She inclined her head to the photographer her parents had hired, who clicked away. "It means a lot to try and keep this traditional."

"We love you, sweetie, and we really like Ben. I wish his parents had showed." She gave Kayla the stink eye. "But you only do this once, so you need to make it count."

"It'll count. I love him so much."

"God's got a plan for you, KayBear. One only He knows. You make your vows in God's house, you dedicate your marriage to follow Him, and you'll be okay." She patted Kayla's belly. "You both will."

"Nothing about this is how I envisioned my wedding, but I'm happy."

"Life hardly ever goes the way we expect." She stepped back and swiped a finger under her eye. "It's time. Are you ready?"

"I am." Kayla lifted her skirt and followed her mom out of the house.

"You pull on that tie any harder and it's going to pop off," Theo said to Ben in the holding room of the church.

Ben dropped his hands to his sides and paced the small

space. “All this waiting.” And wondering if Darcy would show and make a spectacle of herself and him. “I just want to see Kayla and get married already.”

“Looking forward to the wedding night?” His friend and frat brother Skip jabbed him in the ribs.

Ben lifted his brows and inclined his head at Kayla’s brother.

“Oops, sorry.”

“Seriously?” Josh asked. “He knocked up my sister. I know they have sex.”

“Boys.” Theo stepped between the two. “I’m pretty sure it’s unholy to discuss the bride and groom’s sex life while standing in church. Let’s give the man a break.”

Ben wanted to kiss Theo for diffusing the awkward moment. Theo knew he and Kayla had abstained since their one fateful night, but no one else did. He probably should have corrected Josh and defended Kayla’s honor, but he figured he’d simply dig himself into a bigger hole and end up embarrassing them both. Instead, he glanced out the window at the cloudless spring day. It was a beautiful day, and there was a nice breeze fluttering the leaves on the trees.

The community church where Dash worked had a small sanctuary, so their venue was an easy and inexpensive choice—thank goodness, since he’d managed to blow through his meager savings in the weeks since he’d stopped taking money from his parents. His internship with the GBI and the small housing stipend would come in handy while they lived with Kayla’s parents, waiting for the baby to arrive.

There was a knock at the door and Dash, Reagan’s boyfriend, poked his head inside. “Hey, Ben.” He glanced around the room. “Gentlemen. The pastor is here. He wanted me to check and make sure you didn’t have any last-minute questions.”

Questions? No. Nerves? Yes. "No questions. Just ready to get the show on the road."

Dash laughed in the deep baritone of his singing voice, the same voice that made him a popular draw on campus and here in Atlanta. "Soon enough. I think the girls just arrived, so it shouldn't be long."

Ben took his first full breath of air. He'd gone to bed last night worried Kayla would change her mind or that Darcy would show up with his parents and derail their plans. Knowing she was on site and they'd make their union official in the next … he glanced at his watch … twenty minutes meant he could relax and try to enjoy the occasion.

"If you're all set in here, I'm going to go talk to the pastor and grab a seat." Dash held out his hand and gripped Ben's. "I appreciate you stepping up for Kayla. She's a great girl who deserves the best."

Ben put more force than necessary into the handshake, irked at Dash's assumption he'd asked Kayla to marry him out of obligation. "I'm the lucky one." Dash studied him a moment and chuckled, sending a shiver down Ben's spine.

"No, man, I didn't mean that in a derogatory way. I appreciate you and Kayla getting married before I ask Reagan. It'll make it easier for her to walk down the aisle if she's not the first. That girl's a stubborn mess." He tapped Ben on the shoulder. "I'm as eager as you to start our lives as husband and wife."

"That obvious?" Ben asked.

"Dude, if it wasn't written all over your face, it'd be imprinted on my hand after that vice grip."

"Sorry."

"Don't apologize for defending the woman you love. I'll see you at showtime."

Ben liked Dash—liked his easy smile and unabashed love for Kayla's roommate. He liked all Kayla's roommates. After the engagement, they'd welcomed him into their apartment and their world with open arms. Judging by what he'd observed, Kayla wasn't the only one who'd be walking down the aisle soon. He'd bet a million dollars Emily had her wedding all but planned. It eased his conscience to know he wasn't the only one looking forward to marrying young.

The door closed on Dash's back and Ben continued pacing around the room. He passed Josh playing a game on his phone and stepped around Skip and Theo discussing ASU's chance of making it to the college world series. Theo held his hand up to stop Ben from answering the door when he heard another knock.

"Let me," Theo said. "I want make sure it's not you-know-who."

Ben didn't know whether to be relieved or anxious that he and Theo shared the same concerns about Darcy crashing the wedding. After a conspiratorial stare, Theo stepped forward and cracked the door.

"Mrs. Strickland?"

Ben expected his grandmother to be at the door, but his mom entered. She wore a blue dress, patent leather heels, and a please-forgive-me smile. "Hi, Ben."

Theo closed the door, but not before looking past her for others.

"Mom. I'm glad you made it." Ben leaned in to hug her and filled his nose with the familiar scent of her perfume.

She assessed him from head to toe. "You look handsome in your tux."

"Thank you. I'm … surprised to see you."

"I'm sorry I didn't come last night. Your father …"

She let the sentence hang unfinished, but Ben filled in the blanks. *Doesn't approve. Forbade me to come. Can't support your marriage.*

"Dad's not coming."

She shook her head and dropped her eyes. "He's being stubborn."

"I'm glad you came. Kayla was disappointed when you didn't show last night."

"She seems like a nice girl. Your grandmother's been raving about her nonstop."

Ben and Kayla had driven home not long after getting engaged so she could meet his grandmother. It was that meeting and the conversation that flowed easily between his soon-to-be wife and his grandmother that solidified their choice of a name for the baby. Kayla adored his grandmother. "She's the best. You'd like her, Mama. If you gave her a chance."

His mom fluttered one hand while gripping her purse with the other. He'd never seen her so nervous, so unsure. "I wasn't going to come. You know how your father is, but when I got her letter—"

"Who's letter?"

"Kayla asked me to come to the wedding. She wants to heal the rift between us. The gesture, her words, they meant a lot."

Ben's heart filled to bursting. His sweet Kayla and her big, forgiving heart. He loved her more in that moment than he ever thought possible. "I didn't know she'd written to you, but if it got you here, I'm glad. We want you and Dad to be a part of our lives."

"Your father feels he has to remain loyal to Judge Keller. He loves you, Ben, but he's torn."

"I understand he's in an awkward position with the Kellers,

but I won't turn my back on Kayla. I don't expect him to choose between us, but his gratitude can't dictate my decisions."

"Trust me, son, we've been beating that dead horse for months."

Ben hugged his mama—hard and for real this time. She'd borne the brunt of his father's anger and resentment. Her presence meant they had a shot—maybe a long shot, maybe a sliver of a shot, but a shot nonetheless—to forge a new understanding. He'd never felt more grateful to her for all she did on his behalf. "Grandma's seated in the sanctuary. First row. She'll be glad to see you."

"Shocked is more like it. She's been pulling for you, working hard on your dad. She's smitten with your Kayla."

Grandma wasn't the only one. If Ben didn't see her soon, pledge to spend his life with her in front of God and his friends and family before too long, he would wear the sheen off the hardwood floors. "I love her, Ma. I'm sorry I hurt Darcy, but I couldn't have married her. It would have been wrong for both of us."

"Then God had his hands on you both from the beginning. I believe that, son. I hope you do too."

"I do."

She cupped his cheek. "Marriage is full of contradictions. It's wonderful and hard, peaceful and passionate. But most of all, it's forever. You make a vow before God to love and honor Kayla above all else, and I expect you to keep it always."

"I intend to, Mama. Don't worry."

"That's good. That's why I'm here. I love you, Ben. Your father frustrates me, but I love him, too. And he loves you. I hope one day you can forgive us for fighting this."

He'd spent too much time carrying around bitterness and

regret. He didn't want to live that way anymore. Not with so much to look forward to. "You're forgiven."

"Just like that?" she asked.

"Just like that."

His ma stared at him with her lips quirked. "I think I'm going to like Kayla just as much as Grandma does."

"You will, Mama. I know you will."

Chapter Forty-Two

Eight Months Later

Kayla followed her phone's directions from the main highway onto a county road. She pulled her car's sun visor down and scowled into the horizon. Strapped into his car seat, Webb gurgled as he chewed on a teething toy and kicked his legs to a song on the radio, oblivious to his mother's distress.

What in the world was Ben up to, asking her to meet him in the middle of nowhere instead of his dorm at the POST training center? That was where they usually met when they visited his parents. She spotted him in his old barn jacket, leaning against his car at the entrance to another road, huddled against the wind and December's chilly temperatures. She pulled over and rolled her window down.

"Hey there." Ben stuck his head inside and kissed her on the mouth. His face was clean-shaven, and his lips felt cold. "You're a sight for sore eyes." He tapped on the window at Webb, who squealed in delight at the sight of his father.

"I'm a little afraid to ask what we're doing out here," Kayla said.

"There's something I want to show you. Will you follow me?"

She'd follow him anywhere, especially with the glint in his eye that made her stomach curl and her ears ring. He was up to something. It didn't go unnoticed they'd arrived at one of the locations where he'd interviewed for a police officer job.

She followed Ben's car through the downtown area, past a coffee shop and the local hospital—she could apply for a position. Ben had mentioned how this little town, surrounded by miles of farmland, reminded him of home. She knew he wanted this job, not something in Atlanta. Her country-boy husband felt stifled by the traffic and bustle of the city.

He turned off the main drag onto a residential street dotted with small one-story houses built around the middle of the previous century, braking in front of a red-brick ranch with a for-lease sign out front. She put the car into park, stuffed her arms into her down jacket, and got out of the car. After a hug and proper kiss, Ben eased her aside and pulled Webb from his car seat, bundling him inside his jacket while Webb pulled on Ben's ear. Ben smothered his son's face with kisses, and Kayla's heart turned over in her chest. Webb had her hair and eye color, but Ben's lanky build and lightning-quick smile. Both father and son were gorgeous.

Ben turned to look at the house, his eyes sparkling. "So what do you think?"

"Is this your way of telling me you got the job?"

"I got the job, but I haven't accepted. I wanted to talk to you first."

"I already told you if you get an offer and you want the job to take it."

"I know you did, but I also wanted you to have a look at how we'd live—be it here or another place. I can't offer you what you're used to. I want to, but I can't. Not on a cop's salary."

"I don't expect to live like my parents. You know that doesn't mean anything to me." She stuffed her cold hands into her pockets and looked at the house—a little worn, a little dingy—nothing a little TLC wouldn't cure. The challenge of fixing it up, making it home, had her fingers tingling with excitement instead of cold. "This place is—"

"I know it's small." Ben tugged Webb's hands away from his face.

Kayla's heart inflated at the insecurity in Ben's expression. Didn't he know she'd live in a tent as long as they were all together? "But it's bigger than your parents' apartment and certainly bigger than my dorm at the training facility. I know it's ugly."

"I don't mind small." They'd survived sleepless nights and colicky days in her parents' tiny garage apartment, proving what she knew to be true—it wasn't the size of the house that mattered but the size of the love between those who live there. "I can fix the ugly."

Ben reached for her hand and kissed the top of Webb's head before locking eyes with his wife. "We've turned something small and ugly into something beautiful before. I think we can do it again."

Kayla nodded and blinked away happy tears. They'd come so far from those first panicked moments when faced with impending parenthood. Staring at her precious baby boy, she couldn't imagine her life without him or the man holding him in his arms. "You miss the country? The space, the air, the pace?"

"I do. But if you're not on board, we'll find something else. Make other plans."

He would do whatever she asked. Knowing that made it easy to do the same for him. "I love you, Ben. I want you to be happy. I'll take small and ugly any day as long as you're happy. I can work with small and ugly."

"You can work magic with small and ugly." He cupped her cheek and she felt the warmth of him like an arrow to her heart. "I love you, Kayla. There's nothing small or ugly about the way I feel about you. It's big and fierce. If we're not careful, we'll fill that small house with enough kids to need a new one."

Her heart took flight, flapped its wings and flew into the cloudless winter sky. "Sounds like a perfect life."

Please keep reading for a sample of Reagan's story in *Maybe it's You.*

Maybe it's You

Chapter One

Reagan Bellamy picked the wrong night to wear the right boots. Every step she took in her heeled boots shot an arrow of galvanized steel up her calves, past her internal organs, and straight into her cranial membrane. She stopped walking, placed a steadying hand on a nearby tree, and closed her eyes on a deep breath of morning air.

Birds tucked into their cozy nests mocked her walk of shame across Addison State University's otherwise peaceful campus, determined to condemn her with their shrill accusations: Sinner. Hussy. Trash. Reagan shot a regretful glance at the overhead branches, mustered her strength, and limped on.

The predawn sky painted the sidewalk and stucco buildings of ASU with a dull film not unlike the one coating her mouth and her memories. Fitting punishments for her night of debauchery. Why had she inhaled more shots than she had fingers on one hand? More disturbingly, why had her best friends and roommates let her leave the bar with her worst nightmare and freshman mistake? Only now, in a frightening replay of events, the same boy had become her junior mistake. Fool her once, shame on him. Fool her twice …

Reagan was the world's biggest fool.

Some days, like this one, when the morning fog held everything in a tight vise, the sourness of the distant paper mill along Georgia's coastline hung in the air. Off in the distance, the cloud cover was giving way to a headache-inducing glare that would eventually burn away the scent, but not before she'd returned home. She followed the sidewalk into the entrance of her apartment complex and prayed to make it inside before anyone caught a glimpse of her in last night's clothes.

The squeaky hinges of a second-story door proved Reagan had wasted her prayers. She squared her shoulders, flipped her hair behind her back, and winced as the searing edge of the morning's hangover almost brought her to her knees. She tugged on the hem of her sweater dress and tried to pass for heading to church early Sunday morning.

When a pair of scarred leather boots appeared at the top of the stairwell, Reagan bit back a groan. Dash Carter was the last person she wanted to face when feeling her worst. She caught him giving her a full body appraisal before he hiked his guitar case onto his shoulder and descended the stairs with a loose-limbed gait she could only describe as a swagger.

"Rough night?" He eyed her as she worked up the nerve to tackle the staircase, more exposed than if he'd plopped her under a microscope.

"Late night." A wave of nausea pummeled her shaky stomach.

She grabbed hold of the handrail, swallowed back the bile, and closed her eyes.

Within seconds, his minty fresh breath brushed her face. She pried her lids open, but quickly looked away. She couldn't stare into his hazel eyes for more than a second. He had a way of looking at her—with absolute focus—that stripped her bare.

"Whoa there." His tone oozed sympathy, sympathy she didn't deserve. "You okay?"

The gentle hand he placed on her lower back set every nerve ending ablaze. She forced herself to take the next step, and the one after, dislodging his hand and creating some distance. He smelled of soap and sandalwood, while she reeked like a garbage bag left at an abandoned tailgate. "I'm fine. Just got a little dizzy." The throbbing in her head kept her from sprinting up the stairs.

"You need some Pedialyte," Dash said.

She stopped at the top of the staircase and carefully turned in his direction. "What?"

"Pedialyte." Instead of looking at her like a cheap piece of trash, he flicked a lock of chestnut hair from his forehead and pierced her with his calm stare. "It's an electrolyte replacement, like Gatorade. You find it on the baby aisle in the grocery store. It'll help the headache."

"I'm fine." She did little to hide the snark in her voice. Couldn't he just leave her alone?

"No sense hurting when you don't have to."

She'd never disliked him more, and her aversion ran as deep as the string of women who probably fell at his feet. She hoped her closed-mouth smile conveyed her annoyance. She turned around, unlocked the door, and promptly slammed it, sending a shock wave of pain through her skull. What a jerk. He would have been less obvious if he'd asked who she'd hooked up with the night before.

"Will you please stop making so much noise?"

Reagan took two steps forward and found her roommate, Kayla, sprawled on their L-shaped couch wearing a tank top and underpants, her favorite crocheted throw twisted around her legs. Her arm lay over her eyes and she still wore a butterfly barrette in her messy blond hair.

"What happened last night?" Reagan asked Kayla.

"Shh." Kayla held a finger to her lips before gripping her temple with both palms. "Not so loud. It's like an echo chamber in here."

Reagan lowered carefully onto the couch to remove her boots. "At least you made it home. Alone."

Kayla gave a noncommittal grunt before propping up on her elbow. "You're the one who insisted we leave without you."

Reagan's pulse pounded, and her stomach vibrated in response. Leaning back into the cushions, she resisted the urge to pace and argue against Kayla's insanity. "Come again?"

Kayla groaned as she attempted to sit up. "Shelby tried to drag you away from the sweater vest, but you refused."

"Oh no." She dropped her head in her hands as an image of Chad Ferguson the night before fluttered through Reagan's mind like a puff of smoke. He hadn't been wearing the sweater vest that morning, or anything else as far as she could tell when she'd slithered out of his bed. She could barely stand to look at him with his pale chest, spindly arms, and the hair he kept perfectly gelled shooting like bamboo reeds against the stark white pillow. "Why? Why didn't I listen?"

"The same reason I'm lying here in my underwear. The devil alcohol."

"Never listen to me when I'm drunk and insisting I stay with someone you know I detest."

"You're more convincing when you're drunk and lapping him up like an ice cream cone."

"Tell me you're exaggerating."

"I would," Kayla said. "But I'd be lying."

Reagan's head fell back until it nestled against the soft cushion, her eyes drifting closed. Yes, she'd intentionally sought Chad out when she'd found him at the bar. As Professor Atkins's graduate assistant, he had pull in who became the professor's next undergraduate research assistant. Reagan was willing to do just about anything to make inroads with Professor Atkins, but she never thought she'd stoop that low. What a nightmare. "How could I go home with the jerk who took my virginity my freshman year and then acted like he didn't know me the next day?"

"Is he ignoring you now?"

"I got out of his apartment as soon as I woke up."

"Did you …?"

The bowling ball in her stomach nose-dived into the gutter as shame flamed her cheeks. "I don't know."

Kayla's eyebrows disappeared into her bangs. "You don't know?"

"I was wearing my clothes, so I hope not."

Kayla reached a hand over and patted Reagan's arm. "Assume nothing happened and purge it from your mind."

"My mind *is* purged. I can't remember leaving the bar with him. What happened after is a total mystery. All I know is I'm never drinking again."

"Me neither. Let's make a pact."

She shook Kayla's hand, and used her roommate's grip to lever herself off the couch.

"Where are you going?" Kayla asked.

"To scrub every trace of Chad Ferguson from my body."

Reagan clutched the side of the shower, lightheaded from the steam. Or from lack of sleep. She stumbled to her bed and burrowed under the covers but found sleep as evasive as the details of the night before. She'd made a mistake. A big one. She didn't know whether she needed to apologize to Chad or act like the whole thing never happened.

Reagan hated not knowing what to do or how to act after spending her whole life walking on eggshells around her volatile mother and the men who waltzed in and out of their lives. Finally living life on her terms, surrounded by friends, the last feeling she wanted to relive was the sickening dread of not knowing what the next day held. She had a plan, she stuck to the plan, and everything she did was according to the plan. Getting blisteringly drunk and going home with Chad Ferguson wasn't a part of her plan. It wasn't even scribbled in the margins.

Hours later, after a nap and a bowl of leftover spaghetti, Reagan sat cross-legged at the kitchen table, contentedly engrossed in a paper disproving Keynesian economics. She glanced over when the apartment door opened and her roommate Emily walked inside carrying a bottle of red liquid.

Still dressed in last night's clothes, Emily lacked both the hangover and the embarrassment of a night spent away from home thanks to her boyfriend, Dylan. Reagan was still sober enough to remember when Dylan pried the beer from Emily's hand and whisked her out the door. They were disgustingly in love and nauseatingly dependent on one another. Reagan never wanted a man to order her around, but it would have been nice to have someone to run interference for her last night.

"What is this?" Emily set the bottle on the table before breezing past to the refrigerator.

Reagan struggled to remember the point of her half-typed sentence. "What's what?"

"It was on the doormat," Emily said over her shoulder.

Reagan reached for the bottle, turned it around, and nearly choked on the shame of last night's debacle. It had taken hours to expunge her reckless behavior from her mind and find solace in the safety of schoolwork, and the bottle of Pedialyte pulled her back to the present where humiliation ruled.

Her feet hit the floor with a resounding thud, she grabbed the plastic container, and rocketed out of the apartment. Somebody was going to pay.

Discover Other Christian Romance, Contemporary Romance & Women's Fiction Titles by Christy Hayes

Christian Romance:

Maybe it's You

Golden Rule Outfitters Series:

Mending the Line, Book 1, Golden Rule Outfitters Series

Guiding the Fall, Book 2, Golden Rule Outfitters

Taming the Moguls, Book 3, Golden Rule Outfitters

Connected to GRO Series:

Dodge the Bullet

Shoe Strings

Connected Books:

Heart of Glass

The Sweetheart Hoax

Single Title:

Angle of Incidence

Misconception

The Accidental Encore

Short Story:

Good Luck, Bad Timing & When Harry Met Sally

The WG2E's Viva La Valentine Romance Anthology (*Good Luck, Bad Timing & When Harry Met Sally* originally appeared in the Valentine Anthology. The collection of Valentine stories makes a great gift and it's a great way to discover new writers!)

Lost Love Letters: An Indie Chicks Anthology

50 First Chapters: An Indie Chicks Anthology

About the Author

Christy Hayes lives outside Atlanta, Georgia, with her husband and dogs. When not writing, she's reading, walking dogs, or stalking her adult children on social media.

Please visit her website at
www.christyhayes.com
for more information.

Made in the USA
Monee, IL
21 February 2020